WANDERLUST

WANDERLUST

SCIONS
BOOK ONE

EDWARD MCKEOWN

Ad Astra Books

Edward McKeown

6409 Willow Run Dr

Charlotte NC 28277

Printed in the United States of America

Credits:

Author: Edward F. McKeown

Managing Editor: Laura Jean Stroupe

Continuity: Schelly Keefer

Cover Image by Gremlin

CHAPTER ONE

Nineteen-year-old Daire Fenaday wandered the corridors of the powered-down privateer *Sidhe*. For her, the warship was not simply a prize from the long-ago Conchirri War, it was the ship of her dreams. The ship that her father and later her "Aunt" Shasti Rainhell had driven beyond the borders of known space in one adventure after another. Shasti lived on Olympia now, married to its president, where she was chief of Planetary Security. The life of a privateer lay far behind her.

Daire walked on to the bridge, with its spade-shaped layout. Low lights and telltales glowed, but it was otherwise silent, the ship in mothballs now. Private warships were increasingly things of the past, relics of the early days of the Confederation of Species.

Her father, Robert Fenaday, had purchased *Sidhe* from the Navy, to search for her mother, Lisa, lost with her warship in the Conchirri war. Against all odds, he and Shasti succeeded in the near-legendary quest to find Lisa. *Sidhe* became Robert's gift to Shasti, who captained it for the better part of a decade. Now, with Shasti gone to Olympia, the vessel languished in orbit, too expensive to operate for regular cargo runs and not needed to fight.

The years of Shasti's command fascinated Daire. Shasti had the rare privilege of charting any course she chose, on any mission. The intoxicating freedom of those voyages had sparked Daire's soul since she sat on Shasti's knee, hearing of them.

Ironic, I'm closest in spirit to Shasti. Stellan, Shasti's own son, is closer to my mother. Of course, he was raised by my Mom and Dad. The universe really showed its evil sense of humor with all that. Shasti returned from the Evolver War to save Dad from the Othersiders. She found Mom pregnant with me, and it triggered her own dormant pregnancy from an encounter with my father years before. Shasti's Engineered body decided it was time to be pregnant. But it didn't consult Shasti.

She sighed. Stellan had been born only hours after her. Aunt Shasti hadn't been ready for motherhood. She'd been created by scientists in a lab, with no family and an early life on Olympia so horrible she rarely spoke of it. So Daire's brother, which was how she thought of Stellan, was raised by her parents. In return, Stellan treated Lisa as his true mother.

Daire knew that only her love for her aunt prevented Stellan from regarding Shasti as an intruder when she visited. For Daire's sake, Stellan was courteous, if cool to Shasti. It helped that, despite everything, Lisa and Shasti, who had endured much together, were close. Lisa insisted on being called "big sister" by Shasti, who indulged her in any way she could.

Just like, Daire thought smugly, *I'm the big sister to Stellan, even if he is seven feet tall to my five-foot four.*

As if summoned by her thoughts, she heard Stellan coming up the gangway.

"Have you seen enough?" he asked, his voice suited his body: deep, no teenage uncertainty in it.

"No," Daire admitted. "I always dreamt of serving on this ship, by Shasti's side, exploring unknown worlds."

"We have a ship, Sis."

"Yes, yes," she replied. "And she is a useful thing. But…it's not the *Sidhe.*"

"Well hopefully we won't be fighting Evolvers or Voit-Veru cruisers," he replied. "We're going to be traders."

"I suppose so," she said.

Stellan gave a rare laugh. "You often seem to forget about the parts of her stories where they were seconds from death or disaster."

"Yes," Daire said, eyes kindling. "But think of all she did and saw!"

Stellan who took a more sober view of his birth mother's sometimes blood-ridden trail across the stars, merely shook his head.

"I was born too late," Daire mourned. "All the great adventures are done. I could have been a pirate like Aunt Shasti."

"Privateer," he corrected.

"Hah, legalities. We pirates don't need 'em."

"It's the difference between flying space and the executioner's dock," he shot back. "Our dad and my mother needed a slew of Confed pardons to avoid being shot or imprisoned for much of what they did."

"You worry like Mom," she said.

"And you," he said, folding his arms, "are as reckless as Shasti herself." Stellan never called Shasti "mom", only used the more formal "mother", if he had to acknowledge her maternity at all.

"Smile when you say that" she said, assuming a gunfighter's crouch.

"No blasting for you today," he replied. "If you're through walking down memory lane, we have a lot to do before setting out. Assuming our parents don't put an end to this before we launch."

"Dad wouldn't, and Mom can't without him. Besides, Aunt Shasti gave her blessing."

"Big sister," he rumbled, "the galaxy is strewn with the remains of those who underestimated our parents, and Mom doesn't always regard my birth mother's decisions as binding on her."

"You worry too much," she said, starting down the companionway.

"And you never worry about anything," he shot back.

"Not true," she shot over her shoulder, "I keep worrying about where we're gonna find a girlfriend in your size."

"Hah, worry for yourself. Who is going to put up with your temper..."

Amiably bickering, they headed for the launch to take them over to station.

CHAPTER TWO

Farewell parties were long done. As was any last effort by parents, siblings, and friends to persuade the pair that they need not "prove themselves" on the marches of the Confederation. In truth, it would have only been necessary to persuade Daire. She was the restless spirit, the ungovernable fire. Stellan was going because he was as close to his sister as any twin. As children if anyone made fun of him for not being her "real brother" they were immediately set on by a tiny, fearless red-headed menace, who would answer with a barbed tongue, fists, or feet as the situation required. It was beyond question that he would back her to the hilt.

Daire's other siblings—nine-year-old Wulf and seven-year-old Emma had said goodbye the night before and were back in school. Emma had cried, barely able to understand that they were going away and could only comforted by Stellan carrying her around for an hour.

Today, it was only their parents at the dock where their J-class freighter *Wanderlust* waited. The ship looked like a scaled-up atmospheric shuttle, twenty-five years old and hardly sleek. *Wanderlust* was a practical, a voluminous tubular hull with broad, rounded atmospheric wings and a squat tail.

Daire and Stellan had both chosen a color for her scheme, as they would not fly in their father's Shamrock line colors. Daire chose the blood-red of *Sidhe's* hull, Stellan had chosen his normal preference, black. The result was rather ominous for a freighter, but delighted Daire.

Robert and Lisa Fenaday walked their children to the dockside airlock. There was no denying the relationship between Lisa and Daire, who was a smaller version of her mother: fine-featured, delicately built.

Robert had some of the solidity of Stellan but was only six feet tall to his son's near seven. Shasti's genes were dominant in the boy, who was massive and dark of aspect. But Stellan's eyes were the thoughtful brown of his father's and not Shasti's chill, jade-green ones.

Their parents embraced them and stood back. "Time to go," Robert said. "You have an orbital window on Farmoon to make. Time and lunar tides wait for no captain."

"Yep" Daire said, feeling a rare shyness around her father but impatient to be gone. Impulsively, she reached up and kissed him on the cheek. He gave her a quick grin and shook hands with his son.

"I'd say be safe," Lisa began, hugging Daire and giving her a look that bounced off her daughter's bland self-assurance, "but it would fall on deaf ears. At least with you." She wagged a finger at Daire then turned to Stellan and gave the front of his shirt a mock tug. "You, I expect to be the sensible one."

"As always," he said, with a rare smile. She reached up and touched his face. Suddenly her eyes were very bright and full.

"Blue skies and safe landings," Robert managed.

The traditional spacer's goodbye put an end to the leave-taking. With that, Daire and Stellan turned and headed out to the airlock. They knew their parents would not stay to watch them launch. It was considered bad luck, as if you never expected to see them again.

There's truth to that, Stellan thought as they sealed the airlock. *A starship leaves people behind in time as well as in distance. Star jumps removed one from space-time. We won't age, but our parents, siblings and friends will live all the time that we spend frozen between the seconds in jumpspace. Even when we do meet again, we will hardly be the same people. Wulf and Emma will no longer be children but teens.*

"Finally!" Daire said, as they reached the bridge. "You'd think we were going off to war, the way they all carried on."

"Did you expect them to behave differently?"

"Well not Dad, he's a softie and a worrywart. But Mom was in the Academy at my age. Aunt Shasti was already a mercenary. Heck, even Dad had already gone on trade missions. They all did fine on their voyaging."

"Fine?" Stellan asked. "Mom was MIA and a POW for years. Our father touched off a war searching for her. Aunt Shasti fought the Evolvers beyond the frontier."

"Hah, well we'll be lucky if anything more exciting than a tax surcharge happens to us."

Stellan shook his head, then shelved all those thoughts as he helped Daire with the prelaunch checklist. *Wanderlust* was as large a ship as two crew could safely fly and was as automated as possible, so much of the work had been done by the ship's AI, but no flyer worth his fins would fail to check their own ship out.

Both Daire and Stellan had been all but born to space, and each held a master's certificate. Eventually, they planned for more crew but for now, they didn't need the payroll. Checklist complete and exit protocol loaded, *Wanderlust* kicked free of her umbilical and the station. Her drive lit and she began her first outward bound voyage in her new name and colors.

"Look out galaxy, here we come," Daire crowed.

Stellan gave his sister an indulgent look. It was hard not to be caught up in her unbridled joy at doing what she had longed for.

CHAPTER THREE

Daire had selected Serendib for their first port, a primarily human colony world that did not get much traffic despite having been settled a century ago. The colony had a mixed history, opened during one of the ill-considered deregulation binges of the old Confederation. Under-resourced and over-exploited, it was an ideal place to sell their cargo of machine tools, pharmaceutical technology and patents, as well as the luxury goods they'd stuffed in every spare corner.

She hadn't told her parents of her plan to move further to the periphery after that. Both Robert and Lisa knew a small freighter like theirs would have little chance of profit in the well-patrolled and safe sectors where company ships ruled. The place for an independent trader was the periphery, with all its risks. Despite all that, their next destination might have raised an objection. Avanzado lay in a wildcat sector of space beyond Confed jurisdiction, near Voit-Veru space. There were rumors of space-going alien species beyond Avanzado but nothing definite had been found. So naturally it caught Daire's interest.

Wanderlust dropped out of jumpspace in BD+59 87 system, which bore the unofficial name, Beleneus, after an old Celtic god of sun worship and healing, a yellow-orange spectral class.

Serendib was the only world of note in the system, an Earth type planet in a Goldilocks orbit. Humans dominated, scattered in towns and villages about the main continent.

As soon as *Wanderlust* dropped back into space-time, Daire transmitted their manifest and their cargo of space mail. The latter knit together the widely separated colonies of Confederation species and wasn't merely the equivalent of cards and letters. Along with business and personal mail came the latest regulations, court rulings, legislation, patents, copyrights and the formulas for new medicines and other such. Starmail was a guaranteed source of income for any spacer. As they were coming from New Eire, an older colony with an express route to the Star Central, they had an unusually large load of electronic and physical media.

As for the manifest, it's never too soon to start negotiations on cargo, Daire thought. Ahead of them, propagating at the speed of light was their 'open for business' sign. Brokers and merchants would begin reaching out to them as soon as it arrived. When it came to buying from an inbound starship, he who hesitated was often frozen out. Warehouses would compete to store goods for those buyers, and for things being transshipped.

As they lined up for the deceleration to the inner system and eventual landing on Serendib, the first offers came in. Daire considered these, as she also accepted an outbound load of starmail. There had been other ships through the system recently, so the load was small.

The offers on her luxury goods were better than she had hoped, and those were quickly sold. The machinery and other equipment hit a market where other ships had traded in recent months. The margins for those goods, though acceptable, were not as great. She decided to wait until they landed to finalize those. There was always the danger for a ship's captain to be too dazzled with initial offers and lock in too early. Sometimes other buyers who had not heard of the ship's arrival could outbid the first rush.

"Odd," Stellan said on their second morning inbound.

"What?" Daire said, around a mouthful of warm tea.

"I know we're bound headed for the Periphery and Avanzado after this, and we don't have a specific route beyond that. But I have been looking at what cargo has been going outbound and to where."

"And?"

"Well cargoes shipments have been going all over the place but they're all from one company, Nole LLC."

Daire frowned. "That is odd. It's a small colony but there are twenty-seven licensed star-brokers and other merchants. I know there have been starships through here in the last seven months, but it shouldn't have emptied the queue of cargoes waiting to go out. Hell, the Sarmiento Line runs a regular a service here twice yearly."

"Well, it's perhaps a good thing that we weren't dependent on finding any cargo heading for the Periphery," he said. "Cuts two ways though, we might find it harder picking up goods to sell on spec when we are outward bound."

"Yeah," she said. "I'll factor that in when I look at the price of our machine goods. We might do better with them on Avanzado or else-where on the Periphery." It was a gamble, she knew. They were certainly better funded than the normal small ship company, at her father's insistence, but Daire did not want to dip into that cookie jar soon or often. Now, she was even more determined to hold off further negotiations on that part of her cargo until landing.

"We could ask," Stellan said, eyebrows raised.

"And how would we verify anything that we were told? No, something odd is going on, like you said. Let's wait until we land before we ask any questions."

"Wanderlust AI," Stellan asked. "Is there a Confed military base on world? What are the details of Confed presence?"

"Negative regarding a military base," the AI replied. "Confed administration is confined to the 212th Judicial Circuit Court, which meets once every two years for a session. There are consular officials who land biannually accompanied by a Space Patrol cutter. The planetary representative from Serendib is based half the term on world and half at the sector capitol of–"

"Enough," Stellan said to the AI, then turned to her. "It's a typical small colony, settled on a shoestring by a group wanting a different life from the established settlements. There's not much government, and that's only down at the spaceport capitol of Ujain and a few towns local to it. We picked it because it doesn't get much traffic, and lies in the direction we want to go."

"Well, we land tomorrow," Daire said. "We'll go in eyes open and ears sharp."

In the morning, Daire joined her brother on the bridge. Serendib had gone from a small ball to filling the screen and viewports. As always with Earth-type worlds, it was primarily ocean, in various shades of blue. Daire had only seen Earth in holos and was used to the wine-dark seas of northern New Eire. To her, Serendib looked bright and cheerful. The land masses, when they appeared, were scattered. The largest was only a major island, mountainous and heavily forested. Over it hung a surprising amount of atmospheric pollution. The Serendib remit had been for exploitation of the great gem, precious and rare metal natural resources of the world. It seemed that little thought had been given to the effects.

She sighed. At least it was a world with no native species. Living conditions for the immigrant population would grow tougher over time. Back before the war, when the Confederation had been little more than a loose trading association of sovereign planets, the pattern had been common. Discovery, settlement, exploitation, natural disaster, reform and eventual proper husbandry of the colony. At least for those that made it through the disastrous exploitation phase.

Well, I'm not here to settle the place. Just to trade and move on.

She released the autopilot and began lining up for entry. Stellan called in to the Ujain spaceport control and coordinated their approach. There was no other space traffic in the area, only some general aviation that operated on other vectors safely away from their descent.

Daire elected for a nose-down descent and watched *Wanderlust's* prow begin to glow before the automatics sealed the windows. On instruments now, she entered the atmosphere at a gentle angle. Once in atmosphere, *Wanderlust* handled like a piggish airliner. She let the speed drop and lined up on the space and airport. Her freighter deployed its massive landing gear. There was no reason to use fuel in a VTOL let down with so much runway available.

"Do a sweep with our own radar," she said. "I don't trust a spaceport I've never been in with light aviation traffic. There's always some asshole in an ultralight where he shouldn't be."

Stellan grinned. "Already done and continuing. I remember when the *Arvin* landed on New Eire with a glider stuck on her upperworks."

She nodded, pleased. Stellan always seemed able to anticipate her thinking. In truth, she felt that way about him, as if he was another part of her.

Wanderlust bumped and slewed as she hit thicker air and Daire cursed under her breath.

"A bit gusty," Stellan said. "Would have been nice if Ujain control had told us."

"I don't want to think about what they're using for approach radar and computers," she replied. "That's why I set it up myself."

"Yes, Captain, my captain."

The air smoothed out and she lined up on the runway, bleeding off airspeed carefully.

"All is still clear," Stellan said.

"Ujain control," she announced, "SS *Wanderlust* committing to final approach."

"Welcome *Wanderlust*, you are still clear all the way."

Daire applied the retros. As the ship's anti-gravity system didn't work in a planetary field, they ended up hanging against their harnesses as the *Wanderlust* slowed. Small ship that she was, she still massed more than a dozen air-freighters. Vessels larger than her would usually come down in the sea, as could *Wanderlust*, but it greatly facilitated unloading when they could land on the ground. They were fortunate in that all regulated spaceports were built to Confed military standards, with at least one runway capable of bearing immense loads of combat operations.

As they touched down and slowed to a stop, Daire could see the land tugs rolling up, squat, robotic machines painted brilliant orange and black, that were almost all engine. Twenty minutes later, the sturdy machines had them in a dock/gantry. Daire was able to secure the engines and switch to dock power, water and sewage. She stood and stretched out the tension of landing. Stellan, as usual, unaffected by such things, simply continued working his stand-down checklist.

"I'll get ready for port inspection and customs," she said. He grunted an acknowledgement.

Daire went to her cabin and donned her jacket and cap. Petit and young as she was, it always paid to dress the part, especially dealing with locals. She marched down to her cargo deck and hit the servo to lower the main ramp, inordinately pleased by the fact it neither creaked nor groaned as it did so. J-freighters were notorious for noisy hydraulics, but she and Stellan had overseen the refit of the servos personally.

The descending ramp revealed a single port official, though in the background of the dock she could see the usual mix of dock crews, stevedores, robots and other devices servicing the dock. The official was a tall, attractive woman in her mid-twenties, Daire guessed, with short black hair, and dressed in a gray uniform. She looked a little surprised at the sight of a captain as young as Daire, then covered it and walked up, extending a hand.

"Welcome to Ujain Spaceport," she said. "I'm Marguerite Laurent, Assistant Customs Officer."

Daire shook her hand. "Daire Fenaday, ship's master out of New Eire."

"I have your manifest and landing data," Laurent said, gesturing to her large notepad comm. "All is in order. Not that our customs requirements are unusual or strict. All that remains is a physical inspection. Permission to board?"

"Granted. I can offer you some tea or coffee in the galley when we are through, authentic Terran blends."

Laurent's teeth flashed in a smile. "Trying to bribe a customs official, Captain? Well, I'll take you up on it."

For all the woman's apparent friendliness, her inspection was thorough. They ended up heading for the galley a half-hour later, after Daire thumb-printed the inspection. The smell of fresh roasting coffee reached their noses as they climbed up.

Wow, Daire thought, *maybe he really does read my mind.*

As they cleared the hatchway Laurent pulled up short, seeing Stellan.

"Hello," he said, his resonant voice.

"Ah…hi," Laurent said, looking a little overwhelmed.

Daire, so used to Stellan, had forgotten the effect that her seven-foot-tall brother, with his dark hair and eyes, and muscular build had on people, especially women.

"This is my brother," Daire said, "Stellan Rainhell. Meet our customs inspector, Ms. Laurent."

"Brother?" Laurent said.

"Also First Mate, Ship's Engineer, steward and usually cook," Stellan said, "though the latter is more a case of self-defense."

"Hey, I can cook," Daire protested.

"Next time we need something for the reactor, I'll let you know," he replied. "I thought you might offer our company some coffee, so I made some and your favorite tea as well."

"Thank you. We will skip the flogging for insulting my culinary skills then."

Laurent laughed. "I can see this arrangement has its advantages."

"It was especially useful in discouraging unwanted suitors in college," Daire said.

"Very useful," Stellan confirmed. "Take a seat, Captain. I know how you like yours. Ms. Laurent?"

"Oh, please call me Marguerite. No need to stand on ceremony. Cream and sugar for me please."

He nodded. "Then call me Stellan. Please have a seat."

Daire watched as her brother, into whose huge hands mugs, creamer and sweetener disappeared, made them drinks and placed them before them, along with a plate of petit-fours he must have baked when she wasn't watching.

He has none of the clumsiness one associates with big men, Daire thought, as she watched Marguerite watch Stellan. *All his motions are precise, like he always knows where he is. Makes him quite the jeweler. But I bet she's wondering what he's like in bed.*

Stellan served them both, rewarded by a smile from Laurent. He'd made up a mug for himself. But he did not sit and took up his usual position behind her and on her left, leaning against the cabinets. All sipped their fine Terran brews in appreciation.

Daire, under cover of small talk, sought to learn as much as she could of the local situation. Laurent seemed reluctant to talk about off-port news at first. Stellan, sensing that Laurent might be more open to him, finally sat next to her and engaged her. Daire found herself unexpectedly annoyed at the obvious attention she was paying her brother but had to admit he seemed to be charming the other woman.

"How long do you plan to be in port?" Laurent asked.

"Depends on how long it takes us to find a new cargo, or decide to pick one up on spec," Daire answered, when Stellan nodded toward her. "We have no specific timetable or route. This is our initial flight."

"Of course," Laurent suddenly said, "Rainhell and Fenaday. How could I be so stupid? Those names can't be a coincidence. You're the children of Robert Fenaday, Lisa Fenaday and Shasti Rainhell. Oh my God, I can't believe I'm meeting you! Your parents are damn near legends."

"Dad kept telling me that when he wanted me to behave," Daire said.

"I have to ask," Laurent said, turning the conversation to Shasti Rainhell. "Your mother, Shasti Rainhell, what is she like?"

"My mother," Stellan said, "is Lisa Fenaday, who raised me. As for Shasti Rainhell, she is best summed up as: tall, pale and dangerous to know."

"And beautiful," Daire added gently, "and looks scarcely any older than we do."

Stellan raised an eyebrow and seemed amused by Daire's defense of Shasti. It also seemed to soften his mood again.

Laurent, to her credit, seemed to immediately sense that she had reached the edge of family issues, and eased back. "I have seen holos of Lisa Fenaday as well. You favor her; indeed, you look enough like her to pass for her in her youth."

Stellan held a hand level in the air and mouthed, *smaller*.

Both women chuckled though Daire gave her brother a mock glare.

"I can't imagine," Daire said, finishing her coffee, "that between refuel, maintenance and trading that we'd be here for less than three of four weeks."

"Well then perhaps we shall see more of each other," Laurent also finished hers and stood.

"Stellan, why don't you see Marguerite to the ramp?"

"Aye, aye, sir."

She merely rolled her eyes at him.

Stellan left and Daire put away the dishes and remaining coffee, too precious to waste. She waited in the galley for her brother's return. He came back looking pleased with the world.

"So," she said, "I assume you have a date?"

"Why, yes, for two nights from now."

"Learn anything else?"

"There is, as you suspect, something going on here. Laurent mentioned that we might find things…unusual…when looking for an outbound cargo and warned me about the Nole Corporation. The way she looked around when she mentioned that name seems to indicate that this company is a force to be reckoned with even in the Confed jurisdiction of the Port.

"Wanderlust AI," Daire called, "assemble a precis of information Nole Corp and read aloud."

"Nole Corp LLC, founded thirty years ago is a registered mining and export company founded by Goran Nole, age 58, native of New Stockholm, citizen of Serendib by naturalization. Nole LLC is currently the leading exporter of radioactives, gems and precious metals from Serendib. Recent acquisitions and mergers, as well as good fortune in prospecting have made Nole LLC the wealthiest company on Serendib or nearby space. Nole LLC is a privately held corporation with Goran Nole as CEO—"

"AI stop," she said. "Advise negative information on Nole LLC or Goran Nole."

"Nole LLC is frequently cited for violations of environmental and labor laws. Nole LLC has forty-seven active lawsuits against it. Fifteen are for breach of contract or mechanics liens against Nole for funds allegedly owed. Three more are for wrongful termination and the remainder are commercial or land use disputes.

"Ujjain's District Attorney's office was investigating Nole for conspiracy, fraud and tax evasion. After recent planetary elections brought a more business-friendly administration into office, and resulted in the replacement of the DA, these investigations were dropped."

"AI, stop," she said.

"Sounds like a powerful local," Stellan mused. "Someone we may come across in the next few days."

"Enjoy your date with Laurent," Daire said. "But during the pillow talk, see what you can learn about Nole and his company."

"And what of you?" he replied. "Planning to look for companionship ashore?"

Daire reached back and patted a bulkhead. "Got all the companion I need for now, right here. *Wanderlust* doesn't want to tie me down to one place, or to children, or other such nonsense. Besides, once the prospective boyfriends get a look at you, they usually decide to hunt elsewhere."

A more serious expression slid over his face. "Sister, I want you to have all that you dream of. I would never stand between you and anyone who could make you happy. You're a normal girl— you need a normal life."

Daire thought about making a rude gesture then instinctively realized his feelings would be hurt. "I know that, silly."

"And I understand that means you and whoever it ends up being, will quarrel and fuss and annoy each other," he unexpectedly added.

"Such must be expected. I can have no place in such normal disputes. After all, our parents had them."

"Yeah. I've always been amazed Mom and Aunt Shasti didn't fight more. Dad also said the only thing that ever scared him was when they teamed up on him."

"Anything more than normal, however," he continued, "and I will simply make sure that the leftover parts are not found."

She thought about it. "Well, if any boyfriend ever slugs me, I'll help you bury them."

"Burning," he replied. "Much better at disposing of the evidence, especially if we use—"

"Ah, got it. What say we lock up the ship and head into town for dinner?" she asked. "I'm buying."

Like most people who have the responsibility for preparing three meals a day, the prospect of dinner out had an immediate appeal for him. "Wonderful."

CHAPTER FOUR

Stellan let his lungs fill with the new air of a world that he'd never seen before. Even the industrial elements in it didn't reduce his enjoyment of the scents of trees, grass, sea air, all those scents that are either absent on a ship, or so artificial that one wonders "why bother?" All the more so as his sense of smell was far better than a standard humans.

Standard human, that's how Olympians thought of other humans. I will give my mother one credit. She did not succumb to that prejudice. Hell, she destroyed the government that created her and embodied that ideology. I must always remember that I am a human first and Engineered second.

While there were no other starships on the field; though he could see some small tenders and the like, sitting by rocket boosters. They were probably there to maintain the satellite network, as the planet did not yet boast a space station. Small aircraft took off intermittently, their running lights blinking against the dark of the sky and the sea beyond. He idly wondered about their destinations, who was in them and what their lives were like.

On the opposite side, glowed the lights of Ujain, where the first landing had been made and the capitol was founded. A city of about 450,000, it had a decent skyline. Beyond it, he could see the lights of roads and small towns in the foothills that lead out to where mountains were outlined by the last of the sunlight. A river ran alongside the main road, its path over the rocks outlined by a silvery spray.

He waited for Daire at the base of the ramp, under *Wanderlust's* red and black nose. The ship was partially obscured by the gantry's framework of metal and supply pipes. People and machines wandered about —no port or cargo area ever shut down entirely. After a second look from people for his size, he received either friendly nods or busy indifference from passersby.

The cargo that had been sold, or was for transshipment to other destinations, had already left. Stevedores and bots had carried the containers off via the ramp just after Marguerite cleared them for import. He and Daire would inspect the ship and begin refueling and replenishment tomorrow. Tonight, it was the ritual of the first night in port, and relaxation was the order of the day.

Daire came down dressed in a sweater and slacks, looking more like a college student than a ship's captain. He too, had left his ship's uniform aboard, wearing a long-sleeved blue shirt. There was no need to wear the travel cloaks that protected one from giving offense to locals. The culture on Serendib was mainstream and their appearance shouldn't give rise to any unintended offense.

"You look nice," he said.

"Thank you. You, too."

He waved a robotaxi over. The vehicle could hold four but not with him in the mix. Laurent had given him the names of several places but insisted that he reserve the best one for their date. So tonight, he'd chosen a more upscale bar restaurant, outside the port. Automatics logged them out of the spaceport and Confed jurisdiction. Getting out was always easy, getting back into a secured area was the greater chore.

They enjoyed the drive in the cool evening watching the lights and the scenery. Serendib's large moon began to rise behind them, lighting the mountains up.

"Beautiful," Daire breathed. "It's for moments like this that I want to travel the galaxy."

"I know," he replied, smiling at her. "Me too."

Following their local guide's recommendation, they stepped off the tram near the Trans-galactic Pub. A rambling building that incorporated an old cargo landing pod, it stood two stories tall, with a tower that gave it an additional level past that. Like a lot of spaceport bars, it was festooned with balconies and windows, as the people frequenting them spent enough time inside. Party lights hung everywhere. There were outdoor heaters, though the evening was pleasant enough that neither felt the need for jackets.

They walked in and attracted immediate attention in the noisy crowd. Daire was pretty enough to pause conversation by herself but with her two-foot taller brother, they made for quite a sight. They were used to this from their college days.

"Let's not do the bar," she said. "I'm not looking for a date and you have one."

"Suits me. I'm more interested in food and beer."

"Hah, nothing new there."

While they still attracted eyes, Daire wrangled them a seat just inside of the balcony. They got the sight and smell of the world and a little less of the coolness.

Service was by tabletop menu and live servers. Stellan ordered the two largest steins of beer they had and a double helping of angel hair pasta and scallops in a vodka sauce. Meanwhile he made short work of the bread that was brought out.

Daire settled on a chardonnay, a salad, and some baked mountain-stream fish she couldn't pronounce but was made with Indian-fusion spices. The server, a young man in his twenties, paid special attention to Daire, but she was too distracted by the world outside the balcony to notice. When the food arrived, they lost interest in anything beyond their plates.

"Carbs, carbs and more carbs," she teased as he finished the second beer and ordered another. She knew alcohol had little effect on his Engineered metabolism and he could shrug it off at will. "Let a vegetable fall into your orbit!"

"Isn't this pasta made from plants?" he parried. "Besides, I burn everything off."

"Good thing too," she said, enjoying her fish. "Dad used to say that Aunt Shasti's meal allowances were a separate line item on *Sidhe's* taxes, and I'll bet she didn't wolf down as much as you do."

"True," he replied, "but she was notably fond of expensive sweets. So, she was probably the more expensive. You know the type, slender girls who eat salads, fish, then head for the 10,000-calorie dessert menu."

"Hey," Daire said, looking up. "Isn't that Marguerite at the bar?"

Stellan looked up to see the dark-haired customs inspector, talking with a few people in similar uniforms. "Hmmm. One suspects this is more than a coincidence."

"Well, go up and talk to her," Daire said. "It looks like she's just out with some coworkers. She can join us for dessert if you like. Or you can have a drink with her at the bar."

"You won't feel I'm ditching you?"

"Nah, I'm your sister. You'll just owe me a fadeout in case the man of my dreams comes along."

"Fair enough," he said with a smile and stood.

Marguerite spotted him then, if she hadn't before, smiled and waved. Stellan waved back. He felt a little awkward approaching the group, hoping he wasn't butting in where he'd be underfoot. At times like this, his huge size felt like a handicap. There was no way for him to casually sidle up to the bar unobserved.

"Hello," he said to her, and nodded to the others.

"I hoped I might run into you," Marguerite said. She introduced the others, all of whom were older.

"This is Stellan, off the starship that landed today," Marguerite said.

He was pleased she didn't give his last name; it too often required a tedious explanation.

While he answered the usual questions about his home planet and ship, an older man named Fred, bought him a beer. The group chatted amiably before they gave the pair of them some space to speak privately. There was a shaded alcove with a high-top table; and they slipped away too.

"I hope this doesn't seem stalkerish," Marguerite said. "It's not like we don't have a date two nights from now."

"No, not at all," he replied. "It's a small port and a spacer heading out in a few weeks would be a poor choice for a stalker." He wondered if that was quite true.

She smiled. "You're very diplomatic for a young giant. How old are you, anyway?"

"Old enough," he replied.

"Does that come with a number? I don't want to be a stalker *and* a cradle robber."

"I'm twenty-one," he lied.

"Well not too bad," she said. There was a moment's pause. "You're not going to ask?"

"Father said never to inquire about a lady's age or weight."

"Ah, so you inherited his gift for tact," she said.

"I've never been accused of tact before," he replied, "but I'll take it. You seem to have some pleasant friends."

"I need them. I'm the youngest inspector, and Fred particularly has been teaching me the ropes. It's not easy days in Trade just now." She suddenly caught herself and looked about as if fearing to be overheard.

"I get that impression even from just landing, well…before landing," he replied. "The outgoing cargoes have some odd…similarities."

She glanced up at him. "I like smart men."

"And tactful."

A laugh burst out of her.

"Most of the concern," he said, dropping his voice and leaning toward her, "seems to center on a certain four-letter name."

"It does," she whispered back. "A name with a lot of connections, political, civil and other on this planet, Nole LLC."

"All of which seem to center on interstellar trade."

She nodded. "Interstellar and local. You might say they are trying to corner the market by fair means or foul. Watch yourself. Now that you're down on this planet you're going to find yourself right in the middle of it."

The buzz of conversation died down as two men walked into the dining room.

"Speak of the devil, that's Nole," Marguerite said, clearly alarmed, "the older one.

He studied the man. Slim, tall for a standard human, though a head shorter than he, Nole had whitish-gray hair cut close and a similar beard. His eyes were a watery blue. The suit he wore did not fit him well, but he had the air of a man who cared little for appearances. Goran Nole looked older than his recorded age of fifty-eight, enough so that Stellan wondered if he might be ill. The younger, very fit-looking man behind him looked like a bodyguard.

They were making a beeline for the table where Daire sat alone, savoring a dessert.

"Stay at the bar," Stellan said. "Do your best not to be seen or slip out the back and go home. I don't think it's good for you to be seen with me. I'll call you later." He stepped out of the alcove, startling people nearby who had neither heard nor seen him. He resembled his birth-mother in another aspect, when he wanted to be unseen, for all his size, he was good at it.

"You are Daire Fenaday?" he heard Nole say in a curiously accented voice as Stellan crossed the floor, each unhurried stride eating up the distance. The guard noticed him immediately and half-turned to face him, alarm on his face.

"I am," Daire replied, neither rising nor offering a hand. Her eyes flicked to him, knowing that he was coming. Knowing he would not have missed the change in the room.

Nole spotted him, and for a second, something like concern crossed the smooth old face. "Who are you?" Nole asked as Stellan came to stand next to his sister, facing the younger man. He ignored the question, and Nole, and simply stared down at the guard. The man was wearing a closely-tailored dark suit, buttoned in the front.

That means a gun in the small of the back, no other place to conceal a weapon of any size. Tight buttoned suit might be good for impressing wait-

resses, but as mother would say, he might as well have left his weapon home in a drawer. I can hit him three times before he can reach it at this distance.

His engineered body was pouring combat compounds into his body. He felt his vision, hearing, and sense of smell sharpen. His muscles quivered under his clothes, ready to explode into movement. Fear and concern vanished. Shasti had been designed to fight without fear, fast and deadly on a genetic level. That heritage controlled him now. He did not feel like an inexperienced teen facing men. He was a biological superman, totally certain of himself.

"I speak for *Wanderlust*," Daire said, coolly.

"Well then," Nole said, opting for a kind of avuncular tone. "It is you I wish to see. My name is Goran Nole. I am a merchant, miner and shipper. May I join you, Captain Fenaday?" He did not offer to introduce his aide.

"Please do," Daire said. She had been raised by a merchant prince and a Fleet Captain. If she felt any concern or discomfort, it did not touch her face.

Nole pulled out a chair and slid into it. The aide and Stellan remained facing each other.

"Will the young man be joining us?" Nole asked.

"I'll stand," Stellan said. His voice came out in a deep growl. Like every other aspect of him, it too was designed to intimidate. Anyone standing nearby edged away. People at other tables who could not, looked very unhappy. The aide licked his apparently dry lips.

"Tomas," Nole finally addressed the aide. "Go wait with the car. You're making the young giant nervous."

Tomas seemed used to obedience and faded away without a comment. As he did, Stellan took a heavy wood chair in his fingers, reversed it as if it weighed nothing and sat, leaning on the chair back.

"Well, that is more comfortable. You seem to have quite the body-guard there, young captain."

"This is my brother," Daire said, "Stellan Rainhell."

The last name caused the old man's eyes to flicker. "Ah, I see. Yes, a famous pair of names you two bear. One wonders why the scions of such a family are in a backwater like Serendip?"

"I follow the merchant trade as my father did," Daire said idly. "But as my ship's name doubtless conveys, I'm cursed with wandering feet and a desire to see the new and strange. Life on an established line didn't suit me. I aim to carve my own path."

"And you?" Nole asked, looking at him.

"I remove obstacles in my sister's path."

"Very effectively no doubt," Nole returned. "My, my, I did not expect to find two such self-assured young people in charge of such a small ship.

"We've been flying and handling ships since childhood," Daire returned. "Our family thought it necessary to prepare us for the path ahead almost from birth."

And you have no idea what that means in my case, old man, Stellan thought. *Shasti sent the best to teach me, when she did not do it herself. I'm not Denshi but do not take me lightly.*

"Quite," he said. "I am envious. My own start in life was not so well resourced. I clawed my way up on my own."

A warning to us not to take him lightly.

"Since you seem to know who I am," Nole began, "I will not beat about the bush. You both seem quite capable, which allows me to skip a number of tedious steps and assume that you have applied your intelligence since landing. I do so like dealing with intelligent people. It is shocking the number of dullards one meets in trade and commerce. Ah, the time that is wasted."

"By all means then," Daire said. "While I have not set on our next destination, we are very open to offers. I intend to take on some cargo on spec, common enough for small indies like us. But it's always welcome when there is outbound transport cargo as well."

"Excellent. Too bad you have landed here in such complicated times."

"Complicated?" Daire said, feigning ignorance.

Her ploy made the old man smile. "Let me make my meaning clear, young captain. You have landed in the middle of a trade war. The sides are long established, and I am winning. As an outsider, with no interest in the issues outside of a port you will seldom be in, I wouldn't expect this to concern you. For my part, however, well, I have enemies, and they would like to see me out of business. I, of course, feel the same about them. Unfortunately, my adversaries have chosen now to try and resolve things. Foolish, but what can you do?

"My firm is doing very well. We have cargoes to move, though I grant right now we couldn't fill up your freighter. But I have a proposition that has proven to be of considerable interest and profit to the other ships through here."

"You have my attention," Daire replied.

"You'll find what cargoes I have very lucrative. Both the ones I need shipped and material you may buy on spec. However, for whatever space you have left over, I will pay the going rate for break-bulk cargo space. You may fly partially empty, but your bank account will be quite full."

"An unusual arrangement, Mr. Nole," Daire said with a frown. "But surely one that not only involves me in your trade war but seems to have me taking sides. I cannot say that I care for the idea. As an independent trader, we dislike arrangements that bind or restrict trade for obvious reasons. Independents like us are often frozen out when such restrictions begin."

"A point doubtless, though a general one," Nole replied. "Did you plan to do a regular service here?"

"No, but nor have I ruled it out," Daire said. "*Wanderlust* is a new ship and follows no set route, but we are homeported on New Eire. This world is obviously on a jump route that goes back there."

"Though you are not associated with the Shamrock line," Nole asked, his eyes searching.

"I'm on good terms with the owner," Daire stated.

Nole gave a genial laugh. "No doubt, no doubt. Stupid of me to ask. Please forgive me."

"Think on my offer," Nole said, the genial manner sliding off him as easily as it went on. "Sometimes one has no options but to take sides, even where one did not desire or know of the conflict. Mostly, I want you to take your own side.

"I have cargoes going to any of the three jump points you can travel outbound to, or back to New Eire if you wish. And I am willing to pay for your empty hull space to remain empty. Ask about, if you haven't already. Nole, LLC is the largest concern on this world. We have friends in the highest and lowest of places.

"I don't care where you go or what you sell, so long as you're either carrying my cargo or no cargo," Nole said, his eyes narrow.

"You've made your offer clear," Stellan stated.

The old man locked eyes with him.

He's not afraid of me. This is a dangerous man.

"Good," Nole said, with an air of amusement. "Well, I will take my leave of you. Please do consider my offer, most carefully." He stood and left. Stellan watched him go and saw no sign of fear or tension in him.

The buzz of conversation resumed around them, and the pair received a lot of looks from nearby tables, not all of them friendly.

Daire looked at him. "Did you ditch your date?"

"I thought it might be unhealthy for her to be seen near us with Nole around. Though a suspicious part of my nature makes me wonder about this new friendship. Her actions imply that she is not a friend to Nole. It is possible that she is an agent of one of the other parties."

"Ah, good thinking. What do you make of Nole?"

"What you do. Old, tough, unafraid, used to getting his way, confident, but not arrogant. He claims to be self-made and thinks us just some rich kids playing at this. This is not a good enemy for us."

"He's an impediment to free trade."

"Daire, this is not our fight."

"Perhaps. But he may be right. Whatever we do we'll be taking a side."

"The other captains that were through here in independent ships took the deal."

"I looked them up. The first was the *Oriskany*, an old vessel that was being sold at the end of that voyage. She was part of a syndicate, not crew-owned. The other was a Dua-Denlenn vessel that does ply a semi-regular route through here. She's crew-owned but that ship is going in for an overhaul and her finances were strained. They probably couldn't afford to say no and won't be back here for a year or better."

"And we can take the risk?"

"Well, we don't have to say yes. Our coffers are full. This place is on one of the routes home. If Nole comes out on top, Serendib is going to be tough for traders facing a monopoly here."

He sighed. "Daire, why don't you just say that you don't like him, don't like what he's doing, don't like being told what to do in any event, and you are thinking of him as the first notch on your laser."

His sister laughed. "Wow, a laser notch? Been reading those old *Fortune's Starr* adventure books again?"

He merely shook his head. "You want to resemble your Aunt, in more than just traveling the stars. You want to make a name for yourself. I suspect she would warn you against such a thing, as if you'd listen."

"For now," Daire said, "no decisions. Let's just try and find out what's going on. I think you should call Marguerite and make it up to her for abandoning her, you heartless beast."

"If she's even still interested," Stellan said.

"Oh, she's interested," Daire said. "But for what set of reasons remains to be seen."

"I think I might," Stellan said. "After I see you safely back to the ship."

"Oh, come now."

"I mean it. Nole might decide that you make a better object lesson or might be more amenable to reason if you caught an elbow to the head. He didn't like me facing him down and I'll bet his bodyguard Tomas holds a grudge too."

Daire sighed. She knew him well enough to know that he would not yield on the point, and she wanted him to get back to Marguerite. The customs agent knew more of what was going on in Ujain than anyone else they had access to. She also doubted that her interest in them was strictly romantic.

"Very well, after we finish dessert," she said. She touched the pad and ordered coffee and an aperitif for herself and two servings of a fruit pie for him that promised to be just like an authentic Terran apple pie.

Afterward, Stellan carefully delivered his sister back to the ship. Once onboard, he had no worry for her. The ship was persona-locked to them and would not open for anyone else. He had installed the security devices that watched all approaches to the ship and the hatches himself. For good measure he let the ship's repair bot out and had it begin a circuit of the ship. It had no weapons but could summon port police at need. He made a promise to himself to find time to add at least a stunner to its onboard welder and to modify the welder into something more deadly.

If my sister starts collecting enemies, maybe I'll have to see about a combat crab robot.

He called Marguerite whose quick answer showed she'd been worried. As he suspected, she was grateful to duck away from Nole's presence and agreed to have a drink with him in a half-hour.

The evening is looking up.

CHAPTER FIVE

The evening with Marguerite started well and went up from there. The customs officer seemed to have friends and acquaintances in all the places they went. Stellan began to wonder if she was running for union rep or such.

"Or is she trying to show me off for some reason? It's happened before, a girl wanting to impress her friends or family, with the son of a wealthy merchant and two war heroes.

Stellan knew he was both good-looking and far stronger than any standard human, but both his parents and birth mother had long warned him against arrogance and conceit. For Shasti Rainhell, who was even stronger than he was, she called it the fatal disease of the Engineered, hubris. For his father, who had been born to wealth and learned of poverty the hard way, it was to not fall afoul of the disgusting habits of entitlement.

So he examined the situation dispassionately. It could be a mere port affair, common to all who shipped space. Or something more could be going on—for tonight he was content to be out with a pretty girl on the town. The fact that she seemed popular was only a plus.

They bar-hopped and danced at a club. Despite his Engineered grace and Lisa Fenaday's training of him, he still felt like a bit of a bear on a dance floor, but Marguerite's shining eyes were all the encouragement he needed. Late in the night, they ended up at her place.

For Stellan sex was still a new experience and for all the offers he'd had, he'd been careful of who he was with on New Eire. There were always too many eyes and ears, and everything followed him home. Here he enjoyed something akin to anonymity. It added something to the experience.

Marguerite, who it turned out was six years older, was clearly more experienced and delighted with being able to enjoy herself in an unrestrained fashion with him, doing things that would have left someone less strong gasping, or with pulled muscles. She was also patient in showing him what she liked and in learning what he did. They fell asleep with him tucked against her but without any of his heavy limbs resting on her body.

As usual, he did not sleep that long, but lay awake in a kind of peaceful quietude, unwilling to move and disturb her. It had been months since he'd last even kissed a girl, much less more, with all their preparations to leave. That and he'd not quite recovered from Thaliana, a passionate but somewhat unbalanced last girlfriend.

Marguerite was a woman and not a teen. There seemed to be a lot to recommend being with someone more mature. So far, anyway. He lay beside her and studied the nape of her neck; the gentle look of a face composed for sleep.

He also looked about the room, seeing well enough despite the dark. There was some inexpensive impressionistic art on the walls, locally produced, he was sure. One could have enough holos of the work of the ancient masters of Earth but what relevance would they have to a born colonial? There were photo-holos of what he assumed was her family. They were dimmed now but he remembered them from when he walked in. There were also the books associated with her work. Despite the oft-predicted demise of books, written media was still common for such things.

Other curious things dotted the room, stuffed animals and the like. The place was filled with flowers, vases, pottery. Both his mothers and sister were professional spacers and could not abide clutter. But it was better than Thaliana's, whose room looked like explosive decompression had hit it.

The sun rose and he stirred. Marguerite woke beside him. He was too big to slide out of a bed without waking her.

"Coffee?" she asked as she sat up.

"That would be great."

He freshened up while she made coffee and then they traded places. He just threw on his underwear. Even if she had a man's robe there it would be too small for him. The coffee proved to be excellent. He poured her a cup but unsure of how she liked it and left it black.

Marguerite came back out in a robe that came down to barely cover her pert butt. She smiled at the coffee and added cream and sugar then put an arm around him.

"Did I thank you for an excellent night?" she asked.

"No need, it was quite literally my pleasure as well."

"I hope you don't think I jump into the sack with every handsome spacer I see," she added with sideways glance at him.

"I don't, but it would be your business if you did. If it's of interest, I'm not casual about sex either."

"Hmmm, I like the sound of that, though it's not something one expects from a guy your age. Whatever that exact number is."

He smiled. "I'm told I was born old."

She laughed and walked back to the bed, stretching out languorously. He leaned back against a desk admiring the view.

"I can believe that," she replied. "You do have the manner of someone older. I've never met someone so young who was so sure of themselves. Well, no one who wasn't an ass or a poseur. Maybe it's your sheer size and how assuredly you move."

"Well, thank you. It's something I had to master young. I could knock someone sprawling or break things just by brushing against them, particularly anything delicate."

"Like your sister?"

Stellan chuckled. "Daire only looks delicate. She throws a wicked right hand though."

"Oh, at you?"

"Huh? Me? Never."

"What? Two siblings that didn't fight?"

He scratched his chin and sipped the coffee. "We've always been more like twins than like ordinary sibs. We were born hours apart and all my early memories are of us playing together. We must have quarreled some, I suppose, though I really don't remember. While she would roughhouse around with others, it was not something we did.

"No, she never swatted at me, but she's decked more than one boy for saying I wasn't her real brother. Though the last punch she threw was at one of my exes who was badmouthing me."

"She sounds very protective."

"She is and has Mom's temper without her restraint."

"Mom being Lisa Fenaday."

"Yes."

"Can't have been easy," she said.

"Mom managed it. It helps that she and Shasti are so close."

"And you with….Captain Rainhell?"

"Curiosity getting the better of you?"

"Well, I am female."

"Delightfully so."

He could tell by the questioning look on her face that she was still curious and well, it's not like they hadn't slept together.

"Daire is crazy about my birth mother, wanted to grow up and be just like her. While I am not close with Shasti, for Daire's sake, I've always been as easy about her as I can. It certainly makes the holidays easier."

"Again, admirable, not everyone could manage that level of maturity at any age."

"Thank you."

Marguerite seemed to study him for a few seconds as if making up her mind about something. "There's someone I would like you to meet."

Aha, now comes the truth. He leaned back against her counter and sipped the coffee.

"Key Zeong is his name. He's the CEO of Hulu Shipping. Also, he's the leader of the unofficial opposition to Nole's plans to turn Serendib into his fiefdom."

"And why would I want to meet this Zeong?" he asked idly.

Marguerite regarded him from her pile of pillows. With her long limbs and tousled hair, he had to admit she was quite the sight.

"I got the impression you and your sister didn't take kindly to being strong-armed by Nole."

"No," he admitted, "nor would we by anyone. But as traders we have both be flexible and know when to mind our business."

"But this is business," Marguerite said.

"Oh, this here?" he said, with his eyebrows raised with an ironic smile.

She laughed at him. "You *are* very old for your age. I like that. But I'm indulging myself here as well as passing a message along. I like you, Stellan. Not just because you're built like a god. You're smart and you seem good-natured."

"Because I'm not yelling in indignation about being used?" he said, the smile remaining in place.

"You'd be entitled to yell, or to not believe me, but I think you are too grown up for both. How old did you say you were again?"

"Oh, did I say?" he replied.

"Zeong can offer you cargos now and perhaps in the future. This is one of the main routes back to New Eire through this sector. Do you want Nole sitting astride it?"

"The idea of him sitting astride anything is somewhat off-putting."

"So, you'll meet Zeong?"

"I will bring your proposal to my Captain. She will decide."

"From what I have seen of her I think she'll be interested. She doesn't seem to ruffle easily."

"No. Daire is rarely afraid of anything, even when she should be."

"What a nice brother you are." She gave a lazy smile. "Put that coffee down and come back to bed so I can manipulate you some more."

"Ah, I feel myself slipping back under your spell."

They made love again. After, he took her out for breakfast at a small bistro with excellent food and a shaded porch that faced the river. She had a night shift, so they were not pressed for time. It was as pleasant a morning as he'd spent for a long time, even if he suspected Marguerite was an agent for a power intent on reaching Daire and him.

They parted at the doorway, after arranging to go to a concert together. Marguerite did not mention Zeong again, which to him proved again that she far cleverer than most.

He took his time heading back to the ship, enjoying the sun on his back, and watching to see if anyone was following him. No one appeared to be, and he was passed back in through Port Security without incident. The sun was high, though a cool wind from the ocean dispelled the heat as he gained the support gantry for his ship. The ship's bot that he had set on patrol last night was still on its circuit. He patted the small machine, painted as was customary in the same colors as the ship, on its top as he walked in.

About him, vehicles, robots and personnel were busy with the myriad of tasks involved with keeping a spaceport operating. He scanned to see if anyone or anything was taking an unusual interest in him or the ship, but all the activity made that difficult. Finally, he just shrugged and placed a hand on the screen behind the airlock. It glowed recognition and advised that Daire was aboard and on the bridge.

He made his way up the various companionways, grateful that *Wanderlust* was not a tail-sitter, whose interior would adjust from horizontal to vertical. The J-class was designed to be as simple as a starship could be, which wasn't very.

He walked in to find Daire at her boards, doubtless studying trade opportunities. She glanced up at him with a grin. "Well, well I was about to call the Port Police and put out a 'jumped ship' on you."

"And yet here I am," he replied.

"And yet was jumping something I bet," she said severely. "While I was here lonesome, cheerless and slaving away on our future."

"Oh, please," he said. "The only reason you're alone is because you wish to be, and you're never happier than when playing with your ship. Besides, I've already exceeded my quota for being manipulated by women today." He quickly filled her in on Marguerite's offer of an introduction to Zeong.

"So," Stellan said, "there was more to Marguerite's attention than my good looks."

Daire gave him a sympathetic look. "Yes, apparently Zeong thought it would be wise to have a young and attractive contact in Customs. Though for the record, I think your good looks won her over as soon as she stepped on board."

Stellan put his head back and laughed. "Oh, sister, were you worried that my ego was that frail? No, I imagine one form of seduction or other will likely be offered to us frequently on our voyages. This one was rather fun. I even suspect she likes me, but she's surely smart enough not to weigh a passing affair with a trader she might not see for a long time, if ever, against her interests here."

"Well so long as your feelings aren't hurt," Daire said. "I mean there haven't been that many girls, have there? You're sounding kinda jaded there."

"In terms of relationships? Well, you know both of those girls. Noomi was brief and wonderful, but her family moved, and we were too young. The other was the disaster that we both remember too well. They say every man has one where he rides the flaming wreck into the ground. Thaliana was mine."

"Yeah, I don't feel bad about socking her in the nose," Daire said, "psycho liar that she was."

"There have been some...other encounters where I...learned things. I also learned that sometimes sex is simply about sex, or even about manipulation. I learned to enjoy one and not be misled by the other."

"And love?" she asked.

He gazed back at her, a little surprised by the serious turn of the conversation.

"Not that lucky," he said, "time, place and person never lined up."

"Yeah," she said. "Same for me. Plus, I always knew where I wanted to go. Ship masters don't settle young. It makes no sense. I wouldn't start anything serious, because I always knew I was going to lift off for parts known and unknown. It wouldn't be fair. Also, there were too many gold-hunters among the boys looking at me."

"I knew that," he added. "And I knew that you would need me to watch your back. Besides, long term stuff, well it's long term, marriage and all that. Hell, we'll just turn twenty in three months.

"Beyond that…well, our parents came from a great love story. Not everybody gets one like that. Not everyone runs to the horizon with their true love. So, you don't have to worry about me running off with Marguerite."

"Hah, the little spaceport vixen, I wouldn't care if you spanked her bottom pink."

"I'll take that under advisement," Stellan returned. "More to the point, do we meet this Zeong?"

"Oh," Dare said, a wicked light kindling in her eyes. "We do that. We surely do that much."

"Just to spite Nole?"

"Profit, dear brother, we look at profit and reputation."

"Is that all?"

"Well and the fun," she said innocently, "after all why did we come out here?"

He sighed.

CHAPTER SIX

Stellan contacted Marguerite on her private comm and made arrangements to meet this Key Zeong.

"Why don't you take your sister to the Landing Museum on First-in Street," Marguerite said. "It wouldn't be unusual for a visitor to drop in there. There are entrances on two streets. Come in the front and exit on Bleeker Street at 17:00 local time. There will be a white car van in front marked Deeb's Delivery. Get in that."

The siblings, after recording the details of the clandestine meeting on their ship's AI for insurance against any malfeasance, headed out separately. As always, it would be easier for Daire to fade into the crowd, but there were assassin's tricks that Shasti had taught him for staying unobserved and checking for a tail. He used many of them: slipping through buildings and wearing a reversible jacket and sunshields. Because he was so symmetrical in scale, he did not look as large as he was unless he was standing next to others. So he avoided people as he made his way to the Landing Museum, a staple of all colonies trying to engender a sense of pride in their own history, whether that history deserved pride or not.

He arrived at the museum, a rambling, white, three-story building. Casting an eye about he didn't see Daire, so he went in alone.

He saw the usual within, a model of the colony ship that filled most of a two-story room, one of its original small landing craft, preserved in its yellow and white colors. There were also the usual holos of various notables with recorded speeches. To his surprise, he saw a burnt and battered Confed *Tunnan* missile fighter. Apparently, the atmospheric fighter had driven off a Conchirri scout all by itself. Quite an accomplishment in something that was little more than a flying rocket battery. The exhibit honored a Lieutenant Yang who'd fought the scoutship before landing her badly damaged fighter and almost succumbing to her own wounds.

He caught Daire coming out of the bathroom out of the corner of his eye. Lavatories were always a good place to blend in with the crowd. She spotted him immediately, checked her comm for the time and gestured at the exit. He nodded and followed her down the broad stairs at the back of the building.

Daire and Stellan slid into the back of the promised white delivery van, its windows polarized so that no one could see in. The driver, a Morok, pulled away from the curb and into the evening traffic without speaking. In a few minutes it was obvious that the driver was a professional and was changing lanes and levels to make sure they weren't followed.

But a port city like this doesn't have a lot of underground roads, can't do much about drones and satellites.

But there he underestimated their host, because soon after they pulled into an underground garage. "When I stop next to a blue van," the Morok said, in a guttural accent. "You change vehicles. A half-hour from now you'll move on."

He pulled up next to a van that waited with an open side door. The spacers jumped from the original van, which wasted no time heading for the exit. They entered the blue van, its door sealing behind them. A woman sat behind the wheel. She glanced at them.

"Make yourselves comfortable back there," she said. "We're not going anywhere for a while, unless I get the sense that they're onto us."

Stellan and Daire settled in. Both knew better than to try and chat up the middle-aged woman driving the vehicle. She ignored them both. Eventually, she started the vehicle and headed for one of the exits. She too seemed to be watching for a tail but did not use as many tricks as the first vehicle. They drove for fifteen more minutes before pulling around the back of an old building that looked like an ordinary diner.

"Go in through the back," the driver said, "and don't be slow. You'll be met. I'll be waiting for when you are done."

They got out on Stellan's side and two strides took him to the door which he opened for Daire, sliding in behind her. A small Asian woman stood inside and gestured for them to follow. The woman led them to a small room, seated in it was an Asian man, wearing a worker's overall. His hair was dark with only a little grey and his eyes were sharp.

"Welcome," he said. "I'm Key Zeong." He didn't offer to shake hands, but customs varied. Behind them the woman closed the door. Zeong gave them both an appraising look which Daire returned. Stellan kept his face an emotionless mask, which would encourage Zeong to focus on Daire.

"So," Zeong said. "The children of Robert and Lisa Fenaday and Shasti Rainhell. Sorry, there doesn't seem to be an easier way to say that."

"We're used to it," Daire returned.

"I'm impressed. You're still teenagers but have master's license and your own ship. I suppose you were born to the trade, as they say."

"As they do," Daire said. "Your family has been in trade for as long as anyone seems to have cared to keep a record of it."

He nodded, looking pleased. "Indeed, legitimate trade and, if the truth be known, Grandfather was something of a smuggler."

"What trade family hasn't moved the occasionally illicit cargo?" she said.

Zeong looked at Stellan. "No need to play the strong silent type. No one would doubt your strength looking at you, but Margie says you're quite erudite."

"Daire speaks for *Wanderlust*," Stellan said, liking neither the nickname nor the implication, expected as it was, that Marguerite reported their conversations to Zeong.

"As you wish," Zeong said, "but no need to growl at me. I am nothing to her but a side-employer and she was quite discreet in her reports. She probably likes you better than me, anyway."

Daire snorted, but Stellan maintained his stony face.

"You wanted to see us," she prompted.

"Indeed. I, and the consortium of fellow merchants and exporters I represent are very glad to see you. You seem to be as clever as I have heard and I'm sure you have been researching, Nole, myself and other leading merchants probably since before you landed.

"As Nole himself probably put it to you, you've landed in the middle of an all-out trade war. Friend Nole has been working his way up to this for a decade at least. He's bankrolled politicians, a news agency and spread bribes around liberally. Let's also say that he's had a couple of the unwary made examples of. He wants those he buys to stay bought."

"Interesting," Daire said. "He seems to be winning. His candidate is in Government House, and investigations of his organization have been stymied. His bought dogs in the media lie with impunity about anyone who gives him trouble."

"Ah, you've noticed," again came the quick grin. "He's good, the old bastard, and he's decided this year to throw his remaining assets into the fray. Basically, he's trying to monopolize off-world trade. If we cannot ship goods and cargo, he gets that business, and we get extinct, or get crappy jobs working for him. I'll emigrate before I do that."

"You've succinctly explained all the reasons why I shouldn't provoke Nole, and shouldn't side against him," Daire said. "Now tell me what reason there would be for me to not take his deal and rat you out."

Zeong laughed. "Yep, just as clever as I heard. Well, beyond altruism there is the fact that we are on your most direct trade route back to New Eire."

"We're an indie," Daire said. "We don't plan a regular service, and we may not be in this port twice in five years."

"Oh, I think not," Zeong said. "I'm sure your family wants to see more of you than that. But be that as it may, we are prepared to better Nole's offer: trade goods you can buy with no-interest loans, cargoes at premium, not standard rates. In addition to cargo and goods, we'd be prepared to offer you stock in each of the companies of the consortium."

"Giving me an incentive to make sure those businesses don't go belly up?" Daire said. "You're pretty clever yourself, Mr. Zeong."

"Oh, feel free to call me, Key," he said.

"Well, Key," she said. "That's all well and good. But that involves me in a trade war not of my making, against a formidable adversary."

Zeong leaned forward. "Nole is all in on this, trying to finish all of his rivals in one fell swoop. But he's been spending money like water for years. He started with quite a war chest but right now, he's leveraged to the hilt. War is expensive and uncertain, always more than the people who start them think. We, on the other hand, have had to sit on a lot of cash and goods. If we can get a shipload of goods offworld, to wherever it is that you're heading next…well what will sell, will sell, and transshipment fees may make us only break-even, but if it breaks Nole, then it will be worth it."

"Still sounds like a risky plan for beginning merchants like us," Daire said.

"It probably would be, if you were just some kids that had cobbled together some money to buy an old worn-out tub. But you're not. We both know you have backing that you can summon if you get in trouble.

He glanced at Stellan. "The backup you could call would give anyone pause. There are some very quiet places in space that Rainhell's come through."

Stellan nodded.

"But beyond the get out of jail free card you could play," Zeong said, "is your desire to make a name for yourself."

Daire blinked and put a hand to her chest in mock horror. "Why, me? Whatever do you mean?"

"Yes, you," he retorted. "I don't know you well, but I don't have to. I can simply see what's in front of me. You could have stayed on New Eire and had every luxury imaginable. Or, talented as both of you are, it wouldn't have been difficult for your father to justify an early captaincy on a substantial merchant-liner for either of you. Hell, as if he had to even justify it to anyone. Shamrock is a private company and he's the majority owner.

"Bet you hate the idea of trading on your parent's names, or at least you do, Captain Fenaday. You both carry big names and want to show that you are your own people, and it isn't being handed to you."

Daire and Stellan traded glances.

"Doesn't take a genius to see it," Zeong said, waving a hand. "I've been in trade thirty years and the first thing I learned is that it's more important to be able to read people than a cargo manifest."

"Let's say your instincts are serving you well," Daire replied. "You've got a consortium. I don't know who is in it, but I will before I agree to anything. But even with what I guess, you should be able to match Nole with your combined assets. If you can hold your group together."

"Fair enough," Zeong said. "I can arrange a meeting with the principal partners later this week. They're the ones like me that are in Nole's gunsights and are too big for him to swallow whole. Also, they're the ones that he hates so much that he'll never make a deal with them. One of the things I can't respect about Nole. He never can seem to separate business and his personal life. Very unprofessional."

"Why only a select few?" Stellan asked. "Even allowing for security and secrecy, it should be possible for us to meet with all our prospective partners."

"You two are pretty amazing," Zeong said, crossing his arms and sitting back. "You must be the kind of teenagers they have in Hell. But you lack experience and Nole's way in the lead in that area. Someone in the consortium will betray us. Either there's someone here in hock up to his eyeballs with Nole, desperately trying to stave off some personal disaster, or there's someone who will wake up at three in the morning with a quivering gut and run to Nole to cut a deal, so they end up on the winning side.

"Without a clear route to success, I can't completely trust my partners. I need your buy in to make sure that they see a winning hand. The less the weaker players know, the less risk there is."

"I hadn't thought that way," Daire muttered.

Neither had I, and I'm supposed to. Shasti would have. Treachery was second nature to someone brought up in Denshi. Didn't she always warn me about hubris, the downfall of the Engineered?

"What can we do about it?" Daire asked.

"I take it I have your interest," Zeong asked. The glitter in his eyes said he knew he did.

"You do. You weren't far off," Daire said. "I intend to cut my own trail across the stars with my brother's help. There are things I want to do and to be. None of those involve taking a knee before Nole. I can use friends in trade, and you seem to be offering me many."

"That I can promise you," Zeong said. "Help us out now and we will remember you for the future. Having favors owed to the scions of a powerful trading company is an excellent investment. We would look forward to many years of a profitable exchange. Shamrock and your parents have a reputation for remembering those who are helpful to them."

"I don't speak for Shamrock, or my father," Daire said. "You're just dealing with us."

"Of course," Zeong said dryly.

"Back to what you said," Daire added. "What can we do about security? If Nole gets wind of our working with you..."

"For now, we keep our eyes and ears open," Zeong said. "I know all the other traders and I have ears in half their staff, just as I suspect they have some in mine." He handed Daire a data crystal. "Encryption and contact information for a channel between us. Also a list of the others working with me. You give me some idea of what cargoes you're interested in on spec and where you plan to go. We'll make the arrangements."

"I'll be in touch," Daire said.

"Looking forward to doing business with you, Captain. My driver will take you to somewhere you can get public transit back to the spaceport. The less you are seen with anyone on Serendip, the less chance Nole gets suspicious.

CHAPTER SEVEN

Stellan turned to Daire after they returned to *Wanderlust*. "I was embarrassed that Zeong had to remind me of something Shasti drilled into me from childhood, always suspect a traitor. She never forgot the mutiny over Enshar that almost killed her and Dad.

"Zeong is right, we should suspect a traitor in his group, but he's also one of the chief suspects for that traitor. Not to sell us out to Nole though. While it's not impossible, I don't see Zeong ending up as anyone's lieutenant, nor do I think Nole would trust him. But this coalition that Zeong put together is mostly to save his own Hulu Group, and the other merchants are holding on hoping to be dragged to shore."

"And you're afraid that if Zeong makes it to shore," Daire continued, "he'll turn on us. Or blame us if the whole venture doesn't work out."

"Both or either," Stellan said. "We need a counterforce here. Someone whose interest aligns with taking down Nole but could protect us from Zeong or any other traitor, basically to keep the coalition members to their promises."

Daire thought for a second. "The logical place to hunt for them is among Nole's enemies. Chief among those would be the ex-Prime Minister Zuba."

"Yes," Stellan said, "but not directly. Zuba is too high profile. If we head for those political heights, we'll get spotted."

"The former DA," Daire said, snapping her fingers, "Esmerelda Burgos. When I told Dad that Serendip was to be our first port of call, he pulled up his old records. He planeted here twice in his privateer days. Said he had some dealings with a local lawyer named Burgos. The name stuck with me, Esmerelda isn't a common name, not on New Eire anyway."

"Does she owe Dad any favors?"

"No, not after all this time anyway. But more to the point, Nole bankrolled the Freedom Caucus and accused Zuba's administration of corruption. Might even be true, I don't care. Burgos had been investigating Nole. With the change of administration—all of a sudden, she's out of office, the investigation closed."

He stroked his chin. "I see. Burgos would be our back door to Zuba, and a counterbalance to Zeong, or at least another source of intelligence that we could use to check if anyone is lying or setting us up. Pity she's not still the DA."

"Yeah. But no one in power now would have any motivation to help us."

A few minutes of checking showed that Burgos was still living in the capitol and had returned to the law practice she'd been at before Zuba tapped her to be the capitol's DA. Given the size and location of the colony, she had been effectively the lead law enforcement official for the planet.

"I think I'd better make the contact," Daire said, "I'll attract less attention, especially in civies or a travel cloak."

"Agreed."

Daire called and made an appointment to see Burgos the next day. There was no point in Daire concealing her identity, the communication system would inform Burgos of who she was and where she was calling from. Still, she was circumspect about the details, only saying that Burgos had been recommended to her with regard to a trade issue.

The next morning found her slipping away from *Wanderlust* in civilian clothes, looking like any other spacer going into town. She carried a small satchel with her but no weapon. Serendip might not be an inner planet, but it was Confed territory. Daire took the slidewalk out of the port then the tram downtown to the shopping district.

Daire spent some time ducking in and out of stores, seeing if she was being followed. Satisfied she wasn't, she stopped in a bathroom stall and pulled out a light travel cloak. She donned the gray cloak and put its filmy gauze cover over her face, exposing only her eyes. She stepped back into the street, heading for Burgos' office.

Covered by the cloak, she could have been a small member of most of the humanoid races of the Confederation, or one of the human colonies with some taboos about appearing in public. It was considered both rude and provincial to stare at someone in the garment, so Daire became effectively invisible. She walked the concrete streets of the city, surrounded by older two-and three-story buildings, dating from the first landing period. Serendip was not old as colonies went, but many of the structures contained prefab elements and some showed their age.

Further from the spaceport and its noise were the newer buildings: both residential and offices. None went above six stories. There was no need, as land was still cheap and plentiful on the huge island.

Traffic of various sorts moved by her, mostly silent and electrical. Overhead flew the occasional flitter, helicopter and light aircraft. Once, she saw someone in a jetpack, something that would never have been allowed in an inner world city.

Eventually, she stood in front of a four-story building in sight of Government House, which sat on the first set of hills toward the interior. The metal-and-glass façade bore the name she was looking for: *Vassilios, Burgos and Gralt LLC.* She entered the lobby and paused before the AI attendant, a small blue machine of Morok design, and identified herself. The machine noted her arrival and cleared her for the elevator. Once inside, she took off the travel cloak and stuffed it back in the satchel.

A Morok attendant greeted her at the elevator door. The blue-skinned, goblin-like female invited her to follow. They went down a hallway of glassed office spaces filled with associates doing research and into a conference room, with a finely-made wooden table and a view of the mountains. Daire was offered coffee, tea or water, opted for tea, and was advised Burgos would be in shortly.

Burgos entered by the other door a minute later. Daire rose to meet her, sizing up the other woman as she did so. Burgos was middle-aged, dark-eyed, with dark brown hair drawn back in a simple style. She wore a well-tailored navy-blue suit and was taller than Daire, who was used to that. She looked every inch the powerhouse lawyer her resume indicated.

"Captain Fenaday," the woman said, in a well-trained voice. "It's a pleasure to meet you. I'm Esmeralda Burgos."

"And you as well," Daire returned.

"Please sit," Burgos said. "I see you have tea. I think I'll join you in that."

The women seated themselves at the round table and Burgos poured tea into the fine China set.

"I met your father twice," Burgos said. "Back during his incredible quest to recover your mother. A very formidable man. One I believe a number of people underestimated, some of whom didn't live to regret it."

"My mother and father are a great love story," Daire replied, "albeit an unusual one. He was never more determined or dangerous than in relation to Mom, or Aunt Shasti."

"Yes," Burgos said, with a slight smile. "I didn't meet Shasti Rain-hell, she wasn't with the ship yet. But if any of what I've heard about her is true, she is a class by herself. My estimation of your father's skills and luck were vastly increased when I learned that he survived the fact that you and your brother were born hours apart from the two women."

Daire chuckled. "I've always said that Dad would have made the best diplomat in the galaxy. Fortunately for him, Mom and Aunt Shasti are dear friends, Shasti's pregnancy was latent for twelve years and triggered by her being around my mother. Mom felt there was no issue for her to deal with there."

Again came the thin smile. "I doubt it was quite that easy."

"Well, if it wasn't at first, it became more so. Aunt Shasti moved to Olympia and married Mikhail Vaughn."

"And now runs that world's security forces and all its interactions with the Confederation. Meanwhile her husband is standing for the Presidency," Burgos finished.

"You're well informed."

"I have an abiding interest in politics."

"Yes," Daire said. "You're the former District Attorney?"

"Emphasis on the former," she said.

"Yes, the new minister, Oskar Cretan and his party swept Prime Minister Zuba out."

"And me with it."

"And of course this was all engineered by Goran Nole: the political war chest, the alliance with the sleazy Lupus News, all of it.

Burgos sat back and sipped her tea, regarding Daire across the gold-rimmed cup. "Now you seem to have developed an interest in politics."

"What good merchant doesn't?" Daire asked, "if only in self-defense."

"And I suspect that this meeting has some other purpose than a courtesy call on a mere acquaintance of Robert Fenaday's."

Daire nodded and sipped her own tea. "Stellan and I run our own trading company. I don't have to of course; I could have had a nice comfy slot in the Shamrock line."

Burgos studied her. "But you decided you didn't want to be 'Daddy's little girl' who got a sinecure for her birthday."

"Got it in one," Daire said. "I can't and won't deny that I've been set up with a ship and resources through that connection, but we came out here to make our own way and make our own names. I don't think that I came out to the stars with naivete, or childish ideals, but I didn't expect my first port of call to be in the middle of a trade war. Nor did I expect to be all but threatened by Goran Nole if I didn't take a specific cargo, or more, if I shipped anyone else's cargo."

Burgos grimaced. "All but threatened is the operative expression. I imagine he didn't do that in any express or verifiable way."

"Of course not," Daire said. "If he were that stupid, he wouldn't have been able to arrange a political upset and sweep Zuba out of power."

Burgos' eyes glittered. "Just so."

"I don't like Mr. Nole," Daire said. "I don't like being threatened or told what to do with my own ship."

"Why?" Burgos demanded. "What do you care? He's doubtless offered a good price on cargos or just to take off empty. He did with the previous two ships through here."

"Oh, I could take his offer," Daire said. "It would be the smart thing to do. Rake up the easy money and fly away. But I didn't come out here to crawl from star-to-star with my tail between my legs. If I side with Nole, I become nobody. When and if I come back through here, I'll just be his bought dog.

"Now if I can find allies…"

"Allies?" Burgos prompted.

"We've been approached by Key Zeong," Daire said. "He's cobbled together a coalition of lesser merchants to oppose Nole. He's the reason that Nole is so overstretched, battling him, not mention paying off politicians, or buying up ship space."

"If you ask me," Burgos said, "Zeong's only a marginal improvement on Nole. Not so power mad perhaps but…"

Daire smiled. "Zeong advised me to watch for signs of treachery within our little group. I decided that was good advice and to apply it to him first. I need a source of intelligence that's not under control of Zeong *or* Nole. I need somebody who they would both be afraid of."

"And you think that's me."

"I think it's Zuba and you."

She nodded. "And you were too smart to try and approach the former Prime Minister."

"I'd be spotted. Also, I know that you were pretty far along in your investigation of Nole. If I can get a shipload of cargo out of here, well, according to Zeong, he's close to the breaking point financially. If his power is broken, is it too much to hope that there's a chance for Zuba to stage a comeback? Then you could nail Nole's hide to your office wall."

"That would seem for us to be banking a lot on you, Captain Fenaday. While you are out of two lines of very dangerous and influential people, you are, in yourself and no insult intended, merely the extremely young, novice skipper of a small trade vessel."

"If you think that is all I am," Daire said slowly, "and you have some better option available to you, then you should probably turn this deal down. Doubtless your firm has plenty of business coming in through the door."

Burgos snorted. "I see. I'm paid back for my little slight. You're right, a law firm with undesirable political connections gets frozen out of a lot. My partners have doubtless considered whether they'd be better off with one less name on the door. If it wasn't for the fact that Gralt has all the Morok clients sewed up, we'd be in serious trouble.

"Nole and I dislike each other on a personal basis too. He takes every chance he gets to stick it to me and the firm when he can. Can't say that I wouldn't like to get him under subpoena and on the stand. With Zeong's help, I might be able to at least pull his business licenses, or some of them.

"But that's me and I can't speak for Zuba. Politicians play the long game. The current plague of deregulation and conservatism is bucking the trend. He may prefer to wait until the brass ring comes around again."

"That doesn't sound like the sort of man who strives for high office," Daire said. "And will that brass ring come around in time for him? Zuba's not young. A fresh face might appeal to the voters even in his own party. Why back a horse that lost the last matchup?

"I'm not looking for Zuba to do anything until after we lift off with the merchant's cargo and contracts. Then Zeong and the other merchants will have enough money to hang on for the next ship. That provides an opportunity for Zuba to make his comeback when Cole's bankroll won't be available to the Freed World Caucus. If you can work some financial pressure on the banking side—audits, clarifications on Nole's collateral, etc., it wouldn't take much to start the financial avalanche. I'm sure you have other political dirt on Prime Minister Cretan. It might not have been enough during the election—now could be a different situation.

"My father, when he was training us to fight, always said, 'your enemy is never more vulnerable than when he goes flat out to finish you.' Nole's been operating in finishing mode for the better part of year now. If he doesn't finish his enemies now, then he's vulnerable."

"A very impressive analysis. What would you want from me?" Burgos said.

"Zuba's implicit support," Daire said, "and your active backing. I need someone local to keep an eye on our new partners and to make them think twice about selling us out. You'll know who we're working with better than I, and who can be trusted and how far. Zeong will also be careful of screwing with us if he knows we're connected."

"I'm not the DA anymore," Burgos said. "I don't have police or subpoena powers."

"I'm sure you left behind a lot of friends who don't like how this came out, not to mention living with Castro and Nole calling the shots. There's a lot you can do or access—unofficially."

"I may end up being more of a scarecrow than a real threat to anyone," Burgos grumbled.

"That might be all we need."

Burgos sat and thought while Daire refilled her tea, which had gone cold.

"If we're going to do this," Burgos said, "then we're going to do it legally and in proper form. You'll sign a client agreement on behalf of your ship for consultation on trade issues. You'll put up ten thousand credits, which is our standard fee for such an arrangement. That will give us attorney-client privilege. I'll want a full list of who is in your little cabal. Some of them may have done work with the firm and I won't be able to investigate those, but Zeong has never used us, so that shouldn't be an issue. You and your brother will be my only clients of record, so I won't owe the rest of them a thing.

"I'll draw up the papers personally," Burgos added, "and have them sent to your ship for a signature. There will be an invoice with it. After your sign and pay, it will upload an encrypted channel to my office and my personal com.

"I can't promise anything with Charles…Mr. Zuba but I will talk with him and put him in the know. If he's in, he'll begin prepping to take advantage should Nole's situation change rapidly."

"Excellent," Daire said. She took her comm out of her pocket. "Let me send you a list of Zeong's group so far. More as I learn it."

Burgos gave her a code and Daire sent the encrypted information. "Okay, you're a client as of this moment, subject to your signing the forms."

"Excellent."

"I'll bring myself up to speed and brief you on this crew as soon as I can. Meanwhile, I assume you want to get out of here without being observed."

"For now," Daire said. "Later, it will pay to advertise we have your backing, but no point in giving away information today."

"Good," Burgos said. They both rose and shook hands. Burgos tapped a screen on the desk com, while Daire resumed her travel cloak. A moment later, the same Morok assistant who'd led her in, appeared at the door.

"Marish," Burgos said, "please take our client here down the fire stairs. Your car is in the garage below, right?"

"Yes, in my spot."

"Good, drive Captain Fenaday here back to the spaceport. She'll choose where to get out but look for a location that's private. Got it?"

"Got it," Marish said. "This way please, Captain."

Marish led her down the stairwell at the back. Daire was pleased the Morok didn't try to make small talk. They hopped in the woman's nondescript vehicle and motored back to the spaceport. Marish seemed to have a destination in mind and Daire didn't question her, figuring she knew the area better. The Morok pulled up to a spot between the trams and commercial arrival under a shaded overpass.

"Will this do?"

"Couldn't be better," Daire said and slipped out, settling the mask across her face.

The area was full of pedestrians, travelers and workers, even a few other people in travel cloaks. Daire didn't feel she'd attracted any attention as she walked to the secure entry to the spaceport section. Overhead, an airliner rumbled into the sky and a pair of helicopters buzzed over. The AI noted her pass and the guard, a Drisnian, barely glanced at her and she was in, heading for the *Wanderlust*.

CHAPTER EIGHT

Daire settled herself for the call to Nole. *First lure your enemy into a false sense of security.*

She called the Nole Trade offices, where as usual, there was the frustrating interval of wading through AIs and other flunkies whose sole reason for existence was to stop you from talking to the boss. But the names Fenaday and *Wanderlust* worked wonders. In only minutes, she was looking at Nole's bewhiskered face and watery blue eyes.

"Good day, Captain Fenaday. It's a pleasure to hear from you."

"I'm glad that's the case," she replied. "I called to take you up on some of your offers."

"Well in that case, it's an even better day. What may this humble merchant do for you?"

"Well, let's take them in order of importance. The offer you made to the prior captains is of interest to me. I don't want to ship any of your cargo, that's too much like taking sides in your local trade war. But if you want to pay for my holds to leave empty, well, that's your affair."

"Sensible," he conceded. "You have only the smallest stake in what goes on here."

More than you think, you old vampire, and the stake I have may well end up in your heart.

"But you said there was something else?" he added.

"Where I go next is not yet decided, nor would you care, since I'm not going to move any physical cargo for you. But I am interested in buying some precious metals from Nole LLC, platinum, lithium—"

"All the ones that would have value in machinery and refining other metals," Nole said with a smile.

"Of course," Daire said. "Gems and gold travel well and don't take up much space. There are planets far less gifted with mineral wealth than yours."

"Excellent thinking," Nole said.

That began the haggling over the entire arrangement. Nole did not drive that hard a bargain, to her surprise.

I'm probably the last ship he will expects to deal with before he establishes a monopoly here. He wants this done, and I'm only a relatively minor piece on this board. But a pawn can kill a king.

"You are an astute trader," Nole said finally, "or perhaps I am merely too old to contend with such a fiery and clever opponent. I'll have the contract drawn up and sent to your ship."

"Send it to my local counsel," Daire said, letting the bomb drop. "Esmerelda Burgos."

The old man froze and for a moment Daire had the thrill of knowing she had completely surprised her adversary.

"Burgos," he said, his face looking as if he had bit into a lemon thinking it an apple. "How is it that you came up with that...person?"

Daire feigned innocence. "Burgos has had a relationship with my family since my father operated the *Sidhe* out of this world. He asked me to look her up and throw her some business if I could. House Fenaday remembers favors done, and she was helpful to Dad when few were."

"I see," Nole said.

"Is there some issue?" Daire asked. "I was planning on a standard contract."

Nole gave her a somewhat contemptuous look. *I know you know.*

"No," he finally said. "Not for me. I will send the proposal to her. On its signed return, the credits will be posted to your account through the Confed Spaceport Terminus."

"You are a clever young lady," he continued, "be careful that you do not end up being too clever for your own good. Fair voyaging." With that he clicked off.

Oh, I am clever indeed, and you will rue taking me lightly, old man.

Stellan met Daire outside the bar that Zeong had chosen for their second clandestine meeting. Daire had traveled from the spaceport in her travel cloak, checking her trail and changing robocabs. Stellan had been staying at Marguerite's place, and slipped out with her help in the early morning hours.

Daire yawned as her brother stepped from the shadows to greet her. As an Engineered, he functioned with less sleep than a standard human, and rarely seemed tired. She, on the other hand, was missing her bed.

"Zeong," he said by way of greeting, "has been watching too many spy videos."

"Hah," she said. "He's afraid of leaving tracks in the planetary net and what may get recorded."

"That's what we have encryption for," he replied.

She shrugged. "He feels safest face to face. Also why he was so relieved I didn't insist on meeting the others in his little cabal. Three people can keep a secret if two of them are dead. He'll tell who he needs to, and it'll be safer than our making that decision even with Burgos filling in the blank spots."

They walked into the bar, Stellan leading, as he preferred, though she could see nothing around his towering form. It seemed they were indeed expected. The bartender nodded and gestured with his head that they should go to the back. It was after hours, but a few serious drinkers were still present, huddled in small groups talking low over their liquor. That is, unless they were Zeong's men. Most of them chose to ignore the giant and the pretty girl who'd followed him in, which to Daire was much more suspicious than if they had eyed the pair.

A hostess who had seen better days and better dives than this waited for them. She too was silent and merely led them to a small room in the back. There Zeong squatted at a table decorated with a bottle of some clear liquor, looking like a yakuza from an old movie.

They sat next to him.

"Drink?" he asked, holding up the bottle. Stellan shook his head. Daire, feeling the need to be the more diplomatic, nodded. Zeong poured her a shot.

"What is it?" she asked

"Baijiu," he replied. "Hold on to your tonsils."

Daire knocked back her drink, the fiery liquid burned but she let no discomfort show on her face. "Another?"

Zeong grinned and poured for them both. He took his shot, then poured another to keep up with her, but niceties observed, he let the glass sit on the table.

"I've lined up everyone on our side and weeded out some of the unreliable," he began.

"The potential traitors," Stellan said.

"Yeah," he replied. "I'm giving them meaningless tasks to keep them occupied and in the fold, but they're no longer in the know. I've cut everything down to five people like me, who hate Nole's guts and who he'd never consider employing in his organization. It's not foolproof, but it's the best that can be done."

"Good to know," Daire said, "but hardly the stuff for a three A.M. meeting."

"We're stymied," Zeong admitted. "We've got all the background stuff ready, but we don't have the caper."

"Caper?" Daire said with a laugh and sipped the Baijiu. "You *have* been watching old vids."

He shrugged. "Everything is positioned but we haven't figured out how to get it to your ship. Nole has people at the port. Not many, but enough. You start loading our stuff and suddenly there will be port holds and custom issues."

"Undesirable," Daire conceded. "I thought the big hump to get over was getting a captain to take your money and cargo rather than Nole's."

"It was the biggest," he admitted. "But not the only. We have to move before he gets his government friends involved. We are actually more vulnerable to them than you are. No merchant's paperwork is ever fault-free if the government looks hard enough. They may not stop you, but they could stop us.

"We need a plan," Zeong said, clutching his drink, "to get two thousand tons of cargo to you without Noel knowing it."

"In a way," Stellan said, "he's made it easier for us."

"How's that?" Zeong said, eyes narrowing.

Daire answered. "I refused to take any actual cargo from him under his bills of lading. In short, I won't move anything that's material from him. I've arranged to purchase about five tons of precious gems, metals, etc., but that's an outright sale to me. That's my cargo. Otherwise, he's paying a mint for my cargo space to leave empty.

"He's made a mistake there. The terms for breach of a shipping contract are the cost of other arrangements to move physical items and any late fees or interest that a shipper incurs moving that cargo by other means. When I breach my contract with him and return his money, he's left without a claim for damages. No late fees, and since there was never a physical cargo to be shipped by me, he can't stick us with charges for storing it until the next ship.

"Once he gets his money back, and I've left that in escrow with Esmeralda Burgos, he's made whole. He probably thought of changing the standard contract terms, but he'd have to get it past Burgos and didn't want to try it."

"He could file an injunction against your lifting off on a breach of contract allegation, maybe allege bad faith," Zeong countered. If Burgos' name bothered him, it didn't show.

"He could," Daire said. "That's why we have to find a way to get your cargoes aboard and lift off before he does. Burgos can beat those charges after we leave. She says his scheme of sending me out empty is probably restraint of trade, but there won't be much point to him filing suit after we lift off. He may sue you and the other merchants, and I can't do anything about that."

"He can try," Zeong said, "it's not likely to work and would give us a forum to pull him and his dirty tricks in front of the public. The Prime Minister is in his pocket, but the courts aren't yet. I doubt he'd risk it, but we'll handle that problem.

"One bit of good news is that the stevedore's union is with us," Zeong said. "They're getting cut out of loading fees and other work because of the empty ships. Nole may be paying captains to leave empty, but he isn't compensating the union, another sign that we have him outstretched on the money. If he is smart and has the cash, he should be spreading it around there."

Stellan's eyes caught Zeong. "An interesting point, if we could tell Burgos that Zuba can count on trade union support in a bid to force the Prime Minister out...."

"Huh," Zeong said, impressed. "Hadn't thought of that. Most of us merchants regard the unions as a pain in the pocketbook, but you're right. We have a common enemy. The union has a lot of pull in the Worker's Party. The WP is in Cretan's coalition right now. If they were to pull out, the Freed World ruling party might have to call a new election. That would give Nole something to focus on.

"I'll talk to the head of the spaceport workers union. They controls everything from the stevies to the port guards. If they can influence the Workers Party to pull out—"

Daire sat upright. "If we could get the stevedores on your side. No, more, have all your personnel join the stevedore's union for a night. Your people could be in the warehouses readying the goods for transit, even helping with the loading. We could be space-ready in hours."

Zeong snapped his fingers. "Yes. We'd have four times as many people available to help with shipping and loading. Better yet, the warehouses we're storing our goods in aren't ours, for the most part. We could make it look like we've given up. That we're cutting our losses and taking our inventory back to our own buildings for storage or sale on secondary local markets."

"The warehouse crews would have to be in on it," Stellan said.

Zeong shrugged. "They're members of the stevedores union also. If the union leadership sends the word down, they'll go for it. Why wouldn't they? Besides, we only have to tell the higher-ups. The membership aren't going to care what they are moving or for who. They'll just be glad there's some work. Nole has been hurting their trade too. If no one is shipping, who needs warehouse crew? Nole has his own non-union warehouses, he bought them up when the downturn he engineered began to destroy weaker companies."

Daire smiled. "My father always said to think like a Dua-Denlenn in business. Trust is nothing, mutual interest is the only real glue. Nole has been gaining ground but making enemies and even his bankroll isn't enough to feed everyone at the table. He's alienated the stevedores, port officials and other merchants."

"Pity all he has on his side is the political establishment, the executive branch of government and everyone who's knuckled under to him already," Stellan said.

Daire flashed him a smile. "If it was easy, it wouldn't be fun."

Stellan sighed. "I worry about you. Sometimes I think you were dropped on your head as a child."

Zeong gave a rare chuckle. "You two do better than me and my brothers would in business. We'd have killed each other. Anyway, we're burning daylight. Merchant Dural's brother is in stevedore's leadership; I'll get him to make the contacts. As soon as I know anything I'll get back to you.

"Go prime Burgos with word of the union support. They'll need time and money to persuade the Workers Party to pull out of the government. Zuba will need to make the promises necessary to buy that support."

Daire raised an eyebrow. "You're that certain you can deliver the stevedores?"

"We have nothing to lose. It's win or die on our end. Burgos won't commit Zuba until they're assured of union support, but it will save time when we get it if he's ready. If this is going to work, it's going to have to be a corporate and political blitzkrieg."

Daire nodded. "Delay is not our friend. We'll go on a twenty-four-hour countdown clock until you have your end ready. Then we switch to immediate launch status. You have that long to deliver your part. *Wanderlust* is ready to go."

Zeong nodded. "Hold off loading the cargo you bought from Nole. We can pretend to start loading that stuff when we when start moving our own instead. We'll load the Nole stuff last. If you have to run without it, we'll buy it from you. Have Burgos write up a codicil to your contract with us on it."

"I will," Daire said. "I'll call her in the morning."

"From here on out," Stellan said, "we will have to reply on encrypted communication. When this starts, it will move fast. There won't be time to play spies."

Zeong nodded. "I have burner comms at my end. I'll send you an encryption key. I'm sure you have one to Burgos already."

Daire nodded.

Zeong raised his glass. "Fortune to us all."

He and Daire downed their drinks and banged them on the table for luck.

Burgos's reaction was cool but intent when Daire made the encrypted call to her office. It took a half-hour to lay out the entire proposal. The fact that Burgos listened at all confirmed to Daire that her firm was struggling under the weight of Nole's enmity. It also confirmed what Zeong said about the fragility of Cretan's coalition. Assembling the creaking structure of Nole's allies and sycophants hadn't been easy, and apparently some were experiencing buyer's remorse.

"That was a neat trick getting the merchant houses and the unions to talk," Burgos said. "We tried it when Cretan made his move, but he'd been there ahead of us and there was too much animosity between the groups. By the time we realized we were in trouble, it was too late."

"They have a mutual enemy now," Daire said. "They've woken up enough to see it. However, this alliance between the merchants and union may not long survive stopping Nole."

"It only has to last that long," Burgos said absently, "but you've started a stone rolling. Maybe only an off-worlder could have done it, but it's rolling now and an object in motion tends to remain in motion."

"Zeong will reach out directly to you when he has the union support sewn up," Daire added.

"Good," Burgos said. "I will let the Prime Minister...well, former PM, know there is something in the wind. But Mr. Zuba will not be committed to anything before the underpinning are solid. Are we clear on that?"

"We are. That's why you are working directly with Zeong on this part. I don't have enough local knowledge, or pull, to know anything beyond what's being said to me. That's why I hired you."

Burgos grinned. "Daddy shouldn't have let you get away. You have potential, Daire Fenaday."

"I'll tell him you said so," Daire returned, raising and eyebrow.

"Yeah, remember me to the old pirate...err privateer, when you see him."

Stellan who'd been sitting off camera nodded when she ended the call. "I have the link to Zeong. It's in your comm and mine."

"Now all we can do is sit and wait," Daire replied.

"Well," he said standing, "You can sit and wait. I have a farewell date with Marguerite. We may not get time to say goodbye after today."

She nodded.

CHAPTER NINE

Stellan, his goodbyes made to Marguerite, returned to the ship in the early morning hours. He and Daire began the process of going from the twenty-four-launch clock to full launch readiness. This involved finalizing everything they could do internally, topping off fuel and perishables and completing any other business they could, not all of which was tied up in the Nole/Zeong standoff. From now on, neither of them would leave the ship. There was too much to do with launch prep and once the balloon went up, there would be no room for delay.

The only thing Daire held off doing was filing her launch time with Space Control. That would alert Nole. While she had not discussed when she would lift with the businessman, he might think it odd that she would file and not tell him. A launch hold could be dangerous to their plans, so Daire would file it as late as she dared in the loading process.

But they could also not sit there in full launch readiness without raising eyebrows. The gantry would be pushed back in hours. As there was no other space traffic scheduled, they should not have a problem with departure. Large as she was for an atmospheric ship, *Wanderlust* would take off like a conventional plane once the tugs moved her to the runway. Her impellers would gradually build up the speed she would need to fly into space. This was where having the space workers union with them paid dividends. Their contact had the runway reserved, though no formal request for them had yet been filed.

Daire reported their readiness to Zeong, who was working feverishly to cobble together the elements of their conspiracy.

Toward late afternoon both of their comms went off at once. Daire picked hers up. Despite the encryption, Zeong has insisted on code names. His displayed on her screen as Rascal and 'audio only.'

"This is Stormcloud," Daire said, using the code name Shasti had used on her voyages.

"Rascal here. Everything is now set at our end. The Workers Party and the Socialist Party are going to announce they are pulling out of the government at 5PM, in time for the nightly news. There will be accusations of conspiracy and fraud leveled at Nole, Cretan and their allies. Apparently, Burgos and Zuba have been sitting on some stuff waiting for the right moment. They're going to call for the Prime Minister's resignation and a nonpartisan investigation.

"At the same time, the space workers union is going to list all of our staff as union members, even collecting dues for them. We have them near the warehouses ready to go. They will start for the spaceport then. We'll noise it about that we're moving your Nole cargo and move ours first. Merchant Andrus has two big airliners on the pad near you, and we'll claim to be loading them."

"The tugs will start for you as soon as you're loaded. They're too big to leave sitting out there by your ship."

"Ok," Daire said, looking at the chronometers. It was late fall on Serendib; the sun would be setting then. Good, conspiracies needed darkness. They had four hours until all hell broke loose.

"I'll ask for gantry rollback as soon as we're through with this call. I'll wait to ask for launch clearance until we are loaded and hooked to the tugs. Unusual, but I'll just claim I filed for it yesterday and let them worry about it."

"Ok, good. You are a pretty cool customer, Stormcloud. I thought I was just going to sell stuff; never dreamt I'd be marketing a revolution."

"Stay frosty, Rascal," she replied. "This is the fun part." She clicked off and turned to Stellan, who was giving her a mournful look.

"You're really enjoying yourself, aren't you."

"Well," Daire returned, "it's not fighting a monster in a ruined city or wiping out the Evolvers, but I think our parents would be impressed."

"More likely appalled," he muttered.

"Be a good boy and get gantry control to start rollback, will you?"

"Aye, aye, skipper."

At six P.M. Daire and Stellan sat glued to the holoscreen. Suddenly all the news channels began to light up.

"It begins." Daire said.

"They are actually breaking in on streaming services," Stellan said. "Let's see what the live stuff looks like." He waved a finger over an icon. Onscreen two females, one human, one Morok, appeared.

"Shocking news out of the capitol this evening," began the human. "Amidst a cloud of allegations of corruption, insider trading and violations of environmental and financial laws, the Workers Party has pulled out of the government, followed by the Greens and the Socialists. Former Prime Minister Zuba has called for the resignation of Prime Minister Cretan and his Planetary District Attorney Mary Hama and nonpartisan investigations of both, in relation to the Nole Corporation.

"It is fair to call this a government crisis. An emergency meeting of Parliament has been called for this evening."

"In addition," the Morok added, "large scale demonstrations by the Space Workers Union have begun in downtown Ujain and a strike vote is being called for by union leadership.

"There have already been some street clashes between union workers and supporters of Cretan's party. Police are urging calm."

Stellan muted it. "Sounds like Zeong lit off a bigger bang than even he expected."

"All the elements were there," Daire said. "It just required a match."

Stellan studied his sister. Daire was rarely rattled but he was surprised at her calm demeanor, as if bringing down a planetary government was something she had studied in class.

Perhaps in a way, she has. She spent more time with both Dad and Shasti then I did. Both were champion schemers.

Their personal comms chimed. Daire opened the line. "Stormcloud."

"Rascal. The cat is out of the bag, and it seems to be a tiger. The capitol is grinding to a halt. Most of the space workers not engaged with us are walking off the job."

"Excellent, how fast can you get here?"

"Convoys are already heading for you. I have the nearest warehouses emptying into you first, so we don't back up. You should see a company of stevies heading your way any minute to get loading. The foreman, Whan, is my guy. He'll work with you."

"Stellan," she whispered, muting her mike. "Get the cargo bay doors open, all of them."

Her brother moved with his usual speed and economy of speech.

"We'll be ready on this end. I'm going to send my departure signal to launch control right now. With all the confusion, they may just see a frightened spacer, wanting to get out of a city that seems going out of control."

"Hah, I don't want to think of what would actually frighten you. Rascal out."

Daire hit the icon that sent her prepared departure paperwork to launch control. She added a demand that her ship be held safe from the 'riots in the city.' Then she began the internal launch procedures. All the walkarounds had been done. Impellers began to warm, the singularity that would supply AG and later stardrive began to compress. *Wanderlust* was becoming a spaceship again, straining and eager to be gone.

Stellan's voice sounded over the intercom. "Got that company of stevies coming along on buses. I see trucks in the distance. There are three tugs coming as well, with their lights off."

"OK," she said. "We're taking chances in this quick load. Let's make sure we don't take stupid ones. Work with the foreman but make sure it's all secured. We don't need a container breaking loose in the hold during launch."

"On it."

<hr>

Stellan stood on the open deck of *Wanderlust's* main cargo hold, the lights off. The ramp allowed one to drive cargo up into the main section. There were other entrances usable for smaller, break-bulk loads. Further down the field the two big air-freighters serving as decoys, sat with every light glowing. Thin camouflage but all that was available.

He watched union workers pile off the field buses and come running. Daire had provided them with the specs on Wanderlust, but J-class freighters were common, and they would have loaded them before.

An older man with steel-gray hair began barking orders at the crews who separated into units and began to position themselves. Some ran past Stellan into the hold and began working on the cargo straps and tiedowns.

"I'm Whan," the man said, coming up to him.

"Stellan." Neither bothered shaking hands.

"First trucks are five minutes behind me. Turn the lights up, low setting. No need to fuck with people's night vision, and about half my crew are Moroks anyway."

They were distracted momentarily by the rumbling of a tug passing by to take up station under the starboard wing. Another headed for the port side. The last one could not hook up while they were loading.

"We'll move the container cargo in first," he said. "Here's a tablet with load distribution, you better kick it up to your skipper."

"Got it," Stellan forwarded the load schematic and weight distribution to the ship's AI.

The first trucks came quicker than expected. The larger vehicles disgorged smaller carriers, which unloaded standard space cargo containers, each six feet tall, the same across, and about twenty long. These could be stacked three high and five across in the main hold. The cargo had been optimized to jam these as full as could be. Daire had reluctantly passed on some larger farm equipment. It might bring greater profit, but would kill the space of three containers.

Meanwhile smaller containers and boxes began going up hastily erected conveyers, filling the holds further back in the ship and on the next level. Even unused crew quarters were being filled. *Wanderlust* would lift as heavy as her design specs said was safe.

Realizing that the stevies could use his cranes and conveyors faster than he could, he left them to it. But he and Whan raced around checking as much as they could. The Asian man howled abuse at two Moroks who hadn't tensioned a tiedown enough on a container.

Meanwhile, trucks came and went. There was some shouting and scuffling, inevitable as things ended up in the wrong place, but Zeong had planned it well. Computer-controlled vehicles approached from only one direction. They parked in a designated spot in orientation to the ship, then departed from another. The loads inside had been prepositioned with military correctness.

While the merchant's people, temporarily unionized, worked the trucks and everything else, Daire had decreed that only the real stevedores would stow inside the ship. The extra hands would only get in the way and slow them down.

It seemed the supply of vehicles was never-ending, but the main cargo bay load was going smoothly so he decided to do a run around the ship and look at the break-bulk entrances. He also wanted to make sure that no one had banged anything into the *Wanderlust*. Starship hull metal was strong but the stresses it was exposed to were immense.

As he jogged under an impeller, he felt the welcome warmth of the unit above him as it spooled up. Something unwelcome greeted his eyes too. In the shadow of the immense land tug that had hooked up to the starboard landing gear, a man crouched. But Stellan's night vision was as good as Moroks, and it didn't suffer as much from differing light levels. The man's furtive manner aroused Stellan's suspicion. He padded up around the outside of the tug, until he was close enough to hear.

"No, you dumb fuck, get me Nole himself. I don't want—"

Whatever he wanted was interrupted by Stellan's rush from the shadows. He batted the comm out of the man's hand to the ground and slammed a heel on it. The latter gave the man a chance for a barroom swing at Stellan, who merely moved out of the way. He blocked the follow-up jab, grabbed the arm and bridged until he put the sleeper hold his father had taught him on the informer. The man was big and powerfully built, but he wasn't engineered. After a few seconds of struggle, he slumped into unconsciousness. Stellan tucked him under one arm and made his way back to Whan. People stared at his prisoner but didn't stop working.

Whan spotted him coming. "Another one, huh?"

"How many?" Stellan asked.

"Three so far, well four with this guy. Hey, Linda."

A sturdy woman by the nearest loader looked over, cursed and signaled two Moroks to follow her.

"Tape and cuff this asshole and put him with the others," Whan ordered.

Stellan handed the unconscious human to the Moroks, who followed Linda away.

"Make sure nothing happens to them," Stellan warned. "Neither of us needs that trouble, and it would give Nole an opening."

"Yeah, the boss said the same. Normally scabs like them would get swift kick in the ass. Tonight, they'll just get dropped off downtown after you leave. Though if the rioting gets any worse, we may just leave them by the roadside out of town."

"Bad?"

"Worse than Landing Night parties. Nole's built up a lot of enemies and Cretan's fascists like to throw the elbow when they can."

"Union forever," Stellan said.

"You bet," Whan said.

"How are we doing?"

"We're loading the last of the Sheffield stuff and starting on the stuff you guys bought from Nole."

"There's less of that," Stellan said. "We've been moving the precious metals and gems into the secure hold all week, a little at a time. Only the bulky stuff is left."

Whan looked out with a practiced eye. "Give me ten minutes more and we'll be done with the side holds and you can seal them. Five minutes after that and we'll be ready on the main hold. I've been inspecting as we go but this is a rush. Use your time to check in the main hold. Containers are more of a problem than break-bulk."

"Agreed," Stellan raced into the hold and began systematically checking everything he could reach from the back of the main hold to the front. He'd have to rely on Daire to seal the side holds remotely and from the bridge.

"I hope the Space and Aviation Authority never hears of this," he muttered to himself as he tested tiedowns and inspected locking panels.

Whan was as good as his word. As soon as the last load cleared the door, he yelled up to Stellan. "Lock and load, spacer. Black skies to you." With a wave he headed for his vehicle to join the mass exodus.

Stellan hit the main hatch controls. "Daire," he said over the intercom as the massive ramp began to groan shut. "Main hatch closing."

"Get up here. We're moving."

He raced up the spiral staircase that led directly to the bridge. Once there, he saw Daire impatiently staring at the ramp control. It went green just as he came in.

"Tugmaster," Daire said. "This is *Wanderlust*. We are cleared to depart."

"Affirmative. We have you on runway one. It has the longest roll. Starting movement now." *Wanderlust* was too big to jerk when the tugs took hold, but they felt the ship begin to move.

"Tugmaster," Daire said. "I'm running my impellers up to five percent. It will lighten the load and make her a bit frisky, but it could get warm out there."

"Got it. When we get you straight on the runway, we'll join the starboard tug in clearing you to the right. The port tug will clear left. I've made sure he understands not to cross your front."

"Good," Daire said, jaw set. The hours of tension were wearing on her.

Stellan patted her shoulder, and she spared him a half-smile. "I was sure that we were in trouble when Space Control took forever to get back with my launch clearance. But it seems to have been just the wildcat strike thrown at the port. I think they're just as happy we're leaving."

They could do nothing but watch the tugs slowly pull their ship onto the runway. It took an agonizing seven minutes.

"*Wanderlust,* this is Tugmaster, standby for detach in thirty seconds."

"Affirmative. Do you need me to tap my brakes, or are you good to get out of my way?"

"I'm good. We ain't fast but I will give her all she's got. We can replace the transmission later if we have to."

"Roger that."

"Stand by for detach in 10, 9…"

The tugs detached from their three positions on *Wanderlust.* The underwing tugs turned away as planned. The tug in front pulled away from them at an angle in a fast crawl.

"*Wanderlust,* we are clear. Black skies," called the Tugmaster.

"And safe landings," Daire said back. She pushed the impellers to 100% and *Wanderlust* began to roll.

"Radar and all scanners clear," Stellan said. He would not have put it past Nole to run something automated into their path if he had time for it.

"*CSPS Wanderlust,*" came a voice suddenly. "Please abort your take off run."

Daire gave a wolfish grin. "Tower this is *Wanderlust.* Negative, I am at point of no return."

The ship felt alive to them now. She rolled down the miles long, military runway, and with a surge, broke free of the ground, heading out to the oceanside.

The tower came back on, but Daire ignored it as the G-forces built and *Wanderlust* strained to reach the Karman line, the acknowledged border of space and the end of Seredib's jurisdiction. Whoever was calling them, must have realized the futility of their effort, and the channel clicked closed.

They were spacing again.

Hours later and safely above the Karman line in free space, Daire finally relaxed. The ship needed to orbit the planet seven times, building up speed for a fuel-saving launch window to the outer system where jumpspace began. Meanwhile, they watched the news and the confusing political battle for a few hours. Daire slept while Stellan monitored the instruments, ready to power out into deeper space in case a cutter or something else came up at them. They were on their final orbit when Burgos called.

"Thought you would like to hear how it all came out," Burgos said, her face appearing on the main screen.

"By all means," Daire replied.

"Nole was madder than hell, not that he showed it all that much. The banks have called in his loans, given the information that was published on how overcommitted he was and how he had falsified the value of some of the collateral. He'll have to pay a lot more money for loans going forward and has to back out of a number of deals to buy out merchants. It also gives him less money for payola with the Freed World Caucus.

"Meanwhile now that Zeong is flush, he's extending credit to the others. Their window of vulnerability to Nole has closed.

"The planetary parliament is holding a vote of no confidence in Cretan tomorrow. He threw his district attorney under the airbus to try and save himself. But the reform committee is offering Hama immunity if he will testify against Cretan. The whole rotten shambles is coming apart and there's a good chance Zabu will be back in the mansion in a week. With any luck I'll be moving back into my old offices shortly after and getting inditements ready for conspiracy, restraint of trade and tortious and criminal interference in a contract. Happy Days."

"All's well that ends well," Daire said. "It's a pity that Nole isn't bound for a cell."

On screen Burgos grimaced. "Too much to hope for, at least for now. A lot of what he did is quasi-legal or just civil in nature. But he's going have to pull his horns for the foreseeable future. The investigations on him will tie him up and bleed him plenty. I think he's a spent force politically. Besides, too many people work for him. Not good for the planet if his company goes bust, though I personally hope he gets roasted over a slow fire in hell."

Stellan chuckled at the image.

"Smooth sailing to you, Captain. It's been interesting meeting the two of you. I can see in both cases that the apples haven't fallen far from the tree. You're owed major favors here, but try not to burn down too much of the galaxy before you can cash them in. I'll buy you both dinner next time you planet here.

"We'll take you up on that. *Wanderlust* over and out."

CHAPTER TEN

Their contract with Zeong and Daire's original plan sent them to Avanzado, a world only valuable for its location at the junction of several jump points, some of which, when chained to others, would take cargo to markets that Zeong had arranged transshipment for. Avanzado had been on Daire's list of markets, well out into the periphery, near one intersection of Voit-Veru and Drisnian space. The sectors beyond were not explored, and it was in every sense a frontier.

Their landing on this world had been uneventful, although it was less hospitable than Serendib, with smaller oceans. The land mass lay in massive continents, many of which were deserts, or high arid mountains. The one spaceport lay on a southern continent where the Veru had first landed, more arable and pleasant then most of the rest of the world.

It was also the area with the largest native population of pretechnic humanoids. They'd been of little interest to the Voit-Veru, who established their enclaves on world mostly by force of arms. The insurrection that followed made Avanzado an expensive holding for the Voit-Veru, but when they were forced to give up the system, it fell into a no man's land between the Veru and the Confederation. The

Confederation, itself still recovering from the Conchirri War and the Voit-Veru's alliance with Olympia, let Avanazdo slip off its list of concerns, with the result that many of the Confederate species set up holdings there outside of Confed law. It became a freeport, nominally aligned with the Confederation.

After they landed, Stellan had helped Daire sort the farm and light machinery that would be welcome on such a world: solar generators, small engines, machine tools. Given the stock they had not sold at Serendib and what they had picked up there, they were able to supply both corporate and private customers with needed equipment.

A chunk of their cargo was allocated for a Dua-Denlenn named Kelmian, a merchant who'd sent an order to Zeong for water purifiers. While their transshipped cargo was handled smoothly and the machinery cargo was greeted eagerly by buyers, there had been some issue with the purifiers. Daire had gone into the port to deal with it.

Stellan had wanted to go with her but there had been more than the usual share of burnouts and mechanical issues that needed addressing. Everything they could do on their own meant not having to pay a shipwright. While their recent adventures had put them well into the black, expensive problems came up hard and fast in space. They had the funds their parents had allotted them as an investment, but Daire was religious about not touching those unless they absolutely had to.

So, she had gone into port, and he spent hour after hour diagnosing and resolving issues onboard the *Wanderlust*.

The ship's AI chimed. Stellan swore and put his tools to one side, wiping his hands. "Yes," he said, annoyed that he'd have to stop his preparation for removing a servo that was coming up on its max hours of operation.

"Message received from City of Wanger, Central Police."

His heart lurched. "Read it."

"Captain Daire Fenaday was arrested during an altercation in city limits. She has been turned over to Port Police as of eleven PM Local time, charged with assault, assault with a deadly weapon, disturbing the peace and other misdemeanors. Bail is set at 17,000 credits and an arraignment is scheduled for ten AM Local time."

A few curses burst from his lips. Why had he let her talk him into staying behind? Why hadn't he given into his misgivings and called her? Then he seized control of himself. His first job was to get Daire out of custody and back to the ship. They had the cash to do so, and lawyers could be hired later. The immediate need was to kick up enough fuss so that no one thought she was without friends or money. Bad things happened to the helpless on the frontier.

He read Daire's statement attached to the message. She claimed the Dua-Denlenn, Kelmian, had tried to cheat her and his wife attacked with a knife.

Thank God, she was turned over to the Port Police. The local cops might not care much about offworld problems, but the Port Authority would. At least I hope so.

Stellan hurried to his cabin. There he donned the custom body armor his father had made for him, as hardly anything in his life was "off the rack." Then he opened a secure locker and brought out a beautifully wrought metal box. Inside lay his birth mother's sixteenth birthday gift to him.

He paused, remembering the Christmas holiday when she'd given him the box, during one of her rare visits to New Eire. She'd asked him to come up to her rooms, which were held for her use in the Fenaday manor. He'd dutifully followed her. The case had been on the bed, and she picked it up and turned to him. He had not yet hit his full height then, and his eyes were still on a level with hers. His birth mother was beautiful, of that there could be no question. Like all those who transited space, no one could say exactly how old she was. She claimed to be forty-five, but looked scarcely older than when she'd given birth to him.

"You are your father's son," she said, "and mine, though God knows I have done a poor job of that. I doubt you will have a quiet life, if only because you will always throw yourself between Daire and any trouble. I can at least make sure you have the right tools for the life you choose."

He'd opened the finely wrought box to see matching matte-finish pistols. One was a silenced 9mm auto pistol, the other, a laser. Both were made for his oversized hands. Next to them were black knives— a folding one and a heavy-duty blade. All were finely made.

"Thank you, Mother," he'd replied with genuine gratitude. Did her eyes soften then?

"Both pistols are straightforward and completely reliable," she said with a touch of gruffness. "My own field days made me leery of delicate or complicated gadgets that fail under stress."

"Sound," he said, closing the box.

"Never fear to use them, or my name," she added. "Know that should you ever call to me, help will come."

He nodded, feeling confused and awkward. This doubled when she put a hand to his cheek and stroked it. He stood still unsure of what to do, or even what he wanted to do.

The moment passed. "Come on," Shasti said. "We'd better get downstairs before your sister eats all the cake." But his mother had been wrong. Daire had set a large piece of cake aside and was guarding it for him.

Stellan locked the ship, hopped in *Wanderlust's* mule and drove around the squat buildings that seemed a fixture at most space ports. The heat of the afternoon made the antennas and scanners atop them waver and shimmer.

Finally, he pulled up in front of a large gray structure labeled *Port Authority*. An electrified fence surrounded it, and there was a guard post. Neither the natives nor the original settlers were particularly friendly. While the out and out war with the Veru was over, there was a constant run of incidents.

Can't say that I blame the natives, given the sort of ruthless bastards that have descended from the skies on them. Still my job is to trade, not moralize.

Correction, my job is to get my Captain out of the slammer.

He parked in the designated area and walked deliberately up to the guard post, where a pair of guards stood, watching him warily. A Morok and a human wore gray-green camouflage and had holstered sidearms and batons. The Morok extended a barring hand.

Stellan paused a pace away and looked down at the sturdy, goblin-like guard.

"What's your business, Spacer?" the Morok asked.

"I'm here to get my Captain," he said. "You've got her locked up over some problem with the locals."

The Morok considered, his red eyes searching Stellan's impassive face. "Perhaps we better hold your weapons here."

"This is a freeport," he replied. "I've done nothing to allow you to confiscate them."

"Hand them over," the human said, drawing his weapon.

An instant later, Stellan was holding the man's weapon and the guard was clutching his wrist. Stellan ejected the magazine while watching the other guard. The Morok thought about moving, then decided not to as Stellan disassembled the weapon and dropped the parts.

"As I was saying," Stellan continued as if nothing had happened, "under freeport law my weapons are my own, unless you have a Confed magistrate who says otherwise."

"Ain't one here," the Morok replied.

"Then it's not likely to happen. As long as I stay in the Free Trade Zone, only Confed Trade Law applies. If there isn't any law, then I answer to no one."

"Space-lawyer," growled the human, nursing his wrist and glaring up at him.

"Enough guys would make you listen," the Morok said.

"Better bring all of them."

The Morok gave a harsh laugh. "Pretty tough for one so young. What's your name, Spacer?"

"Rainhell."

The Morok's eyes widened slightly. "Not a name to be bandied about."

"I'll tell Mother you said so."

"Fuck," the alien said, stepping back.

"You're just gonna—" the human began.

"Shut up, Gwent," the Morok said wearily. "It's not my fault you don't know shit, but this is trouble above our paygrade."

Stellan nodded and walked around the pair, leaving the human to scramble in the dust for the pieces of his weapon. The doors auto-opened and he stepped into cooler, dryer air with relief.

Stellan was not his mother, raised from infancy as a trained killer but he had her tailored genes. Shasti had been bred to dominate, to destroy without fear or pity, the strongest and fastest human ever created or born.

He strode past people of many species, most of which gave him a wide berth and a wary glance. No one impeded him and he stopped before a second-floor door marked *Port Manager* and opened it. Inside was a large room of desks, monitors and holo scanners, the staffers looked up in annoyance. The buzz of conversation dropped as he walked in.

He walked to the biggest desk at the far end, before a more ornate glass and wooden door with brass knobs. A dark-skinned human male sat at the desk in front of it. He looked up as Stellan stopped in front of him.

"Welcome, Spacer," he said in a voice devoid of welcome. "What can we do for you?"

"Stellan Rainhell," he announced, in a deep voice that made people shift. CPSS *Wanderlust* out of New Eire. You're illegally holding my captain, Daire Fenaday."

The man flicked a holo up. "Says here she busted a chair over Good Merchant Kelmian's head, slugged his wife for good measure and resisted arrest."

"My captain said Kelmian tried to renege on our contract and that his wife pulled a knife on her. We're in a freeport and we're Confed citizens. Without a Confed Court here, you can declare her persona non grata and kick us off world, but you can't hold her. Neither course of action is an intelligent one for a colony that wants to do business with independent traders."

"Now look you—"

The door behind the man opened and a Dua-Denlenn female in a dark red suit stepped out. Everyone stopped moving and talking. The elfin female, with her golden skin and eyes, blue from lid-to-lid, stopped behind the human.

"Please forgive the ignorance of my staff," she said in a musical voice. "Only sheer ignorance, or an equivalent degree of complete stupidity, can explain the failure to appreciate what the names Rainhell and Fenaday mean in conjunction with New Eire."

There was a visible wince in the room.

"I've already sent for Captain Fenaday to be brought here immediately, where I will, of course, release her to you. Please come wait in my office, where we may begin to rescue your opinion of us." She gestured gracefully and Stellan walked into her office. The buzz of conversation rose. People began to scurry.

As utilitarian as the outside room was, the inside was the picture of comfort: sofas, cushioned chairs, ornate but elegant furniture, including the desk the Dua retreated behind.

"I have not introduced myself, I'm Revol, the Port Manager of this unfortunate piece of real estate."

Stellan knew a Dua would only give her individual name to an alien but gave both his. "Stellan Rainhell."

"Yes, of course, son of Robert Xavier Fenaday and Shasti Rainhell, now head of security on Olympia, which means head of Olympia. You favor your mother."

He nodded.

A side door opened and another Dua female in a port uniform stepped in. She brought a tray of drinks, cakes and cookies. These she placed between Revol and Stellan, turned and left without a word.

"Will you have some refreshments?" Revol asked.

He allowed himself a smile. "Would a Dua have even slight respect left for a fool who took food and drink from an unknown party?"

She gave a delicate chiming laugh. "You are familiar with our customs, I see.

"Well, we are a suspicious people but not a stupid one. The

refreshments are quite safe. You bear names that would urge one to extreme caution. I may well have them tattooed on the backsides of those who have put me in this position. I am not grateful."

"Nor should you be," he replied, "both lines of my heritage have a long memory for offenses."

"And one hopes, favors too," Revol said. "All charges and specifications in this matter are dropped. No fines, attachments or any other form of annoyance are contemplated. Indeed, your landing fees and any port charges will be waived for your stay.

"While there is no Confed Authority on the world, we run it in accord with Confed regulations in the hope of eventual association. You are free within the port, and I will see that there is no nonsense about a *persona non grata*."

"The matter of Good Merchant Kelmian's dispute with you captain is not so easily disposed. That, I regret to advise, falls under the civil auspices of the planet currently headed by a human, one governor Langhari. However, I will be certain to put a word in with my fellow Dua. I find myself shocked and embarrassed by his poor judgement. Alas, he married poorly and has never had the good sense to remediate that error."

"We'll work it out," he said. *I hope.*

"There was a quick knock at the door. The same Dua who had entered before led Daire in.

He controlled a flash of rage at the site of her bruised face and black eye. Some of this must have reached his face despite his mother's exhortations to always keep his thoughts from his face. The Dua placed her hand on a sidearm. Revol's disappeared beneath her desk.

"I'm fine, Brother."

"I will be the judge of that," he growled. Both Duas flinched. He rose slowly from his chair. Starting something was pointless and risked Daire. He walked over to his sister who looked tiny and fragile in his eyes.

If I can get my hands on who struck her...

"Really," she whispered. "I'm okay. Just like to get back to the ship."

He looked at Revol. "We will remember your efforts."

If the inherent ambiguity in his statement bothered Revol, it did not show. She rose. "My assistant will see you out. Black skies and safe landings to you both."

The other Dua opened the door and the siblings followed her downstairs to an exit.

"Your vehicle," the Dua said in a whispery voice, "is best accessed by going around the building to the left to the employee exit. You will not encounter the same guards. I shall remain with you if you wish."

It was a Dua's way of reassuring them that no ambush awaited them.

Stellan shook his head. "Good day." She took it for dismissal and vanished back through the door.

"Can you walk?" he asked.

"Yeah," she replied, subdued.

They made Daire's best pace and exited through another guard post, whose occupants studiously ignored them, back to the Mule. He quickly drove them back to *Wanderlust's* landing spot on the hard-packed dirt of the field. Once there he scooped his sister up in one arm, despite her protest and took her to their small infirmary.

"I said I was fine," she said, as he gently deposited her on the treatment table and activated the auto doc.

"Quiet," he growled. Daire looked startled and he felt a stab of remorse. He'd never raised his voice to her.

He heaved a great sigh of relief when the medical scanner showed nothing more than surface bruising on her face and, back and upper arms.

Daire, who wouldn't admit to any weakness under torture, looked at him with full eyes. "You're mad at me."

He gently ran a huge hand over the unbruised side of her face. "I am never mad at you, Big Sister. Only terrified of what could have happened to you and grateful it is not worse. Why would you get into a fight without me to back you up?"

"It was a setup," she admitted. "That sleazy Dua thought he could cheat us by renegotiating the contract. We're a brand-new ship, wouldn't do to get a bad reputation. His wife and he staged the argument. Guess, I made that too easy.

"They'd planted some witnesses in the crowd. When I tried to get away, he grabbed me, and I broke a chair on his head. The bitch tried to stab me. I'm glad for all the training Dad gave us. I blocked it and smacked her with a bottle, then… well, you know the rest. The porties were all on their side, of course. It got a bit rough in the van."

His gut clenched at the thought of what could have happened to her in the van of so-called police on this unregulated world. Only her status as ship's uniformed officer had saved her.

"What would Mom and Shasti have to say," he asked, carefully running a regenerator over her bruises, "about getting egged into a fight on the enemy's terms?"

She squirmed a little. "A lot, I guess."

"Yeah," he added, finishing with the regenerator. "Deserved too."

She sighed. "The Port Manager who intervened in my favor, Guild?"

"Doubtless."

"Not good that we ran into them so early in our voyages."

"This one is sensible. She knew who we were and was not happy to be involved with us. Hence the impressive concessions. A more ambitious or less sensible person might have thought of kidnapping you or seeking to ingratiate themselves with the various of our parent's enemies. Some of whom are quite powerful and not easily daunted. As for the rest, no indie trader goes long without contact with the Guild."

"Worse," she said. "Now, we might be seen to owe them a favor. I hate trading on our parent's accounts. We came out here to make it on our own. I wonder if we should consider aliases."

"Well, not here," he said. "The impression we have made locally will last longer than the dent you put in Kelmian's head. But even should we change our names and the ship's, the Guild and any decent intelligence service will always know who we are."

He surveyed the result of his ministrations. "You look much better already. I'll make you something to eat, then you should get some sleep."

"Hey," she replied with more of her old spirit. "I'm the big sister here."

"Tomorrow you are. Tonight, you take it easy and leave things to me."

CHAPTER ELEVEN

Daire rolled over in her bunk. A sudden throb in her cheek finished waking her. She sat up slowly, feeling for injuries. The regenerator had worked its medical magic, but it would still take some time for the aches to go away from the blow of the local cop's gauntleted hand. She breathed carefully; her ribs were still tender as well.

It could have been much worse. Out here, I'm no longer the instantly recognized, privileged daughter of a wealthy and powerful family. By the time they figure out who I was, I could have been hamburger. Or worse, they could have raped me.

God, I must have scared the hell out of Stellan. She slipped out of bed, used the shower and took some of the pain meds he'd given her. *I can't give him any more reason for worry. He's burning under that calm exterior.*

Stellan had questioned her about the officers who beat her. Though it hurt her to do so, she'd lied to him about not seeing their faces. Her brother combined a streak of her father's tenacity with his birth mother's unforgiving ferocity. He'd been as strong as a grown man when he was twelve, as the variety of school yard bullies who tried him found out. All their father's training had been for control, not strength. Stellan had never needed to strike anyone twice, but avoided fighting if possible.

Unless it was over me. There her brother showed neither restraint nor mercy. When she was ten, a group of boys had surrounded her on their bikes, shoving her around until she fell and cut her knee. Stellan had fallen on them like a bear, flinging three of them, still on their bikes, into the river.

Kinda put a kink in my dating life later, she thought as she pulled on a fresh uniform, *but I was more interested in ships and voyaging than boys, anyway. Still, I'm glad we're getting off this rock soon. Stellan is smart enough to find them, given enough time. We don't need the trouble.*

She checked her face in the mirror, then put a little makeup on the bruised area. *Good thing Dad isn't around. He wouldn't be happy with me having taken a contract with a Dua I didn't know without better references and security deposits. How many weeks did he spend hammering into me the need to deal differently with different cultures, particularly Duas? And I went alone, just a first-time trade with the very young captain of a small indie ship Kelmian wasn't likely to use again. That was practically inviting Duas to try something. Maybe that's why it got out of hand so easily. Kelmian couldn't resist and he threw the frame job together on the spot. Bad move by him, a smarter Dua wouldn't have taken that risk. They'd have fixed it post the deal.*

Still, Dad would have given me a failing grade on this trade. Then he would have found the port officials and reminded them that the last time a port held a Fenaday unjustly, he arranged a 20-kilton sunrise for it. Everybody always talks about Aunt Shasti, but Dad was the one you really didn't want to push when it came to family. He carries that streak of Irish bloody-mindedness just below the surface.

Satisfied that nothing was visible, she came out of the cabin. It was only a short walk to the bridge where she found Stellan engaged in the endless maintenance and checking of the ship. He popped his head out from under a panel, hearing her as she came up the corridor.

"How are you?" he asked, putting his tools to one side.

"You mean, other than annoyed with myself, grateful to you, and kind of pissed at the universe?"

He gave one of his small, serious smiles. "Other than that."

"Well, you're as good a ship's doctor as a cook. I'll have to remember that at your performance review."

Now he did chuckle. "I'm glad." But he came up to her, put a hand under her chin and studied her face, his dark brown eyes filled with concern. "It looks good. One doesn't want to overdo a regenerator treatment—there can be side effects. Ribs?"

"All good."

The grunt he gave conveyed skepticism.

"Honestly, only slightly sore, and I took a pill. I'll be fine."

"Shouldn't take those on an empty stomach. Come down to the galley—I made an egg casserole."

Daire sat at the table while her brother fixed breakfast for them both. Her plate looked tiny by comparison when it slid in front of her. One downside to his Engineered genetics, Stellan ate like an Okaran. They talked only of the ship and the profits to be made in their new venture while they ate.

A chime sounded. The AI's neutral voice came on. "Attention: we have received a summons to the Planetary Governor's office for two P.M.

"Display," Daire said, with a sinking feeling in her gut.

A woman's face appeared on the screen. "To Daire Fenaday, you are commanded to put all business aside and appear at the offices of the Honorable Vam Langhari at two P.M. to discuss charges and specifications arising out of an assault on Merchants Kelmian and Devia. Failure to do so will result in your restriction to the freeport limits and denial of trade rights. If you have any questions, please comm this exchange."

A flashing light indicated a rider. Annoyed Daire touched it. "This is governor Langhari's assistant, Barslow. I am authorized to assure you that you will not be detained during the hearing and will be allowed to return to your ship and the freeport, though you will not be allowed out again if the hearing goes against you. You may bring your crewman but will not be allowed to appear before the governor armed. Either come without weapons or be prepared to surrender them." The message was accompanied by a digitally secure copy of a safe conduct pass for both of them.

Stellan looked at her. "What do you make of that? An interview with a planetary governor?"

"Odd," she replied. "Even in a shithole like this, why would a governor make time to meet with the captain of a small indie over a port dispute. He wants something. Something he thinks we can deliver, or he wouldn't call on us. He thinks we're in trouble—"

"—Which we are."

"Don't interrupt when I'm captaining...as I was saying, he sees us as in distress and needs a favor. Interesting."

"Our alternative is to lift off and move on to another port of call."

"With no cargo, and taking a loss both fiscally and reputationally on this dust ball? No."

"Daire, I will not allow you to be jailed or manhandled again on this planet."

"We can't call Mommy and Daddy every time we get into trouble."

"Sister, I will not change my mind on this."

She raised a placating hand. "Let's go see what the bastard wants. We'll just check out stunners like nice merchants, so we have something to hand in and don't look like easy marks. Don't bring any of the assassin stuff Aunt Shasti gave you."

He sat back. "Dishes are yours."

"Fair enough."

They readied themselves for the interview at the governor's office, filing their safe conduct with Revol's office, though hearing nothing back.

Daire set up an interstellar mail transmission to be fired off if they did not return in twenty-four hours. The message would go up to the Confed mail computer on the orbiting space station. Interfering with Confed Starmail was virtually impossible, and the penalties were draconian. It was, after all, the glue that held the Confederation together. She blessed the days her father had spent with her on space law and the practical aspects of getting around in trade.

Thus protected, they boarded the mule and drove into the jurisdiction of Avanzado. There was a checkpoint at the port exit, where Stellan showed a comm of the summons and they were let through.

The governor's mansion was not far from the spaceport, which seemed logical given the hostility of the natives. The area outside the port was mainly occupied by Confed species but she saw a few natives who had chosen to do business with the otherworlders. Tall, slender creatures, muffled in flowing robes and headscarves, it was difficult to get much a sense of what they looked like, save that their bone-white faces held two pale eyes under a sensor organ that saw into infrared.

At the mansion they faced bunkers and fences and the occasional blast wall. Guards passed them in, after confiscating their stunners. They frowned up at Stellan, who clearly made them nervous. Her brother glowered down at them.

Good, she thought. *We must make quite the pair.* Stellan, like Shasti, was so well proportioned that his size was not so apparent until he stood next to something for scale. When she stood next to him, she looked like a child's doll.

Good things come in small packages, she thought, then squared her shoulders.

An aide, possibly the same one who'd left the rider message, greeted them at the door. While he did not introduce himself, he advised that they were expected and would be having a private conference with the governor.

Daire wasn't surprised when they were conducted to a meeting room instead of the governor's office. *He doesn't want it known that he met personally with us, hence the unnamed aide and the offside meeting. This could be useful.*

"The governor will join you shortly," the aide said and closed the door.

Shortly turned out to be thirty minutes later. Daire found herself amused at the crude power play. Finally, the door at the back of the room opened. Guards stood outside but they did not follow the bearded man who entered the room and closed the door.

Daire and Stellan both rose.

The look he gave them was not friendly, nor did he offer to shake hands. "Have a seat."

She could not place his accent, nor tell what world had given him birth. He looked as if there had been some genetic drift from the original Terran stock in him, which could mean one of the older colonies. His brow ridges were pronounced and there was a greater than usual length to his arms. A strange tattoo she didn't recognize covered half his face.

"I'll get right to the point," he said. "My time is precious."

The planetary governor glared at Daire. Stellan shifted slightly but the energy in it caused the man to break off and look at him, sitting back in his seat. Under the desk, Daire reached a hand across and placed it on his curled fist. Her brother slowly and deliberately relaxed.

"Alright, listen," Langhari said. "You two are in deep trouble here but I have a solution for it."

"We're listening," Daire replied.

"The freighter-liner SS *Alamy* left here on its regular run twelve months ago galactic standard time. She was an old R-class freighter, crew of sixteen, hauling cargo and twenty-seven passengers. She should have returned four months ago. *Alamy* does a circuit of Barnard's Star, Lyare A, Monceros and Algol B. Confed Navy found a buoy in Monoceros indicating that the captain had found a new jump point somewhere."

Daire's eyes widened. "You think he jumped an uncharted point? Hell, and people call *me* reckless. How did a madman get in charge of a line-freighter?"

"By being the son of the owner," Langhari said. "Sometimes parents show more love than sense with their children. You know the type: overindulged, spoiled—"

"Now listen…" Daire growled.

"You were saying something about a means to resolve our present situation," Stellan added before things could entirely come off the rails.

Langhari and Daire broke off their collision course. "*Alamy,* is a single ship company," Langhari said. "Only a small firm would have service this far out of the frontier. Isn't that why you're here? Anyway, the economic downtown hit the *Alamy* pretty hard. They took a big loss on their last cargo run here.

"Captain Hara is a headstrong man and apparently took that chance to reestablish their fortunes. The gamble is unconscionable with passengers but the bounty for discovering a new hyperspace route is in the billions. More if it leads somewhere economically viable. He may have made a deal with his passengers and crew, or he may have simply hijacked them."

"Hard to spend it," Daire mused, "if the route brings you back thousands of years in the future, if at all."

"Just so," Langhari agreed. "Not to mention other unpleasant ends. No hyperspace route has come out in a sun or planet, the gravity gradient would prevent it, but some have opened in dangerous areas swept by radiation. There is also the prospect of encountering a new civilization with the unforeseeable consequences of that."

"So, what do you want us to do about it?" Daire asked.

"The Confed transport was on a mission. It had neither the time nor equipment to search more than briefly. The buoy did not say where in Monoceros system the jump point was. Doubtless Hara wanted to protect his bonanza from claim jumping. A jump into a new hyperspace point was out of the question for the transport in any event."

"For them and us," Stellan said. "Survey ships do that sort of work. The equipment and crew are expensive and specialized. They might examine a point for years before attempting it."

"Understood," Langhari said. "But Hara-san, some investors, and the insurance company have put together enough money to have a simple probe made. One that could jump through and return after some basic scans.

"Your mission would be to find the jump point, see if it is feasible to go through and return. If it is possible to go through, jump out and determine *Alamy's* fate. She is well over her life support failsafe, the route was always at the high end of her capacity, so a rescue mission is unlikely."

"Unlikely? It's impossible," Stellan stated, "with a class J freighter like ours we don't have the space, or life-support capacity."

Langhari waved a dismissive hand. "No one expects you to find anything beyond the frozen dead. But Hara-san wants her son's body back and the ship recovered if it can be. If there is a jump point, the bonanza will sooth her losses.

"What's in it for us?" Daire asked, before Stellan could stop her.

"This little contretemps disappears off all records, a standard finder's fee on all salvage and a two percent share in the jumping fee from Confed."

"Bah," Daire said leaning back and looking at her nails. "Get Survey to do it. Suicidal risks are in their department. Course, you may have to wait a few decades…"

"I could impound your ship," he said.

"I could call home and have my father send a freighter full of lawyers," Daire replied. It was a bluff. Daire would do anything to avoid calling on her father for help, but Langhari would not know it.

"Then there's jail time for you," Langhari snapped.

"Then I call Shasti Rainhell," Stellan said, who was not bluffing. "I leave to your imagination what follows."

Evidently Langhari had a vivid imagination. "What do you two young pirates want?"

Stellan sat back, arms crossed over his chest, this was Daire's province.

An hour later, they sat in a coffee shop looking up at a building topped by a minaret. Daire looked uncommonly pleased with herself.

"It is possible," Stellan said, "that piracy is your true calling."

"It bothered me to play the parent card," she admitted. "But it's all we have going for us, at the moment. Still, our record is now cleared, regardless of what we find. We have a contract to move the cargo that *Alamy* should have boosted to Monoceros. If we find the point, we get two percent of the upfront fee, one percent of any additional bonuses and a million credits for jumping through ourselves."

"I don't like the idea of boosting through an unknown jump point," he said.

"Nor I," she admitted. "But we only have to do so if the probe indicates less than a year out of space-time round trip. Otherwise, we get one hundred thousand for getting the probe in and back."

"But if it *is* less, we have to jump in," he said.

"I can't bear the thought of going back to New Eire admitting we couldn't hack it out here," she said. "I'm already ashamed that we had to pull so much on their names."

He considered. Like Daire, he had a drive to prove himself on his own. Possibly even more so given his neglectful mother.

"There is something to what you say. By using them as a weapon, we become bigger fish, surely, but we'll also inherit their enemies. Perhaps your idea of *nom de guerres* is worth considering. Not here or now, clearly. We've made an impression in this port similar to the one you left in that cheating Dua's head. Neither will fade quickly"

"We'll need to leave some word here in case we don't make it back," Daire said. "I hate to think like this but, well, it's a good thing that they have other kids."

"More sensible ones too," he added.

Daire snorted in irritation. "I'm gonna record something for Mom, Dad and Aunt Shasti."

"I'll do the same for Mom and Dad."

She looked at him.

He sighed. "You want me to leave a goodbye for her too?"

She just continued gazing at him.

"Do you think she cares that much about me living, that me dead, will be an issue?"

"Yes," Daire said quietly, still holding his eye.

"You want me to do this."

She nodded.

"For that reason, then."

"I'll take it," she replied.

Daire left to take care of some port paperwork and other issues relating to their cargo. Stellan resumed the never-ending duties of checking over the ship and making sure that space would not kill them next time they set out. It was always a point of pride with him that no official had yet found fault with the ship's condition or records. But first he took the time to leave messages as Daire requested. The ones to Robert and Lisa were easy, full of love, gratitude, and assurances that they should not worry about him and that he would protect his sister with his life.

Next, came the one to his birth mother Shasti Rainhell. He could not think of anything to say and returned to the engine room to recheck the sealed casing of the Cherr Drive. Finally, he could put down his portacomp and picked up his personal comm. He has promised Daire he would do this. In nineteen years, he had never broken a promise to her.

"To Shasti Rainhell," he dictated. *"To be delivered in the event of my confirmed death, or if SS Wanderlust is overdue past its life support capacity.*

"If you receive this, then I will likely have fallen to one of the perils of space travel. Know that I was doing what I wanted to do. I suspect that, in some way, you will grieve for me, for all that we have never been close.

"The one thing I will ask you to do is to reach out to Lisa, who raised me. Comfort her and Robert, who gave me a home when you did not. I have held this against you in the past. I will not do so now. I have learned from Daire, who seems as driven to space as you were, and as little interested in a domestic life. Maybe she has helped me to understand you a little better. Farewell, Stellan."

Satisfied that he'd done the proper thing, he returned to his work in a better mood.

CHAPTER TWELVE

Despite all that had happened, there was still trading to be done. They had a lucrative outbound venture. Because of the nature of that venture, they would carry no freight dedicated to a specific port, as it was possible that they would have to jump into the unknown. Like the ancient sea traders in the time of wind and sail, they shopped for those novel and unique items that would make them a profit no matter where they landed. Unlike with a shipped cargo, where they were only transport, here they had to use their skills to locate, evaluate and bargain, placing their capital on the line. Unfortunately, there was little that made Avanzado a trade mecca.

Daire found a locally made Voit-Veru liqueur that she enjoyed, and thought might travel well. There were native handicrafts and jewelry, including some unusual stones that Stellan selected. Only the unique, the utterly necessary and valuable paid to ship through interstellar space.

"We're not going to fill a cargo hold with liquor, trinkets and local handicrafts," Stellan muttered as they left a small shop run by one of the natives who'd resigned themselves to the alien presence. The alien had offered them a substantial supply of native rugs. Privately, Stellan thought them ugly, but tastes varied, and Daire thought they might appeal to the Morok market.

"No," Daire admitted. "I've a mind to take on a cargo of local lumber. That could appeal to crafters and furniture makers. Exotic woods from the frontier."

"Yes," he said. "That's a good idea, lightweight and the cost at this end will be low. But that is a very speculative market."

"It's little risk, given the outlay," she replied, "and will leave you with a bigger budget for gems. But we can keep looking."

They stopped for lunch at a restaurant run by a Drisnian. The small, grey-skinned humanoid recommended dishes other humans had found palatable. In the distance, a noisy demonstration was going on. They could see a group of Voit-Veru, waddling around with signs and banners. A few hopped into the air, waving their signs and looking like angry kangaroos.

"What's that about?" Daire asked the Drisnian.

The alien looked at the Veru with disdain. "Who knows? Damn Veru are always protesting something. You'd think they'd won the war. Pity they didn't all take ship and leave after it ended. They're half the trouble we have with the natives."

The dishes the Drisnian selected were good and they took their time at lunch. The demonstration was still going on when they left, and they gave it a wide berth. As they reentered *Wanderlust,* a bong on Daire's comm made them pause,

"Revol," she said to him, then opened the channel. "Greetings, Port Manager."

"Fair day to you as well, Captain Fenaday," came the Dua's voice. "One hopes you are in good health?"

"Much improved, thanks to you."

"I am gratified. I call with more good news. Our office has unofficially remonstrated with good merchant Kelmian about the effect his foolish incident has had on our interstellar relations. He has repented of his errors with you and agreed to pay the full contract price for the goods in the warehouse. He will also pay the warehouse fees, as he is responsible for the delays. There will be further trouble from that quarter."

Daire looked at him and shaped the word *Guild* with her lips. "We are most grateful for your assistance."

"We wish you safe voyaging and to have a better opinion of our little operation. You may even remember us to your parents sometime. Farewell."

"Well," Daire said. "All's well that ends well. Kelmian is sorted. We have a commission and there's nothing holding us on this rock now. I'm going to finalize our purchases on that wood. You do the same with the gems now that we are getting paid by Kelmian.

"All we need to do is wait for the Syndicate to get that probe and the sled ready, and we are out of here."

"A place I will not miss," he said. "Though I fear with our travels, we may end up looking back on this dust pile with fondness."

The probe arrived by tractor trailer, was inspected by them both thoroughly, as was its supporting software. With the machine safely secured in their main hold, they lifted off. Once in orbit, they passed close by the small and very basic space station that serviced the planet. Recyclable boosters were temporarily added, as Avanzado did not have an accelerator. These would boost them up to speed for the trip out to jump space without need to use any of their own fuel. A robotic commercial sled would accompany them, full of supplies to allow them to loiter near their destination.

They traveled out without event. The booster pack detached and would make its own way back, looping around an outer planet to return some months in the future. The sled, its rudimentary AI slaved to their own, fell into station behind them. It was expendable and didn't even possess a stardrive of its own. The close proximity to *Wanderlust's* Cherr Field would allow it to ride through essentially in their wake. Beyond food, fuel and water, it carried a few cold sleep tubes. There was no way to carry enough, nor was there any real possibility of finding survivors but they would also serve to return a few bodies, notable Hara's, at his mother's insistence.

Wanderlust herself ran mostly empty of cargo; other than some small high-value items they had traded for. The voyage would pay for itself by salvage, not trade goods and risk of loss was the syndicate's problem.

All *Wanderlust's* holds were packed with life-support supplies, fuel and material that might be useful should they need to make some repairs to *Alamy*. Stellan thought it foolish to carry much of it. They were not a repair vessel full of engineers and shipwrights. But the machinery could be sold should it not be needed, and the loss to the syndicate would not be much.

They began the series of jumps to take them to *Alamy's* last known location. This too, was unusual for a freighter, usually only warships jumped space multiple times in succession. Stellan weathered the jumps as best he could and was grateful when they finally reached Monoceros. For several weeks now they would ride in normal space.

Monoceros system held little to excite them: fourteen planets circled the blue star. Only on the moon of one gas giant had Survey found life. Mere microbes that needed a few billion years evolution to be interesting. The other planets were baked or airless rock.

They decelerated as soon as they reached the area of the outer system where Survey found the *Alamy's* buoy before she passed out of anyone's knowledge. Daire managed a station-keeping position near the buoy, then they set about hunting for the jump point itself. The Navy transport could have done it, but it would have meant missing a rendezvous with the fleet, something no commander cognizant of his chance of promotion would do.

For them, it was mostly a matter of searching on instruments, they knew something was there and suspected the buoy was not terribly far off. *Alamy* had made severe inroads into its life support and energy by this part of the voyage and would not have gone far to dump the buoy. Daire believed that they had only gone out of immediate detection range and her suspicion was well founded. They found the roiling disturbance in the gravity field after only two days. Now it was the probe's turn to take over.

Stellan worked on the probe, readying it for the plunge. It and he were in the main hold with its capacious hatchway on the lower hull of *Wanderlust*. The other cargo lay around it in space-tight containers. The probe was an unlovely thing, a thirty-five-foot instrument shaped like a torpedo, with sensors instead of a warhead. This one had seen better days from the cuts and welds made in it. The probe was in perfect working order but unlike during its service days, no effort was made at "spit and polish."

Stellan checked it over, humming an old New Eiran tune about a Galway girl to himself as he used the diagnostics in the inspection port and supplemented those with a scanner. Finally satisfied, he snapped the inspection port closed. "Probe ready, Daire."

"Great. Come on up. We can watch it launch together."

It was only a minute to reach the bridge up the companionways. *Wanderlust* was too small to boast turbovators. Daire sat on the left side, the traditional place for a captain in this format of cockpit. He slid into the right and tapped a holo screen. "Probe control on the bridge."

She manipulated controls. "Depressurizing hold. Cycling outer hatches."

"Probe on internal power," he added.

"Outer doors open. Clear to deploy probe."

He nodded. "Nav is online. Grapples released. The launch mechanism is pushing the probe out."

On the screen, they watched the probe, physically shoved by its cradle, move slowly forward toward the yawning hatch. The cradle pitched the torpedo far enough away so that the engines could be fired. The bay was brilliantly lit but they could not see the stars and only a yawning blackness seemed to await the probe.

"Closing hatch. Engaging engines," he said. "Probe is on its way."

On screen, the engines lit, and the probe slowly pulled away. As a torpedo, it would have vanished in a blaze of speed but there was no need for a probe to do so.

"Switching to your board," he said. "Your ship now."

"I have the probe," she advised. "On course for jump space entry in nineteen minutes and eleven seconds. Setting up remote sensor for jump."

She looked over at him. "This is like planetary flying on instruments at night."

He nodded, a good pilot not only used the ship's sensors but while in connection with them and the actual field of jump space, they "felt" the best point for entry and triggered the jump. But with the probe, they would be out of the jump field. She would have no feel and have to rely on her instruments alone, which Daire, a natural flyer, hated. Stellan himself preferred instruments and lacked his sister's ability to sense jump space. He had to concede pride of place to her as a pilot.

They waited patiently as the probe closed on the unknown jump point.

"It's never how I imagined it as a kid," he said. "No whirlpool of light, no flashes, just one instant a ship is there, next, it's not."

"Yep," she replied with a smile. "Not like in the *Fortune's Starr* movies at all. On approach now. Five, four, three, two and jump."

The probe simply vanished.

Daire stood and stretched; her shoulders must have been unconsciously tense from remoting the probe. "Well, it's away. God know when or if it will ever come back—a month, a year, a thousand years? At least we only have to wait for two months before we get to return and resupply."

"Feel like some dinner?" he asked.

"Sure. No autochef? You're cooking?"

He nodded.

"Watcha making?"

"Beef Bourgogne."

"You are the most wonderful brother ever."

"If you could learn one end of a ladle from the other..." he teased, then laughed at the face she made.

CHAPTER THIRTEEN

They settled in to await the probe's return. Days passed quietly, in maintenance and other work. With the ship in a long orbit of Monoceros, there was more than the usual downtime. Like all spacers, they had hobbies that whiled away the time spent in space. Stellan worked on martial arts, especially with Daire showing a renewed interest. The beating she had taken on Avanzado was not far from her mind.

But the mind as well as the body needed stimulation. Stellan spent the time crafting rings, brooches and necklaces both from stock he had brought on board and materials he'd traded for, including oddities from Avanzado. Daire watched in fascination as his big hands worked on the delicate metal and gems.

As for Daire herself, while she joined her brother's practice in striking and kicking, her love was dance. And she would practice for hours there as well. Her other interest was hydroponics and gardening. The ship's trays of renewable plant life did more than renew and refresh the air. They provided flowers for the table and vegetables for the pot.

Not that she did much with the vegetables. Daire had not inherited her mother's cooking skills or interest in it. Fortunately, Stellan enjoyed the additional time spent with Lisa, and had become an excellent cook, a skill much prized among spacers. They always sat together for dinner, with a tablecloth, cut flowers and all the propers. The ritual was comforting and gave them something to look forward to on the quiet days of waiting.

"Surely Hara must have been mad to take a liner on a starjump through an uncharted port," Stellan murmured after dinner, staring out at the stepped-down glow of the blue star.

"You're thinking of what happened at Beta Lyare?" Daire said, as she loaded the washer.

"The scoutship, *Silver Chalice*," he said, nodding, "went into a point there and was presumed lost. Then the Denlenn translated an "Old Empire" map the Culcacs made and found out that the outward leg of the Beta Lyare jump was 1037 years long. There was no information on the reverse leg. The *Chalice* won't even reach their destination for another six hundred years. If the poor bastards return, it will be to what? Everyone they ever knew will be gone for centuries. Will our civilization even be here?"

"True," she replied. "Beta Lyare is the longest jump anyone has ever found, though. Most jumps are under five years. And one leg is usually shorter than the other. So mad as it was, it's not utterly irrational."

He looked at her.

"Alright, even I wouldn't do it."

"Better."

I'd better watch it, Daire thought, as she finished washing up after dinner. *He's big, tough, kind, and can cook. The right woman comes along, and she might snatch him off my ship. Then where would I be? He's always been popular with the ladies, though he showed little interest in getting serious with anyone. Well, not after Thaliana anyway. I know he wanted to get out into space as much as I did, but it may not always be that way.*

She sighed, and as she always did with any problem without a quick solution, shelved it for the future

They prepared to spend the month that they'd contracted for, after which they would return to Avanzado and resupply for another trip.

The sled with its supplies and equipment would remain in-system in event of further need, sacrosanct, unless they jumped out after *Almay*.

The first week passed and they were well into the second before things changed.

"The probe," Daire shouted, racing past his room, "it's back!"

Stellan stood from his jewelry-making. "So quickly? Amazing." He chased after her to the bridge. They leapt into their seats. Daire quickly tuned to the probe's frequency. They could bring it aboard, but patience was not part of her character. The download of data began.

"The probe reached a brown dwarf system. Spectral Class L, so it would look more orange-brown than brown. It's got a chart name only, mass of numbers and letters. It's not on any known hyperspace route. It's a short jump in distance as well as time, 6.934 lights, a week out and three back on the hyperspace currents.

"Stellan, it's doable!" Daire's eyes shone. "Think of the money to be made and the fame for being the first ones through."

"Second ones through," he corrected. "Remember *Alamy*? Remember that they *didn't* come back?"

"We'll be more careful," she promised.

Stellan sighed mentally. There was no chance that Daire, living up to her name, would back out now, even if they hadn't been under contract.

"We must make preparations," he insisted. "In addition to leaving the probe here in case we don't come back, I want to broadcast the data on the twenty-one-centimeter band in real-time. That way no one can cover up the fact that we found the entrance and went in. It might be convenient for us to disappear rather than be paid all that money. We'll leave a disaster beacon here too. They can destroy that, of course, but a message propagating at light-speed can't be interfered with."

"Sensible," she agreed.

The pair spent the next few hours rechecking all systems in their ship. They were far from help now, and there would be no possibility of aid on the other side. Daire, as ship's master, prepared the message and broadcast it, staking their claim in the indelible fabric of the universe itself. It would be twelve years before it reached a transmitter across normal space, but it served as insurance of a sort for them.

Then it was time for the jump. They parked both the drone, its fuel nearly exhausted, and the disaster beacon. They'd recover both on the way back—if they made it back. The supply sled would again ride through on their wake.

Stellan prepared their jump drugs, as even a short hop in hyperspace could be debilitating. Their little freighter lined up on the coordinates the probe brought back. Daire nudged the freighter toward the spot in the firmament where energy roiled and twisted apart the fabric of space time.

Daire was in communion with their instruments. Good pilots approached the transition point armed with math and the best computers. Great pilots were able to "feel" the jump point. As they meshed with the electronics that resembled the synapses of the brains of intelligent life, they could sense more than the instruments provided.

Daire was a great pilot. Her eyes snapped open. "Jumping now."

There came a twisting sensation, colors tumbled, scents became strange. Stellan felt the plunge, then nothingness.

Suddenly the universe was back and in order. Stellan steeled himself with the discipline of a spacer and a martial artist. Breathe. In for four through the nose, out for eight through the mouth. Center yourself. Very deliberately, he reached for the vial of restorative. The jump hadn't been bad but like Shasti Rainhell, he was more sensitive to spatial-time disturbances than standard humans.

Next to him, Daire was scanning her instruments. As usual, the jump had less effect on her. She was only absently reaching for her vial. Even if the jump did not make one queasy, it depleted the body, so she drank the lemony fluid, making a face at the taste.

"No return on near-scan," she said. "Sled in formation with us. Wow, we are way in-system for jump space."

"Stands to reason," he replied, scanning the ship's systems. "A brown dwarf would have vastly less gravitational force. Any jump points could be further in than normal, less field density and gravity distortion."

"Thank you, Dr. Science," Daire said cheerfully. "There's the star." She rotated *Wanderlust* slightly and the so-called brown dwarf came into naked-eye view.

"More of a dull orange," she said. "Looks like a burning piece of coal."

"Kinda is," he replied. "Records say a mass of about seventy Jupiter-size planets. Too small to quite light up on its own. It may have accretion planets, but there shouldn't be any gas-giants in system."

"This one didn't miss star status by much," she replied. "If there are any small, rocky planets, they'd have to be in close to be habitable."

"Habitable? In this system? Dream on, Big Sister."

"My dreaming got us here."

"Well, that's true. Now let's hope it gets us back."

"Not before we look for *Alamy*. Scan is propagating. Still nothing near."

"They should have emerged from somewhere near our position," he said.

"Roughly, but that can still be light-minutes away. He may not have been as good a pilot as I am and mushed out somewhere else."

"Maybe he was better," he teased.

"'Nother word and I will clap you in irons—then it's bread and water for you."

"And I have to make the bread…I'm tuning for any radio messages on the usual frequencies," he said. "Hey, I've got something. It's a marker buoy."

"Yeah," Daire said. "Wow he did mush out—2.3 light minutes behind where we emerged."

"Do we drop one?"

"Nah, I'll just use his and allow for the time. Nice of him to light up the exit sign. But we'll park the sled here. Firing retro rockets to slow to station-keeping on that buoy."

"Wonder why he didn't make it back?" Stellan muttered.

"I wonder where he went?" Daire asked. "We came through with full tanks and extra life support. Hell, extra everything on the sled. He was would have started at about 50% life-support capacity and 43% fuel. Dumbass."

"He would have headed system inward," Stellan said, "to see if there were planets or anything else valuable. Getting anything more on radio or telemetry signals?"

"Only background so far. He was probably running as silent as he could, doing more listening than broadcasting. Should we do the same?" he asked. "We could send out a signal from here, just like we did in Monceros system."

Daire shook her head. "From the point of insuring that people know where we went and why, the Monoceros signal will do that. Here, well, we don't know who or what is listening. If we hear an SOS from *Alamy* that changes things. Right now, let's not draw attention to ourselves."

"I'm computing the best course he could have taken with his fuel and life support for a run into the inner system," Daire added. "Logically, he should be somewhere along it."

"Logic doesn't seem to be Captain Hara's strong suite," Stellan said.

"Well, if he deviated off that course," she said with a shrug, "then we'll never find *Alamy*. Maybe some survey cruiser will in the future."

"Anything on scan?" he asked, still worried about uncharted rock or even a thick belt of dust.

"Nope. I'm using the spare computer capacity to check for objects by occlusion, but you know what that's like."

"Needle in the haystack," he said. "Well, scan is out to 13,000,000 now. That gives us a big enough sensor envelope for the automatics to evade any asteroids at this speed. Brown dwarf systems can be lousy with rocks and gravel."

"Nothing like it so far," she said. "Changing course to follow

Alamy's best estimated. Go get some rest, I want one of us on the helm at all times. This is a new system. Anything could be here."

They adopted six-hour watches, usually just sharing one meal together. *Wanderlust* continued to gather information on the new system as they traveled inward from the jump point. They had no way of knowing how far in *Alamy* had gone, so they did not alter their speed. Nothing threatened their course, though a small comet provided a light show for them. They hadn't bothered to name the system; the syndicate that had sent them would claim that privilege. When they needed a name, they just called it *Alamy* system.

"So far," Daire said, around a mouthful of pasta, "this system doesn't seem worthy of a name. No planets yet, just some nickel-iron rocks and comets." With the scan building a better map of the system every second, they dared be off the bridge for brief intervals now.

"Don't be so quick to judge," he countered. "There may be planets we haven't found, asteroids with valuable minerals. The fact that there are ice comets means basing here is feasible. There may also be jump points to more exciting systems."

"Hah!" she said. "What has happened to my doomsayer? From whence comes all this optimism?"

He smiled. "You're rubbing off on me. I must seem giddy and dewy-eyed."

"Well," she said. "Me for some sleep."

He eyed her plates. "Guess I'll do the dishes—"

A bong brought them both upright. "Contact ahead," the neutral voice of the *Wanderlust's* AI sounded. "Extreme range."

Dishes forgotten, they raced for the bridge.

CHAPTER FOURTEEN

What *is* that?" Daire muttered. She tweaked the scanner, but *Wanderlust's* basic sensor set was unable to give greater clarity to the huge metallic blob ahead.

"It's not *Alamy,*" Stellan added. "It has more than a thousand times the volume and a million times its mass. Spectrography shows it to be refined metals. Doesn't recognize half of them."

"A ship?" Daire said. "Nobody builds them that big."

"That we know of," he said.

"It's not radiating much, no UV. There is some indication of infrared that could be secondary to power generation. There may be some lights that aren't visible at this distance, but it looks derelict."

"A space station?" he wondered.

"Unlikely," she replied. "It's in orbit of nothing. There's no obvious reason for it to be there, nothing to guard and nothing to service. Why would somebody build that much metal for no purpose in a system like this?"

"The only good news is that we've not gone far on *Alamy's* estimated course. We can use the fuel to slow for a rendezvous without cutting into our safety margins at all."

"If *Alamy* came this way," Stellan said, "they would have come within sensor range of it. They would have made for it."

"Agreed," she said. "Brother, this is a family choice here, not a Captain's choice. I say we go for a rendezvous, land if possible."

He looked at the mysterious contact on the screen. *I do not fear you,* he thought. "We're more than just merchants. We came out into the galaxy to make our mark. Let's start here."

"That's the spirit," she said with her usual wild grin. "Let's go get 'em." Her fingers flew over the instruments and *Wanderlust* rotated, her impeller drive beginning the most efficient deceleration manage-able. Meanwhile, they watched the information flow in on the object and the visual begin to grow more distinct.

"If that is a ship," Daire said, "it's like nothing I've ever know of. There's no design philosophy among the species that would yield that."

"Indeed," he replied. "It looks as if someone crashed a fairy-tale castle into an asteroid."

"And yet there is a faintly organic look to parts of it," she said, "as if it was somehow… woven?"

They looked at the vast bulk of the object occluding the star. Some lights shone on it, visible now that they were closer, mostly pinpoints of various colors that illuminated little. It seems a random collection of spires, towers, rounded hills of metals ending in ziggurats. The metal it was made from, and it did not seem painted, was a mixture of copper, bronze, dark browns and grays and the glitter of the occa-sional brighter metal or transparency. Clearly it had never been intended for any atmosphere. The vast structure rolled, not fast enough for any centrifugal gravity effect and for no other apparent reason.

"A mad being's sculpture?" Daire joked.

He shrugged, raising both hands. "It doesn't *look* like a warship at least. But it is alien. Daire, this is a fantastic discovery."

"Getting a heat reading finally," she said. "Inconsistent. The outer parts of it are space normal. I am getting some indication of more heat inside. Check the E-5 unit. I should be getting much more definite data than this at this range."

It took him a few seconds to do the diagnostic. "E-5 is nominal."

"Then our sensors aren't penetrating the exterior. I'm going to try signaling it. Radio first. I don't want anyone to get nervous about our communications laser."

They beamed messages in Galactic standard for twenty-minutes. Neither expected the denizens, if there were any aboard the vast alien hulk, to reply in standard, but it would show they were trying to communicate. Only the hiss of background radiation came in over the speakers.

Now, Daire began using the communication laser at a low setting. The flashes should get the attention of anything looking in their direction. Only stillness greeted them. They and the great bulk of the alien structure, slipped silently through the space of the brown dwarf, as if they had always been there.

"Derelict for sure," Daire said. "No space-faring people would ignore a signaling object so close to their hull." She slapped her hands together. "Free space salvage, and nothing about it in our contract. This baby is all ours. A bazillion tons of refined metal and who knows what else?"

"Shall we do a flyby?"

"Yes," she said, "slowly and at a reducing tangent, making several orbits of it. There may be some active systems aboard that could take issue with us being on an intercept or collision course. We'll sidle up to it."

For all her reputation as a reckless hellion, Daire was no fool. Space gave no second chances, and they were far from home. She set up the course and they closed on the object; soon it would be in visual range. Daire used the comm laser to signal and the ship's own lights to illuminate the massive structure ahead of them. They began to circle it.

"I thought it might have been a hollowed asteroid," Stellan said, "but it's all made of metal. You can see a sort of weird logic to it now.

This was built of a piece—" He paused as a large rent appeared in the ship. "Weapon fire?"

"Doesn't quite look right for that," Daire said.

As they rolled on, they saw more signs of damage, other rents and cuts in the ship's hull, some bigger than *Wanderlust*.

"Doesn't some of this look like it, I don't know, melted almost?' Daire asked. "Especially those towers there, they almost look like they became liquid and refroze again."

"This thing looks old," Stellan commented. "More of an impression than anything else."

"Yeah, I feel it too."

They were so lost in their contemplation of the hulk passing below them that it took a few seconds for the prosaic, clean-lined white and silver hull to register on them."

"That's the *Alamy!*" Daire cried.

"But what's happened to it?" he asked.

CHAPTER FIFTEEN

lamy lay below them, not so much sitting on the surface of the alien object, as sunken into it, as if the derelict had been soft mud that the ship had unwittingly come down on. About a fifth of the vessel lay embedded in the alien ship.

"How is such a thing possible?" he muttered, mostly to himself. Daire killed their forward motion leaving them a thousand yards over the other Confed ship.

"I know one thing," Daire said. "We're not landing on the damn thing."

Alamy, a mixed-use vessel, was, like *Wanderlust,* built to land horizontally on land or water, so they were looking down at the top of her. Her lights were on, but it was the wan disaster lights, casting a reddish glow on her hull, a visual warning to rescuers that something was terribly wrong.

"The bridge is in the center of the top deck of *Alamy,*" she said. "Just below us. Signaling now both comm laser, ship lights and radio.

He nodded and attended to the radio. "CPSS *Alamy,* this is CPSS *Wanderlust* out of New Eire, respond." But as before, the minutes ticked by, and the ship below yielded up nothing.

He leaned back and looked at his sister. "The table stakes keep rising, Sis. Do we fold out of this game and head home, or call? We've found more than anyone has any right to expect."

"And yet we know nothing," she replied, glaring at the ship below. "It's like space itself is daring us. Here are the big leagues, are you up to it? No, we investigate. Two reasons, I'd lose my self-respect if we just scampered off. Second, but more important, there's power left on her. Someone could still be alive. Maybe they have been surviving inside the alien derelict. We can't scan through its hull metal, we don't know. How could we voyage space if we left here without trying?"

"No argument from me," he replied. "But now, we broadcast all we know, eventually it'll hit Confed space somewhere.

"Yep, I'll broadcast our log and the images of the alien, now."

"Daire," he continued unexpectedly. "I too wish to explore this, but I will not allow foolish risks. You take too little notice of danger."

She looked as if she might argue the second point until she saw his set face. In matters of her safety, Stellan, who would normally indulge her any way she wanted, was immovable.

"Okay, if we are going aboard, we go everywhere together. Ya got that, brat?" When she called him that she was playing her high card, older sister and captain.

"Aye, aye, Skipper. You do the message. I'll get the gear ready."

They tight-beamed calls at *Alamy* for an hour, scanning as best they could with instruments not designed for this job. The vast alien bulk around them did not react to their efforts. It simply lay there, the movement of the stars showing its random, rolling motion. They had matched it, so the structure was motionless relative to them. But the few lights did not change, and the electronic emissions coming from it did not alter. They were ignored, not perceived or perhaps no one was aboard.

"The only thing to do is board her," Daire said.

"Please tell me that we are only talking about *Alamy*," he groaned.

"That depends on what we find," she said. "Start putting together food, first aid, water and tools. No telling what we may need."

"Weapons and armor as well," he cautioned.

"Yeah, that too."

Only Daire's deft touch on the controls made the docking possible. Once again Stellan marveled at his sister's ability to handle a ship, outstripping even their father. Daire's legendary impatience always disappeared when it came to ship handling. Still, it took forty-five minutes of slow and incremental maneuvering before she managed the hard-dock.

They came down atop the hull of *Alamy*, as far away from the area where the liner and alien ship seemed to fuse together as possible. It put their lower personnel airlock next to the big cargo doors on *Alamy*'s dorsal, an area designed for small ships such as shuttles to dock with the liner. *Wanderlust* came within a whisker of being too large, but she too had been designed to lock with a wide variety of ships, despite her ungainly design. They sat essentially piggy-backed along the raised spine of *Alamy* alongside a corridor running through the crew section abaft the bridge.

Stellan waited by the airlock, watching the umbilical auto-lock to the outer door of a personnel airlock on *Alamy's* starboard side. The interior of the tube was bathed in green light signaling it was safe.

Daire appeared at his shoulder.

"Spacetight," he said, "all the connections are made. I'm not getting any AI acknowledgement though, which is stranger than hell. No comm signal from a person either. All I can tell is that there's gravity and pressure on the other side of the lock according to the sensor on our side."

"The AG field is still working," she muttered, "but that's always the last thing to go when the ship's singularity fails."

"Unless it's the alien ship's field," he added.

"What's the reading?"

"On gravity it's 75%; atmosphere is 14.7 standard."

"Consistent with a ship on power save," she replied. "I don't think it's the other ship's field. Can't rule it out, but nothing points defini-tively that way."

They spent some time caching tools, food and water by the airlock door.

"Ok, gear up," she said. "I'll keep watch."

He returned to his cabin, donned his mother's gifts, then his custom body armor. He drew his spacesuit from its locker taking time to add the armored panels to its exterior.

"Hey, what's holding you up back there?" Daire's voice came over the intercom.

"Coming," he said. He returned to the bridge only a few steps away.

"Ok, watch everything," she said. "I'll get in armor too." Hers was kept in her space cabin off the bridge, little more than a closet.

Stellan stared at the silent freighter and the immense, oppressive bulk of the alien whatever it was. It did not look like a ship, more like someone had torn out a piece of a city and flung it into deep space. Lights shone in odd places, seemingly with no relation to each other. Most were pinpoints of dull orange, mirroring the coal-like local sun. But a few were a chill blue, or an unhealthy-looking green.

Don't let your imagination run away with you. They're just lights.

Daire returned in armor over her suit, with a stunner on her hip and a small laser in a shoulder holster. A multitool hung from her belt.

"Ready?" Daire said, clearly impatient to board *Alamy*.

"When we open the *Alamy*, I want you to stay behind me. There's no telling what could be on the other side."

Daire smiled and thumped him on the chest. "What sense does that make? Can I shoot over your head? Can I see through you? I should go first, and you cover me. I'm actually safer in front of you. Your hearing is better, and you'll sense something sneaking up behind us before I would."

Nonplussed by the good sense in her argument, he hung back as she cycled the lock open. He had the big bore pistol in one hand and had to admit that he could certainly see better over her than she around him. Not that it made him any happier.

The hatchway cycled open. Though they were in suits, the ship had atmosphere, and they had their speakers on. But the only sound was that of the hatch servos. They leaned in, Daire looking left as he scanned right, pistol in front of him. The corridor stretched away on both sides, ending in closed interior partitions that cut off the view. Some debris lay on the floor, a tray, a food packet, a single sock.

This was not the hallway of a ship in good order. Sloppiness on a starship was a symptom of system failure at least, and possibly disaster. The floor looked dirty, meaning the ship's servitor machines were offline. That meshed with the wan lighting and the minimum power mode.

Daire used a small scanner designed for atmospheric samples.

"What do you think?" he asked. "Suits on, off, or just use the local air?"

"Local air," she said. "The scans didn't show anything inimical. We can save the air in our suits for depressurization, or some other danger. It's going to take a while to search this ship, not to mention if we decide to search in the alien one. We can't carry enough oxygen if we use it here."

"Very well, but I should take mine off first—"

"—Because I can carry you if you go down?" she interrupted. "Stellan, you're half-engineered and big as a house. If there's something here it will affect me first. It might not affect your engineered interior at all, and you can carry me under one arm if you need to. I'll take the first breath."

"Damn," he said. "I don't like this one bit."

"I know," she said, "but it provides the best safety for us both."

"I liked it better when you screamed and cried to get your way," he replied. "I could ignore that."

She smiled at him. "Let Big Sis take the lead on this one."

He racked his brain for a sensible counter argument and came up with nothing. All he could do was nod.

"Okay, I'm going to do a quick sample through the test port in my helmet."

Stellan could only stand helpless and watch her as she opened the port, took a breath and closed it.

"How do you feel?" he demanded.

"Fine. Nothing unusual, the air was a bit dry but nothing else. No weird smells or anything like that. The life-support plant seems to be working within normal limits. It's cold but you'd expect that in a ship in powersave. I'm not feeling anything, let's give it a couple of minutes. Meanwhile, we can check this corridor."

With Stellan watching her and everything else, they headed right, toward *Alamy's* bridge. This was senior crew quarters. All the cabins were unoccupied and showed signs of people leaving them hastily. While personal possessions were there, what was missing gave some clues: clothes, shoes, toiletries, as if the crew had to go somewhere.

"*Alamy's* armory is just off the bridge, forward of that sealed bulkhead," Daire said.

He nodded. "Infirmary is aft of the other one, as would be the other-deck access. The only elevator is through the main hull top hatch and runs to the bottom. No access in this corridor."

"Well, we won't be using that anyway," she said.

When they reached the forward bulkhead, before the bridge, it failed to open. They backtracked to try the sternward one. It too, failed to respond to their proximity.

"More of the powersave?" Stellan said, "all auto systems are off. Still, these should react to touch if nothing else." He examined a telltale on the bulkhead. "According to that, it's normal pressure on the other side. I can use the manual and crank it back."

"Hold off. Time for a more serious whiff of the local atmosphere." She opened her faceplate as Stellan watched anxiously. After a minute of breathing, she nodded.

"I think it's ok," she replied. "We can move with the faceplates retracted."

He opened his. To his nose, the ship's air was both dry and a little stale. He checked his meter again: carbon dioxide and other gasses were nominal. But with the ship on minimum settings, the air wasn't being stirred much.

He gestured at a comm set in the bulkhead.

"Go ahead," she said.

"A female voice might be more reassuring to someone listening."

Daire touched the voice tab. It didn't respond. "No power, or the circuit is fried."

"They may have prioritized air and light and cut off everything else," he said. "They are well over their life-support endurance capacity."

"Which means that they are getting O^2 and maybe power from somewhere," she said, "maybe the alien ship? She's a fifth sunk into it. The lower cargo bays may be open to it."

"Or maybe a lot of people stopped breathing months ago," he replied.

"Let's go back and get our supplies," Daire said, "then we'll see if we can get through these bulkheads."

They walked back to the airlock. He picked up the cutting torch he'd positioned in case of need. Daire lifted the first aid kit, food pack and water canister they'd prepared. "In case we find anybody alive."

He nodded. "Set the ship to persona lock. Your or my living hands to unlock it."

"Already done. Nobody will be hijacking our ship without us."

"Good, it's a long walk home."

"Let's do the bridge first. If there's information to be had it should be there, even if we have to go back and lug in a portable generator to get it.

CHAPTER SIXTEEN

I'm betting that they entered the alien through the lower ramps," Daire said as they walked toward the bridge. "*Alamy* is designed to land horizontally. Her passengers and cargo could depart through the large ramps that formed part of the lower hull."

She carried a portacomp which she hoped would open some of *Alamy's* sealed compartments. They had already tried the access codes the owners had given them. Evidently Hara, the only one who could alter those codes as ship's master, had done so. Behind her, Stellan lugged a power jack and a plasma cutting torch.

The process was frustrating, with multiple trips back to their own vessel to get additional tools or more gas for the torch. They forced their way through the sliding bulkhead that led to the bridge and the armory. A quick look showed the armory empty. Then they opened the bridge using a manual override. As Stellan cranked back the door, Daire peered around it, a stunner in her hand. She whistled.

Stellan let go of the crank and his hand snapped to the autopistol. "What?"

"There was a firefight in here. Somebody voided a lot of warranties."

He leaned over Daire and surveyed the room. The equipment

inside showed damage, clear evidence of laser shots had left some plastic melted and cracked. Others might have been shot or struck with improvised weapons. Mercifully, there were no bodies.

Daire slipped in before he could stop her, and he had to crank the doors three more times to admit his larger bulk.

"Huh," she said, looking at the main panel, which showed considerable damage. She's already connected the portacomp. "No logs, no manifest. Looks like someone either buried it, encrypted the files deeper in the system or purged it. Probably Hara with his computer access. He was hiding a lot."

Stellan looked about. "The engineering panel is trashed. The fire protective foam triggered on it."

"What happened here?" Daire murmured more to herself than to him. "Was there a mutiny? Did the passengers rebel against what Hara was doing? Did someone from the crew have enough and decide to turn back?"

"My guess is that whoever started it," Stellan said, "Hara's faction probably won. Anyone else would have wanted those logs and entries to justify what happened. The ones with the command access would have been Hara, his First Mate and maybe the Engineer."

"Likely."

He knelt on the floor. "It's been cleaned but there's a lot of dried blood on this floor. One or more people must have died here."

"Damn."

"Yes. Let's get a scan of all this for the authorities."

She nodded, stood and used her handheld portacomp to get the necessary video.

"We should get down to sickbay," Daire said. "If anyone was doing science, their work might be there and maybe we can find out about casualties."

Since they were inside the bridge, it was now easier to get access to the lower decks. Daire didn't alter the settings and return power to the auto doors. It might alert someone or something below them. With the signs of violence on the bridge, simply announcing their arrival seemed less of a good idea, so Stellan opened each door with its manual crank.

Each corridor or compartment revealed seemed ordinary, but to a spacer showed signs of panic and disaster: compartments handing open, doors not secured, personal possessions and such lying on decks.

When they opened the hatch to the small medical bay, this was confirmed tenfold. Used medical supplies were strewn over what had clearly been a bloodied deck.

"Somebody here was working on a number of casualties," Daire whispered. "Check the autodoc. *Alamy* was too small for a ship's doctor."

"You do that," he said, weapons in either hand. "Let me check the adjacent rooms." He walked forward and around the diagnostic bed and the autodoc, which hung from its ceiling track where it could move about the room.

Daire walked over to a screen and pulled her portacomp off her belt. She used this to initialize the autodoc, which always had power priority on a ship. Stellan glanced over as the screen lit, then turned his attention to the corridor outside and the other entrances. Satisfied after a minute's search that there was no immediate threat, he returned to Daire's side.

"They didn't wipe this one," she said grimly. "It's showing treatment of twenty-two people, everything from laser and projectile weapon injuries to skull fracture and other blunt trauma. Seven of them died or were already dead when the autodoc checked them. It did some surgeries and recommended evacuation of three of them. They didn't have a cold sleep chamber so no option of a badly wounded person being frozen."

"Does it say who the injured were?"

"A mix of passengers and crew. The dead included the third officer of *Alamy* and two brothers who worked as space hands in asteroid mining. One of Hara's relations, an able-bodied spaceman, was among them too.

"Maybe the Third took a dislike to Hara's way of doing things and found a couple of miners to back him up?" he asked

Daire threw up her hands. "No way to tell, but Hara and his core of crew and relatives were largely intact. Only one of them died and two were injured. Most of the injured were passengers."

"Daire, if we run into Hara or any of his, we may have to defend ourselves. This is murder one way or another."

She looked up at him, a pensive expression on her face. "Agreed. The passengers would have had little say in this. As Captain, Hara was responsible for their lives and safe transit. He seems to have wiped his ass with that obligation. Until I see evidence otherwise—that makes Hara and company all suspects."

"They may have had allies among the passengers," he said. "The amount of money involved in finding a new jump point is fantastic. People have been killed for a lot less. We'll have to be careful if we trust anyone at all.

"What does the autodoc say about bodies?" he added.

"There are none in deep freeze. More proof to me that Hara and the baddies came out on top. They must have spaced the bodies. A hard shove or using a cargo handler and they'd have been tossed into the dark. Even if this thing's gravity pulls them back eventually, the corpsicles would fall far from here."

"Okay," he said. "Nothing more to learn here."

Again, Daire scanned the room on her portacomp for video before placing the small device back on her belt and pulling out her stunner, leaving the more lethal laser holstered. He thought about telling her to change weapons, then decided it might be better to have the nonlethal option and be able to shoot first and ask questions later. Daire might hesitate to kill someone. He wouldn't.

They continued to search the decks, finding nothing new and arriving at the deck above the cargo bays where *Alamy* had sunk into the alien. Stellan slid open a view panel. They could see the interior of the cargo bay, but the angle didn't allow him to see the front of the hull. Nothing moved in the minutes they studied the cargo well, with its bulky containers and webbed cargo.

"No one seems to be home," Daire said. "Let's drop the supplies we brought here and return to *Wanderlust*. We can get some food and EVA this from the outside before we open this sealed deck. We're far up on *Alamy's* hull, but I want to make sure there are no surprises with our own ship before we go further."

"Sensible." They dropped the food and water they'd brought down along with their O2 packs. There would not need them on *Alamy* so there was no need to carry them back. While it had taken many tedious hours of effort to get all the way down in *Alamy*, it took only twenty minutes to regain *Wanderlust*.

Stellan sealed their hatchway with no little relief at putting the ghost ship and the alien whatever-it-was behind them. They ate quickly, then Daire suited up for an EVA. Small and nimble, she would go much faster without him and use less life support as well.

He watched from the bridge as she exited a personnel airlock with a jetpack and a retractable tether. She first checked *Wanderlust's* exterior. Finding nothing amiss, she worked her way forward on *Alamy*, having sworn to not touch the alien ship. Daire reached a point where she could examine the join between the ship and the alien artifact. *Alamy* had sunk nearly eight feet into the alien in perhaps nine standard months. The atmospheric breach was clearly closed but even had the alien not trusted to that—it would not need to have drawn the Confed ship so far into its embrace. This was more a capture.

"Hara," Daire said, shaking her head in either awe or disbelief when she returned. "He must have used his communications laser to cut into its hull. He ran power from his engines for an arc cutter after that. Then he docked and put a soft seal around the area he cut, docking the *Alamy*."

"He probably figured it would facilitate looting the derelict," Stellan speculated. "Hara'd cut into his life support time badly and wanted to get as much as he could. Wonder how much of this monstrosity's internal atmosphere he vented while slicing into it?"

"Whatever damage he did, has mended, at least outside," Daire said.

"So, they did a soft seal on the inside at first," he said. "They must have, to stop the atmosphere loss. Then they went in, eventually all of them. I don't know how soon *Alamy* started to settle into this thing after that, but it was evidently too much for them to overcome. Or something prevented them from trying.

"We'll have to cut *Alamy* free, if we can, to return her with us. I don't think we have the laser power. I'm not keen on running power taps from the reactor to here either. We don't have that sort of equipment on board. We'd have to use theirs if they left it behind in working order."

She nodded. "I don't think we can cut her free. She doesn't have the energy reserves for it. If we just used *Alamy's* engines, she'd tear apart. Salvaging *Alamy* isn't an option just now."

He nodded. Daire knew ships better, if she said it could not be done, that was it.

"Let's get a few hours of sleep," she said. "I want to be fresh when we open that cargo deck."

"I've set the AI to alarm if anything moves in the umbilical or outside of the ship."

"Nice," she said with a smile. "Tricky programming that. But knowing you, I bet you started on that program before we left New Eire."

"You grab some shuteye first," he said. "EVAs are exhausting."

Daire nodded and headed for her bunk off the bridge. He stretched out in his custom-made bridge chair. Since they had to build it for a man his size, he'd made sure it would double as a decent bed. Daire, he knew, would fall asleep as she always did, like brick dropping off a building. He would doze lightly, in the way of the Engineered, asleep but aware. When Daire woke, he would slam down into REM sleep for a better rest.

CHAPTER SEVENTEEN

Seven hours later, rested and refreshed, they returned to *Alamy*, lugging more supplies, but now going down through the central shaft that ran adjacent to the liner's turbo. It was narrow for him, but it saved time.

Finally, they made their way to the cargo level. After checking the gauges that showed breathable atmosphere in the bay, some adroit hacking by Daire caused the door to roll back without a struggle. As the interior lights came on, Stellan leaned in, laser in one hand and big-bore pistol in the other. The cargo deck lay a level below them, with its containers and break-bulk packages secured by webbing filling it.

"Look," Daire whispered, her own laser in hand. "They did it. The cargo ramp is down and open to the derelict's interior." Beyond the clean white light of Alamy's ramp, lay the alien's dimly-lit and cavernous interior. They watched intently but nothing advanced out of it.

"Daire," he said, "back the lighting down forty percent, the differential in light is making it hard to see out there. It will save power too."

With the light dimmed, Daire could see he was right, the white light of the cargo bay had washed out all detail. But even now it was hard to know what to make of the greenish-gold space beyond the ramp. The interior of the alien boasted light, but it seemed an almost random assemblage of colors and placements. The deck of the alien was not like *Alamy's* level deck, with tie-downs and other provisions for cargo. It seemed to pitch oddly, containing bumps and hillocks, some of which were crowned with equipment. The area near the ramp was flat and contained some tables and other detritus off the *Alamy*. Hara must have set up a collection point for artifacts here.

They came down the broad stairs that led to the cargo bay. Daire unhooked a large light from the wall and shone it into the space beyond. It gave a view of the dark-toned bulkheads and things that were recognizable as hatches beyond. They saw no sign of Alamy's crew.

"Where the hell is everyone?" Stellan muttered. He holstered his laser but kept the pistol in his hand. They walked around crates and containers.

"Stay on the *Alamy's* deck," he warned, "and do not go close to the alien metal."

Daire nodded and paused well back from the ramp.

"Whatever is pulling *Alamy* in," Daire said peering, "isn't dissolving the metal. It's just sinking the ship into itself."

"That is good so far as it goes," he replied. "I prefer not to be dissolved by some weird alien metal if possible."

Daire waved a dismissive hand. "The tables and other stuff off Alamy are right there and are fine. No, this is either a damage control measure, or it's a way of capturing ships."

"A flytrap," he said sourly.

"Just so."

Daire squatted on the edge of the ramp, well back from the alien metal and peered into the poorly lit and cavernous space beyond. "It's not a total derelict. There's power, there's atmosphere and it's active enough to begin to absorb *Alamy*. There have to be people in there somewhere."

"Yet they haven't come out to meet us. Daire, this place is old. I feel it. There may be no one left. Perhaps there never were. Don't discount AIs or robots."

"Things are not right out there," she waved an arm at the darkness. "The people that built this would have no need to be afraid of two small civilian ships. What happened here? Warfare, system failure, plague?"

He shivered. Stellan was afraid of few things, but illness was a particular horror among Engineered. If their enhanced bodies failed, medicine was unlikely to help. "There's never been a disease that has jumped different star species, not even among the Denlenn and Dua-Denlenn, who must once have had a common ancestor."

"If it did," Daire mused, "there'd be no stopping it. It would be virulent beyond any measure we know. But I don't think it was unhealthy people that went into this thing. If the *Alamy* crew were sick, they'd have stayed here, near their ship with the autodoc. No, somebody thought their best chance of survival was going out there."

"There wouldn't have been space suits for everybody on *Alamy*," Stellan said.

Daire nodded. "Only the regular crew. There'd have been emergency bags for passengers but they're just good for a few hours and no one would want to walk around in one. So when they entered the ship, the passengers would have been unprotected."

"Makes you wonder if they entered voluntarily." Stellan wondered.

"Hara's crew had a couple of hard cases in it," Daire said, "and most of the rest of them had served with him for a lot of years. A lot of them were related."

"Meaning that he probably didn't have that much trouble keeping his own in line."

"Yeah."

"So, Sister, do we explore or pull out?"

She looked up at him as if he was crazy. "We board of course. This is the discovery of a lifetime. I mean, what did we go into space for, if not this?"

"I thought it was to sell overpriced trinkets to the natives?"

"Hah! That's just what you have to do to keep flying. No, this is what I was looking for, an adventure worthy of Aunt Shasti. Besides, if there are any survivors out there, they'll need our help. We can take back a few. If there's more, we can leave enough supplies until we and the Navy return."

Stellan sighed inside. Sometimes he wished she'd spent a little less time idolizing his birth mother and a little more time listening to their father. Robert Fenaday always hedged his bets where possible, and thought like a chess master. Daire seemed born to play poker.

They took light space suits, weapons, tools, food and water for several days. The thing they were to explore was immense. The space suits they would probably cache somewhere after they were sure they did not need them. It would be impossible to spend days in them and would just exhaust the suit's power and air as well as their own strength.

They could do little about securing *Alamy* behind them, lacking the proper codes. Nor did they want to risk closing the ramp for fear of being unable to open it again. They would rely on the persona lock on the *Wanderlust.*

CHAPTER EIGHTEEN

They stood on the ramp with all their equipment, under the clean white light, which Daire backed down to minimum settings. Again, Stellan held his pistol. Daire left her laser in its holster but carried a hand light and stunner. They stepped onto the alien deck, looked at each other and suddenly laughed, dispelling the tension.

"Well," she said. "No wave of alien horrors."

"And we didn't dissolve or anything," he replied.

"Looks like it's going to be a good day," she said, with a grin. "Gravity is a little higher. She consulted her portacomp. "About .90 of standard."

"Huh," he said, annoyed at himself that he hadn't noticed.

"If you weren't all made of muscle, you'd have felt it."

"Whoever these people are," he said. "They have far greater mastery of AG fields than we do. Ours are internal to the ship's AG grid. There should be a conflict zone where *Alamy's* and its meet. It should have overpowered *Alamy's* field since she's sitting on this with minimum power. Their machinery has incredible discretion."

"Yeah," Daire seemed, the avarice of a born trader glowing in her eyes. "Think of what that patent would be worth!"

"Doubtless Hara thought the same."

"Killjoy," she replied.

They moved forward, peering around. Of *Alamy*, they could only see the hatchway and its soft seal, and a little of her hull. There did not seem to be space enough for the ship to be drawn entirely in, but somehow Stellan did not doubt that it would happen. There was an almost organic and malleable look to the alien's interior.

"Conduits and air vents," Daire said, pointing up to large openings high in the bulkhead facing them.

Underfoot, the surface was pebbly in places and smooth in others, following no pattern Stellan could fathom. The air was cool but not biting as they moved around shapes and things that might be machinery. He found the random assemblage of lights and colors a bit disorienting save where dispelled by the clean yellow of their own lights.

"Some of it's familiar," Daire muttered. "Those are surely cranes up there. I see conduit, rounded, not square, like ours. Those grilled openings toward the upper deck must be air vents."

"Yeah," he said, sparing a quick glance upward but otherwise watching for anything that might conceal an enemy. "There's air circulating. And it's not steady. It pulses, probably at random. Somebody gave thought to simulating planetary atmosphere. That's good, as far as it goes."

"Which isn't very," Daire replied. "I think these were a big people." She pointed to what seemed to be the split doors of a main hatchway. "Even allowing for this being a cargo area, look at how high that hatch is."

"Yeah, but it could be for heavy equipment, or even small space-craft," he said. "Don't make assumptions, it colors your thinking." Privately, he thought she was right. If so, these aliens would have been larger than the bear-like Okarans, or the extinct Conchirri, the largest aliens anyone had yet met. It was a sobering thought.

They split at the door, moving to each side and looking at various protuberances and shapes trying to sort out some sort of control. Stellan also looked for some sign of a personal port, which would allow passage without opening the massive hatch. Not finding one seemed to support Daire's idea that the aliens were large.

Hope nobody is at home.

"Hey," Daire called. "I found the control. Form follows function. Boost me up there, I think I can open it."

He nodded and stepped back and lifted his sister to his shoulder keeping his auto-pistol ready. Daire manipulated whatever she'd found. The hatch opened, slowly but with no creaking, groan or other sign of disuse. Lights flicked on, a mix of greenish-yellow, blues and the occasional red or orange. Beyond, lay a trio of passages branching off from a round room with grooves on the floor.

"Hey, those grooves go up two of those passageways," Daire said as she hopped down. "A rail system maybe?"

"Maybe," he said, eyeing the passages which ran out of sight. "Do you see an identical set of controls on this side?"

"Huh? Oh yeah, let's not get locked in. Yeah, they're here."

"Good," he said, "wasn't planning to close it behind us anyway but some automatic might."

"Look," Daire said pointing at the floor by the one passage without grooves, "meal wrappers, plastic utensils."

"Yep, litter. Humans were here."

"And then they went on," Daire said, a touch of impatience in her voice. "Let's see if we can find them."

They entered the room, walking up to the litter.

"They must have used this as a base for a few days," he said. "There's a fuel cartridge from a portable stove. Plastic pads they may have slept on."

Daire looked at the three passages, the ones with groves on the floor were larger, the ungrooved one in the center seemed to climb in a spiral. She looked at its surface. "Pebbly for grip."

"And the grooves might have been for some form of transport. I think we should go up the center one. Wouldn't want to get hit by a cargo bus in these others."

"Agreed," Daire said. "Let's leave our suits here. I don't want to risk getting them torn and they're a pain to move around in."

They shed the suits, along with some of the equipment, and placed them near the entrance. Stellan rolled up one of the memory-foam mats *Alamy's* crew had left and bungeed it to his already stuffed backpack. If they slept here, it would keep Daire warmer.

Stellan wanted to precede his sister but knew she would again argue she couldn't shoot over him, so he settled for side-by-side. They walked up, staring at the lights which seemed placed randomly.

The halls of the ancient alien structure seemed endless, a labyrinth of green-gold metal lit randomly by lights of varying sizes and hues. Floors were neither even nor level. Nor was it entirely quiet. Some machinery circulated air, sometimes briskly, sometimes in a sluggish and irregular breeze. Any object made of metal made sound as it was irregularly heated and cooled. The sun might be a brown coal, but it emitted heat and radiation and space was always sucking both out of any object. So, there were irregular pings and bongs. Metal groaned and moaned like a distant soul in torment.

Watch that last, he thought, remembering what his father had told him, *imagination makes you jumpy. Jumpy gets you killed.*

"I have no idea what I'm looking at," Daire complained. "This thing is spacetight—which can't be an accident, but it's like nothing I've ever seen or heard of."

"Knowing how you love ships, that says a lot," he returned. "It's not compartmentalized like a normal ship, much less a warship. I'm not even sure these are corridors or passageways. What are all these bumps, structures and openings on the floors and walls? The lighting is spotty, bizarre and conforms to no pattern. Most Confed lighting is in various shades of yellow or white, for the suns that we all developed under. Even the Moroks, who prefer blue lighting, developed under a yellow star. They just prefer low light and evenings."

"Yeah," Daire said. "It's like a Christmas decoration designer went mad in here. I guess they saw best in this yellow-green light. It dominates."

"Some space stations have engine power, to change their orbits but this has to have a stardrive," he added. "Clearly, it never came from here."

"It may have fallen into the system," she said, examining a sweep of metal form that had no obvious function but towered over them.

"From another star system? That's millions of years of fall, maybe billions. And the lights still work, and it holds air and power? That's asking a lot out of even automated self-repair. Our technology couldn't do it."

"Well there," she replied, "is part of the answer. It has a stardrive, and it's functioning at least intermittently. It can't have moved far at normal space speed and has drifted into this system."

"Who's steering?"

"Maybe no one. That might be automatic or AI. Still any half-way decent AI should have noticed us closing on its position. Unless it too, is only working intermittently."

"None of this gets us any closer to finding the *Alamy* crew." he said, peering into an adjoining corridor. Daire was using a torch, but he preferred his Engineered vision which saw further into infrared and ultraviolet if he wanted to.

They entered into a large space with circular levels above them that were colored like the inside of a layer cake.

"We've stayed on the one passage so far," he said, "and the porta-comp has mapped it but I'm reluctant to rely on something that may get scrambled."

"I left my ball of string back on the ship," Daire said.

"I packed some tubes of ranger markers," he said. "At any turning, I'll make a mark on the wall. Any light will cause it to fluoresce."

"I knew I brought you along for more than lifting heavy objects."

The space around them was filled with boxy shapes that had no obvious function and varied from suitcase size to that of a small car. Some had smaller pieces on them, like tools or ornaments.

"Do we take some samples?" Daire called from halfway across the space.

"How do you know they won't explode if moved?" he countered. "We can souvenir hunt later."

They soldiered on another thousand yards up the pebbled corridor when Stellan pulled up. "Odd smell, not good."

Daire sniffed, but she didn't have her brother's Engineered sense of smell. "Yeah, getting only a whiff."

"Now, I go first and no arguing," he stepped in front before she could object and knew his long legs would keep him there. He heard an irritated "hmph" from Daire, but she fell in behind him. A minute later they reached a cross passage, in the smaller passage to the left was the source of the smell.

A pile of… something lay in the passage. Stellan made himself go closer and put out a hand when Daire tried to follow.

"This was a body, I think," he said, fighting nausea. "I don't know what happened to it, it looks like it's been ground up. There's bone bits, fabric, and hair. It's not a full body— God, Daire, were there children—"

"No, no," she said, shaken, "no children on the manifest."

"Something died here, something organic. It smells like human blood but it's dry and old. I'm guessing it happened soon after they arrived."

Daire scanned the area. "No sign of a firefight. No scorch marks on the walls or expended cartridges, no weapons on the ground."

He backed away from the mess on the ground. "There were no heavy weapons on *Alamy*. She had the usual stunners, and there were three lasers for the officers. No projectile weapons."

"Yeah," Daire said, "but the inventory doesn't always tell the tale. Does it?"

"Wish ours didn't. I wouldn't mind a triple-auto just now or an even heavier laser." He quickly changed magazines on his pistol. The new mag had a mix of armor-piercing and explosive bullets.

"What do we do?" he asked.

"We go on," Daire said, "people were here, and they were in trouble. Maybe they're dead, we don't know. But if it was us, we'd want someone to come looking."

"Daire, we're not Navy or the Patrol. We're merchants, and we've found this thing. Maybe we've done enough."

She was silent for a few seconds, looking at the desiccated remains that had been a person, on the deck. Then she shook her head. "Brother, I feel we have to go on."

He knew that she was asking herself what "Aunt Shasti would do?" Stellan had a far less idealized view of his birth mother and knew her ruthlessly practical streak. He wasn't sure she would have explored more.

"Very well then, on a little further." He wanted to say that if they saw much more of this, he'd get her out if he had to carry her kicking and screaming under one arm. But something stopped him as he looked down on her. The determined jaw, the resolve in her eyes, all were Lisa Fenaday's.

One day, my little sister will command fleets. My part will be to have her back, not to make decisions for her.

"But not down this passage," Daire said. "Let's stay on the main one."

"Aye, aye, Skipper.

She stuck her tongue out at him. He used the ranger market on the wall, drawing skull and crossbones for the body.

They proceeded, but now Stellan fell in behind his sister, judging the danger of something coming up behind them to be the greater. He strained every sense, but the vast structure was filled with the noise of its own existence. In this unfamiliar place he did not know what sound he could safely disregard. All now sounded ominous.

They spiraled up the passage, occasionally coming across some evidence of Alamy's crew: a lost glove, a food wrapper, an ejected mini-battery. At the next branching passage, they covered each opening but saw no additional signs of what had destroyed the presumably human body they'd found, nor any other sign of a casualty.

"Maybe whatever ground up that person was working off a dead body," Daire said.

"One can hope, Sis. One can honestly hope."

At the third crossing, they found a machine of some sort A dark-green barrel with three copperish tentacle arms lay on its side. Scorch marks on it and the bulkheads spoke of a close-quarter combat with lasers. More, the machine was physically battered.

"Someone had a projectile weapon, despite what the manifest said," Stellan judged. "Those are slugs—shotgun or particle accelerator. Hara was stacking his deck."

"So they fought this…thing," Daire said. "I don't see any… human stuff lying around. Looks like they won this round. What is it?"

"It doesn't look like something designed for combat. Could be a cargo droid of some sort or a maintenance machine. It might have had secondary security function. They took it down with small arms and maybe bashing it with heavy tools. Comforting."

"We know they came this far," Daire said. "It's been a long and tense day. We have to decide whether to go back to the ship or grab some sleep here."

Stellan considered. The security of returning to the ship appealed to him. But it meant a trek back. Then they would have to recover ground they'd already traversed. "If you're determined to go further…."

She struck a heroic pose. "Daire by name, Daire by deed."

"Then we make some food and crash here for a few hours, before going on," he said. "let's see if we can find some safer place than this open hallway."

"We'll take turns on guard," she said. "Surprises around here are apt to be unpleasant."

He gave her a fond smile. "I'm hardly tired. You can sleep."

"You may be Engineered but you need rest too," she said. "I need you alert and at your best."

"As you say. But I need only an hour for every three you do, and this cold is more draining on your tiny body—"

"Tiny! Ok, I'm a little short—"

"—I only meant in relation to mine. I weigh three times what you do—"

"And eat four times as much!"

"Too true."

Mollified, Daire edged past the dead machine into the side corridor in hope of finding a room or some more defensible space. But they only came to another smaller round room with spokes coming into it.

In the center there were structures on the floor. Of what, he had no idea. To him, it looked like a badly made sculpture of metal boxes. There was no sign that any part of it moved. Nor did their few basic instruments show any sign of energy or radiation. It was large enough that they could lie down inside of it, and it would provide some concealment and cover. The lights in the area were the warmer yellow green and abundant enough that they could see easily.

"It will have to do," Daire said. She shed her pack inside the sculpture.

He dropped his next to her then dropped the mat, which she looked at gratefully before folding it in two and sitting on it.

"Let's look around a little first, make sure all is well," he said, light in one hand and weapon in the other.

She nodded.

CHAPTER NINETEEN

While Daire unpacked their little microwave pad and some rations, he checked the area, looking over alien objects. There was the occasional small machine or tool that he did not disturb, but the area was devoid of any indication that it was used for living quarters. He suspected it was some sort of maintenance runway.

He leaned into the hallway that extended from it. These were almost as well-lit as the hall they were in, and he didn't need the light, so he hung it back on his belt. His hand ached a little from holding his pistol so long, so he holstered it. His instructors might have mocked him for having it out so long and gripping it so tightly.

Nervous in the service, that's me. The scrape of a booted foot to his left brought him around in an instant

Standing in the last of the passages into the sculpture room stood an alien. Tall, lithe, her skin was a deep red, contrasting with her long silver-white hair and eyes like burnished copper in a symmetrical and attractive face. He was so captivated by that face he barely noticed other details like the bronze jumpsuit, belt, a half-cape. Her hands were empty; arms held well away from her body in an odd posture. So, he removed his from his weapon.

The alien looked at him. And he at her

"Daire," he called.

At that, the alien bolted. Her speed startled him. "Wait," he called, knowing there was no way she would understand and started after her, unsure if it was wise but unable to stop himself. They pelted down the dark-green corridor of odd shapes and disorienting lights. But Stellan found himself outpaced even at his best speed, something that had never happened before. She gained with every step, sailing over any obstruction.

"I'm a friend," he called after her fluttering cape.

He heard Daire yelling after him on his com but could not stop to answer. The alien leapt over a divide, like a slash in the floor and onto something that looked like a cargo net. She scrambled up and out of sight before he reached the divide and stopped.

Am I so ugly that she ran? Has she seen a human before?

Stellan knew he could easily jump the distance over the floor divide, even from standing, but at his weight, there was no way he could equal her speed in climbing. She'd be long gone before he could reach the top. He looked down at the gap in the floor. It dropped away to an unguessable depth.

"Stellan, Stellan," Daire shouted both over his comm and from behind him. He could hear her running feet. Sudden remorse struck him at how he must have frightened her.

What was I doing running off like that without support? My birth mother would have laughed at me for a fool.

"Sister, I am fine. Only a little ahead of you. I saw an alien, but she ran away before I could stop her."

"Don't move," she ordered.

Oh, she is going to be very angry, and deservedly so. If she had done this, I would have ragged on her for days.

Daire appeared around the bend, eyes blazing and weapon in hand.

"All is well," he said soothingly.

She holstered her weapon, but he could see she was shaking with anger.

"You need not say it," he began. "I acted the fool and apologize. I should not have run off without you backing me up."

His sister put a fist on his chest—she didn't manage to speak. Her breath was coming hard and fast from the run and fear.

"I'm sorry," he said. "Truly."

He heard a sniff, then she thumped him hard with the fist. "If you ever—

"—This will not happen again. My word on it."

She relaxed, looked up and smiled at him, though he could still see her eyes held unshed tears.

"Let's get away from here," she said, looking around. "Tell me about her as we go."

Engineered senses alert, and looking in all directions, he walked behind Daire as they headed back. Though his hand rested on the butt of his weapon, he left it holstered, and Daire did the same. There was no hostility shown them yet, and it would not do to provoke it by appearing like pirates. They were traders. Drawn weapons were no way to greet potential customers. If there were locals and their prior experience of humans was Hara and crew, he and his sister might need to show they were peaceful.

Daire peppered him with questions as they walked. He was surprised at how vividly the alien remained in his memory.

"She was no human, nor any mutant variety that I have ever heard of," he said. "Humanoid, skin of a deep red, silver hair and copper eyes. She was athletic and fast."

Daire cast a glance over her shoulder at him. "What makes you so sure it was female?"

That brought him up short. "It was… just an impression. She was beautiful."

"So was Darren from high school. He was prettier than I was."

"You do well to remind me not to rely on assumptions when dealing with a new species," he admitted. "Appearances can not only be deceiving – they can lead to deadly mistakes."

Daire grinned. "Well, I hope for your sake she is a girl. You seem rather smitten."

He snorted but wondered if Daire was nearer the mark than he wished to admit. He could not get the alien girl, and girl he was certain she was, out of his mind.

"Well, a humanoid, anyway," Daire said. "Most of the known galactic species are. The existing ones anyway. The Voit-Veru are an exception. Historically, the Culcacs were avian. There's evidence that at least one of the Old Empire species looked like some sort of six-legged crustacean but all the current ones are bipedal, one head, two arms.

"That covers a lot of ground, Sis. You hardly resemble an Okaran or a Morok. It would also mean that ships, stations, anything built by such a species would largely conform to ours: rectangular doorways and hatches, stairs and the like. The interior of this place looked like a syndust junkie designed it. She was shorter than I, but not by much."

Daire shrugged. "She might not be with the original owners, or they might have been multiple species."

"So far, she's the first lead we have," Stellan said.

They regained the chamber where the sculpture sat. This in itself made Stellan uneasy, as Shasti had drilled into him, *"When you break off contact with an enemy, move to an unknown location. Don't appear in the same place twice."*

But was the alien girl an enemy? She'd been unarmed and seemed only concerned with getting away. Which didn't mean she wasn't rousing soldiers to come after them.

Daire seemed to divine his thinking. "We came here to find people. Well, one has found us. We've got to take some chances—"

"Some!" he said, giving her a wide-eyed look.

"Don't interrupt your captain while she's pontificating. Running back to the ship won't get us anywhere. What do you think our rep would be if we come back saying we found evidence of survivors and then fled after we saw one unarmed alien?"

"That we were too smart to die uselessly?"

"Think again."

"So?"

"Back to Plan A, you warm me up a nice dinner and I get a nap. If they don't come looking for us. We go looking for them."

While Daire kept an eye, Stellan heated rations for them. The small microwave pad could warm, boil water or cook depending on the setting. They enjoyed their prepared dinner of chicken and vegetables. He always had a few days' worth of meals stored aboard ship in preserving bags. They tasted better than regular field rations though they had those in their packs as well.

Afterward, Daire made an accidental but useful discovery when she twisted a nob on one of the small boxy shapes of the sculpture. Fluid spilled out as she yelped and dodged away. But a quick scan with their scanner showed it to be pure water. It flowed to a catch basin that opened. A quick twist the other way stopped the flow.

"So at least part of it is a fountain," Stellan said. "This will make for a more pleasant morning. Try not to twist anything else."

Daire stretched. "I'd leave it on, but the water might run out."

"Not to mention the sound might cover something creeping up on us."

"That's my brother, always walking down the sunny side of the street." She touched the nob again and the water stopped.

They stretched out on the highest flat part of the fountain. The sections around them would make any rush on their position a dangerous proposition for attackers. Daire gave him a bright smile when she lay on the foam pad he'd brought for her, and fell asleep instantly.

Stellan sat nearby, his large body and higher body temperature warming the semi-enclosed space. He was keyed up still and determined to let Daire sleep. When she woke, he might grab an hour. But right now, the alien girl dominated his thinking. Could she be quite as beautiful as his memory painted the fleeting figure?

She probably has a mate among her own, he thought. *Hell, she might be male for all I know. Why am I thinking this nonsense?* But it did make the hours in the alien sarcophagus pass more quickly.

Daire woke five hours later, fussing at him for not waking her earlier, then demanded he sleep. He dropped off for an hour and a half, then woke refreshed to the smell of coffee. Daire had taken advantage of the free water to make both coffee and hot water. He didn't need a shave with the depilatories he used but washing appealed. His sister had apparently bathed while he slept.

"Wonderful," he said, "had we been attacked you would have been the image of a heroine of the spaceways, laser in hand, naked and wet."

"Smile when you say that. The mere sight would have conquered the aliens outright."

He sighed. "Ok, how about some privacy, while I do the same." He cleaned up and dressed quickly, while Daire packed up their small campsite. Afterward, he shouldered the pack and they refilled their water containers.

"Time to go looking for your girlfriend," Daire teased.

He merely grunted and marked the wall showing the way back to the ship. They started down the corridor the silver-haired alien had fled. When they reached the place where the cargo net lay, Stellan stopped.

"There was an opening in the floor before," he said. "She jumped it before she swarmed up that net there.

"You're right, there was," Daire confirmed. "I saw it too. I didn't look down but—"

"I did. I could not see a bottom."

"What the hell sense does that make? Who puts a pit in a corridor?"

"A trap perhaps?" He took some rope and tied it to his pack which was the heavier of the two, then tossed it ahead to see if the floor opened up. Nothing happened.

"Tie it to me and I'll secure another rope to that cargo netting," Daire said, shrugging out of her own pack.

He considered, stilling the "Hell, no" that was behind his lips. He finally nodded and securely tied his sister to one line, leaving her the other to secure on the net.

"Leave no slack in the line," he said.

Daire made it to the cargo net with no issue and examined that netting for so long he grew a bit impatient.

"These are plant fibers," she called. "This was something made and relatively recently." She swarmed up it and shone a light inside. "Hey, there's planks of light metal up here. Enough to build a footbridge. More proof that the pit is a known feature."

She tied off to the cargo netting. He slid the packs across, then with the rope secured to the netting, he quickly joined her. The floor did not open even under his weight. If it was a trap, it was for something far heavier than he was.

"It can't be a trap," he muttered aloud. "No one would put a pitfall in a spaceship. There has to be some other logical use." But for the life of him he could not imagine what it was.

Daire went up the net, and he tossed up the packs and joined her. Then after making his ranger marks, they set off at a brisk pace down the hall. He wrote "trap" on the floor where the divide had been.

At first it was more of the same, halls and corridors, strange machinery, some of which they could intuit the function of and some not.

"I think we may be hitting a more residential area," Daire said. The hallway had opened up and the roof receded. The light over them was brighter. Once they passed under an immense canopy of some clear substance that revealed the brown dwarf, burning like campfire coals.

"It must be a transparent metal," Daire said. "It's insane to have such a vulnerable area over so much open space."

"Sanity and the makers of this place may have had only a nodding acquaintance."

They paused before one open door to look in at something that was clearly an apartment. A table and some tortuous looking chairs stood in one area. The beings that would have sat in them would have been twice as tall as Stellan. The table had square plates and cups, the latter big enough for a bucket. Lamps stood in the corners. There was debris and dust underfoot, perhaps from clothes, drapes, pictures and other things that made of less sturdy materials had decayed over the ages. The chairs and table were of metal but when

Stellan climbed up to the tabletop, the cup he reached for crumpled as he touched it.

"Some form of plastic," he said, "so old it just about dissolved." He peered at some bunks on the wall of the inner room. "Their consumer goods were probably like ours, designed to be recycled. But anything they made for the long run, their metals and machines, just bounces age off."

CHAPTER TWENTY

Seven hours later, they entered a large room, different from any they had been in before. Piping of some sort ran through the walls. As opposed to the more organic and greens and golds of much of the alien monstrosity, this room seemed made up of many panels of differing grays, from anthracite to a dove gray. It was one hundred yards to the far side, which held a similar opening to the one they'd come in through.

The light was dimmer here and both resorted to their torches as they cautiously moved in. The floor was dotted with small square and rectangular shapes about Daire's height, laid out in rows but with lanes between them which might be walked down. She went up to one. It held a grill and had the look of a burner or such. Cool air was wafting out of it.

"There's an odd smell," Stellan commented on. "Kind of like when you're standing next to the impellers when they're warming up."

"I wish I had any clue as to what the hell this is," Daire said. "This is maddening. We're both damn near born spacers; we should be able to understand *some* of this."

He shrugged. "How well would the astronauts who landed on

Mars in the twenty-first understand an impeller or a Cherr drive with no one to explain it?"

"True," she said. "Stellan, I am beginning to think this a fool's errand. We've been in here most of two days and only seen one unknown alien. There's no sign of any of *Alamy*'s crew, or any power that runs this place. The one alien…well I don't know what to make of her but if her kind ran this thing why would they need to improvise a cargo net and some rails to cross a divide?"

"What do you want to do?" he asked. "We've been keeping a map on our comms, and I have been ranger-marking our path, but I am also growing concerned about the distance back."

She thought. They had food and water for another day, two if they stretched it though that was hard on her brother with his accelerated metabolism.

"Let's check this space out and see how far we can see from the other side. If there's nothing exciting ahead, well, this is as far as we go. We may be as likely to bump into the red girl on the way back as forward."

"No argument from me."

They started across, keeping to the edge, with Stellan in the lead. About halfway, Stellan stopped to examine something that might be a control panel on a raised dais.

"The panel is still active," he said. "Some parts look burned out. Others look as if those telltales have been on so long, they've partly melted or affected the material covering them. There's some knobs and switches up here, though they would be big for an Okaran."

"Knobs and switches?" she said. "That sounds out of place and primitive in here."

"Maybe," he said. "Low-tech takes less maintenance and if it does the job, why go high tech? I'm not going to touch anything but since this looks like a control, I want to record and study it a little."

She nodded. It was too far over her head for her to see, so she flashed her light toward the center. There she saw what looked like a globe on a pedestal.

He was engrossed in his study of the panel, and its faint lights. She moved down the lane leading to the center, carefully shining her light about. Now she could see that the pylon and ball stood in the center of a disc of multi-colored metals. The pedestal was twice her height and the ball on it was ringed, and seemed to be blue, white and green.

Could that be a representation of the planet this thing came from? Maybe a solar system map? This could be a museum or a monument?

"Hey. Stellan," she called. "Forget that panel for a moment. Come take a look at this."

"Daire," he called, starting toward her. "Don't get so far—"

As Daire's foot came down on an anthracite panel on the floor of the circle a dull, base and bone-jarring noise sounded, freezing them in place with its sheer volume. Daire jumped back, but around the room metal panels were moving, one nearly at her feet, tumbling her away.

"Daire!" Stellan shouted, racing toward her. But fast as he was, the metal panel dropping from the ceiling was faster. He brother looked up and threw himself backward in a roll to escape the falling metal.

Daire clambered to her feet, looking about frantically at the moving panels with no clue as to what she had started. She looked back the way they had come but could no longer see the entrance. She dodged panels of metal, some descending, some shifting or rising from the floor. Stellan was nowhere in sight and she could only desperately hope he'd escaped being crushed.

She jumped an opening that appeared in the floor and noticed that while the grated rectangles before had been emitting cold air, now warmth flowed from them, increasing quickly. Racing and dodging, she tried to get out of the center.

A panel moved, and behind it lay the sanity of a green and bronze corridor lit by yellow-orange lights. She dashed for that opening, throwing herself across the last yards into it. She hit the deck, fortunately in a smoothly floored section, but fetched up painfully against a raised section of platform in its middle.

Daire looked back. The room behind her had closed up. As soon as she could catch her breath, she pulled her comm. "Stellan, Stellan, are you alright? Where are you?

There was no answer, only the hiss of the open channel.

––––––––

Stellan cursed at the wall that cut him off from Daire, but his strength availed nothing against it, nor could he find any mechanism that had triggered it. He listened but could not hear his sister on the other side. He tried to comm his sister but the portacomp showed no connection. The section of hull that moved had been thick, nothing either of them was carrying would have made a dent in it.

The moving panels around him revealed a room and in the increasing heat of whatever the gray room was, he raced into it. Now he prowled around the inside of the large room he'd become trapped in. It looked like some sort of crew quarters for something larger than himself. Bunks stood on the deck, though there were no mattresses on them. There were lockers but no clothes in them. He saw something he thought might be a water fountain and sure enough when he trod on a plate in front of it, clear water fountained up. He stretched up and quickly refilled his canteen.

At least I won't die of thirst in this nightmare.

As he looked around, he realized that one of the walls of his prison did not go up to the ceiling, it stopped at least three feet short. Instantly, he turned to one of the metal bunks. Like most furniture in something in space it had tie downs on it. It took only a few seconds to understand the latch and use the prybar on his tool belt.

The bunk came loose, and he wedged it between the low wall and another. He holstered his weapon and the pry bar. In seconds, he'd climbed the bed's metal rails and reached the wall top, broad enough for him to balance on and look down into another room.

The next room was lit by cool green lights. This was clearly a mechanical room. Some of the equipment, lathes, grinders and such, he recognized. Form follows function. Others, he was clueless about. Most important to him, it was open at the far end. He looked down, there was a metal table below with enough clear space that, if he were careful and lucky, he could drop down without risking an injury.

Stellan maneuvered himself and hung on to the far end of the wall with his hands then balanced on his elbow. He tried to hang from his hands on the inner side but slipped on the smooth surface of the wall top and dropped, landing with a bang on the table, which mercifully did not collapse. Stellan took the drop in his knees without coming off his feet. He snatched his pistol out.

Nothing charged out at him or otherwise reacted. He hopped off the table and ran to the entranceway, lest something seal him in again. Looking out both ways, he found himself in a long straight corridor, lit with yellow-orange lights that made it easier to see. The corridor was wide enough to have flown *Wanderlust* through. Two sets of tracks ran down the center and as far as could be seen in both directions. In the distance to the right sat something that might be rail cars. The light down that way was dimmer.

"Daire," he called on his comm. "It's Stellan. Come in." He called repeatedly, but nothing came back. He tried to reach the *Wanderlust's* AI and could not. In a way, that was reassuring, it meant that there could be a benign reason his sister did not answer. The mass of unknown metal might be interfering with her communication or possibly some energy source was as well.

I will find Daire. If it takes the rest of my life in this hulk, so be it. I will find Daire at all costs. Dad never gave up on finding Mom, well, either Mom, I won't give up on finding Daire.

He reviewed all he had done and how he'd moved. The left-hand way took him back in the direction he'd seen Daire. As there was no cover, he simply stepped out, pistols in hand and began jogging at a ground covering pace. There would be a hallway or something that could take him in the direction he needed.

Be alright, sister, be alright. I will find you.

As Stellan came out onto a balcony, he saw what looked like miles of machinery below him. It put him in mind of a giant tank factory he'd seen holos of from the Conchirri war. Lights flashed or pulsed. The air was filled with the hum of machinery, the snap of circuits opening and closing and the scent of ozone. The hair on his arms rose.

Lot of static electricity, not a good place for life.

He studied the area and saw movement, but it all appeared to be mechanical in nature, cranes, conveyor belts and the like. He guessed this was a repair and manufacturing center for the great alien machine. The prospect of going down among the machines and power conduits was unappealing, and Daire certainly wouldn't have if there'd been any other choice.

As he turned back into the corridor, he spotted something at the far end on his backtrail. He quickly faded back, opting for the laser, which would not be heard over the din of the factory space behind him. A picture of the alien girl came to mind.

That would be too much to ask of luck.

Slowly, he leaned out, laser down but ready. At the last cross passage, something stood, a bipedal alien, a strange almost avian shape, with a nodding head. It was difficult to see, perhaps it wore some kind of pale clothing?

Then it moved more into the light, and he realized why he was having trouble seeing it. It was translucent, the amber light permeated it. He'd swear it was wearing something like a spacesuit but without a helmet over the crested head.

A projection? A ghost?

The alien image wavered and was suddenly further down the hallways. He wasn't sure if it was walking or drifting, but mercifully it was headed away from him. A moment later, it winked out. Whether it had gone into another corridor, or simply into the wall, he wasn't sure. But he had no desire to follow it and find out, nor to appeal to it for aid. While it had not seemed aware of him or hostile, he had to fight a shudder at the thought of approaching it more closely.

A quick shock of static electricity interrupted his observation as his shoulder touched the wall. He cursed and decided to move away from both the factory and the image. Quickly, but looking about for ambush, he left the area.

The hallway branched into what appeared to be the entrances to enormous storerooms, possibly for the goods, or supplies for the factory. One contained acres of what he thought were compressed gas cylinders, another held drums of liquids which could have been for anything. All were larger than he could manage by himself, more confirmation of the alien's size.

Yet another storeroom held immense skeins of fabric of various sorts. He saw some that were so fine that he made a mental note about possibly finding them again, leaving a ranger mark there. The fabric puzzled him. He'd seen no fabric in use and no bodies to wear clothes, beyond the one ground-up human. Yet machines worked as they were programmed to do, possibly making and recycling fabric for their dead owners.

But it was the next one that proved a treasure trove. Precious metals of various sorts in large ingots, arrays of gems, some bigger than a man's fist lay in open trays in front of containers that promised even more wealth.

A sound made him duck into cover. Further into the room was a machine, twin to the shattered one that *Alamy's* crew must have fought. It appeared to be working on a machine, similar to an industrial drill press. It took no notice of him, though any half-decent AI should have noted his entrance into the room.

So the treasure has a guardian, he thought, glad that greed hadn't overcome his caution and he hadn't reached for any of it. He backed out and continued on his way.

Ghosts and machines that have been doing their programmed work for God knows how long? That thing I saw couldn't have been one of the original crew unless we were totally off about their size. I don't think it was as big as me. Could it have been another castaway? If so, what the hell happened to it?

None of this is helping me find Daire. Time to move on.

As he passed through what looked like crew quarters, he was struck by a sudden overwhelming sense of déjà vu, as if he'd been there before and knew the place. It was so overpowering that he swayed. More, he was almost instantly certain this was not his memory. He was seeing it from a greater height, and his senses were... different. As quickly as it came, the intrusive memory faded.

"What the hell was that?" he muttered and stared about wildly. In one corner of the room, he saw something and approached it slowly, then drew back. Something had died there, long ago. He saw the husk of something vaguely like a lobster, larger than man but with fine digits on its appendages, though there were also large fighting claws. Its softer parts had long disappeared leaving only chitin and rusted metal. It had not been an animal, but he doubted the desiccated corpse was one of the ship's original owners. It did not seem that ancient. He wondered how long the alien spacer had lain there in neglect and what he had died of. As he studied it, he noted something that looked like a weapon, though not for a human hand. The conviction grew in him that this being had ended its own life.

Why whatever kept the corridors clean hadn't attended to the alien's corpse, he had no way of knowing. Perhaps given the feeling that this place was an ancient device–that it was kept both clean and working ought to be more the surprise.

Stellan was not religious in any formal sense, for all that his father at least nominally followed the cultural norms of an old Earth religion. Lisa had too. Shasti never had, nor had it ever seemed to concern her. Sometimes his birth mother seemed to lack imagination and her mental force was only expended on the tangible. Perhaps because she had met godlike but living beings, it had cost her a belief in the divine. For himself, he was not sure what he believed but he felt some need to acknowledge the spacer who had died here.

"Sorry old fellow, whoever you were. The breaks in space come hard and cold, as I'm sure you knew before you lifted off, but it's certainly hard to land alone and far from home. Peace to you."

He wondered if his birth mother would have laughed, but knew Mother Lisa would have understood.

CHAPTER TWENTY-ONE

Daire wandered down the hallways of the giant alien structure wondering how to get back to Stellan. Despite her best efforts, she'd become disoriented in the endless passages and could find no ranger marks, nor signs that she was in the areas they'd traversed before. No effort on the comm and no shout had gained her any sign of her brother. After a while the wisdom of giving her position away seemed to outweigh the faint chance that he might hear her.

We both have our packs, weapons, food and water. I know he got out of the way of the descending wall. I saw him do it. He wasn't crushed. A tiny, frightened part of her mind said that she had no idea of what happened afterward.

It wasn't a trap. A trap would have been more lethal, more efficient. The wall moved because of some need of this giant machine, whatever that was, we just happened to be in the way. Besides, anyone who would spring a trap would follow up. All this did was separate us, but we're both armed and unhurt, at least I am, and I would surely be the easier target.

He'll be searching for me frantically. I have to think like he does. He lost me near here. He will stay as close as he can searching in as systematic a way as he can. As a last resort, he'll find his way back to the ship. So I should circle out and see if I can pick him up. I have no idea which way the ship is anyway.

Face it, Daire, you're lost, you're scared and right now you don't feel like Aunt Shasti at all. 'Course, there must have been times when she was scared and alone. She was by herself on Mounus being hunted by Voit-Veru infantry when she found Mom, right? Aunt Shasti didn't crumble right? You want to be able to hold your head up when you see her again.

The pep talk did a little to restore her courage. She'd always imagined herself at Shasti's side in desperate battle. Now was the first time she would have to prove, even to herself, that she was worthy of that position. Weapon in hand, she crept along, quiet now and listening for any sound that could be Stellan or anything else in the immense space. But the strain of the quiet and the fear that some other part of the alien structure would suddenly shift wore on her.

She found another layer cake room and raced in but there was no familiar fountain in the center. This one had a winding staircase in its center with steps almost three feet high for the huge feet of the alien's builders.

Up, more toward the alien's exterior.

As she began to climb, a scent reached her, tumbling down the stairway. A scent known to any gardener: plants, open earth and water. She continued up, quickening her pace as much as she could on the huge stairs. As she reached the third level, the area around her brightened considerably, not full sunlight as she was used to it, but enough that her eyes had to adjust. Encouraged, she climbed in almost frantic haste.

The next level of the spiral staircase opened onto a sight that stunned her. A vast cavernous space, filled with plants; a thousand acres and more. Above it hung huge lamps of glowing yellow. She even saw clouds of water vapor rolling slowly across it. One began dropping its load in a fine sheet of light rain nearby, stirring the fronds of trees.

Daire stood taking it all in, trying to make sense of what she was seeing: trees, bushes, flowers in every hue. Everywhere she looked, there was some form of fruit, nut or grain. She breathed in the riot of scent, which even had she not been used to the sterile air of the giant artifact, might have been overwhelming. It reminded her of her own tame little hydroponics garden back on *Wanderlust*. For a second, she had to fight off the shameful sting of tears at the thought that she might never see it again.

Aunt Shasti wouldn't cry! She shook it off and looked about. The area she was on was a platform above the dirt level of the surrounding area. She could see that the fields were not as level her eyes had first told her. There were very small hills and some thin streams running.

You're a gardener. Think. Not all your plants need the same moisture, and some will rot if it is too wet. But this is cultivation. Where are the farmers?"

Daire tried a few more stairs to see if she could see further. A scent tickled her nose, and she sneezed. As she wiped her eyes, she saw movement in the plants, a rustle that was more than wind. Something was watching her.

She waited, then looked down at her weapon. It might be a predator, or an enemy, but she was too far above the ground for anything to rush her before she could hit it.

Face it, you need help and if there's someone there, they aren't going to come out into a weapon. She placed her weapon in its holster, briefly considered drawing the stunner instead but realized that it wouldn't help.

If I'm wrong, I'll get to practice that fast draw Aunt Shasti taught me.

"Hello," she called as calmly as she could. "I come in peace. Please come out. I have put my weapons away.

For a minute, nothing happened, and she began to wonder if she had imagined the rustling.

"I speak your language some," a voice called. "Some, a little. Not enemy."

The voice sounded female to Daire, a little high, but that could mean nothing.

"Yes. I am not an enemy. Please come out. I will not harm you.

"No fight."

"No fight," Daire repeated.

A large bush rustled, and the alien stepped into view. She was either the same one Stellan had seen, or her twin. Her skin was deep red color, her hair silver and falling over her shoulders. Her large, slanted eyes reflected the light with a coppery hue. The alien's human-like hands were out and empty, held in the classic gesture most species used for *"look, I have no weapons."* She wore clothes of what looked like a metallic fabric in earth tones and a half-cape.

Daire mimicked her gesture. The alien was taller than her, perhaps six feet, athletic, graceful in appearance. Like Stellan, she felt it was female, but that concept might not even apply. For now, it was simply easier to think of the alien that way.

The alien turned slowly to a nearby tree and picked two pieces of a yellow fruit.

"Food," she said. "Safe food. Others of your type ate. When they came. I learn their talk…no, I learn their speech. Some of. Food is safe."

She advanced slowly. Daire was above her on the unrailed spiral staircase. The alien slowly placed one piece of fruit on the stair near Daire's feet and then took a bite of the other.

"Who are you?" Daire asked, looking down at the silver-haired alien. "I assume you learned Gal-standard from the crew of the *Alamy*? Where are they?"

The alien looked back, cocking her head at Daire as if to look at her from each eye separately.

Odd. Her eyes are wide set but like any omnivore they're together on the front of her face. She should have binocular vision. Her odd stance, arms akimbo didn't strike Daire as natural for some reason. Yet she didn't give the feeling of being hostile.

Daire picked up the piece of fruit and with misgivings took a small bite. It was often dangerous for a trader to refuse hospitality. The fruit was tart but refreshing. She liked it but limited herself to the bite for diplomacy's sake.

"Who am I?" the alien said, again cocking her head in short, quick movements. "Good important question. Bad answers only. Name is…

my name…me… original not oldest, original me. Name is Tifra il Edil. That one. Yes, that one.

"Job, yes, job," the alien seemed to steady. "Philologist. Yes, that word, knower of many languages. Translator. Scholar. One of great memory." Her body seemed to shake for a few moments.

Bitter laughter? Daire wondered, *seizure? How the hell to know?*

"One with an excellent memory," Tifra il Edil said. "A curse here, as you will find out."

"What do you mean?"

"Hard to explain. Start with who are you? Who is the big one?"

Daire drew a breath. "I'm Captain Daire Fenaday, freighter *Wanderlust*, out of New Eire."

"Names of nothing meaning to me," the alien said. "My name il Edil. Means Edil clan, born into clan --so il. If come into clan another way would be, fa Edil. Do you wish to speak formal?

"You mean names? No. Captain is my rank, master of the ship. Daire is my individual name, and you may call me that. My clan is Fenaday. New Eire is my birth world."

"So, Daire. To speak informally, I am Tifra. Mid-formal Tifra-Cha. Formal is full name. My species…Mefal."

"The big man, as you called him, is my brother. He is…" she paused, first mate might confuse the alien, "also my crewman. His name is Stellan Rainhell. His clans are Fenaday and Rainhell. Birth world New Eire."

Again, the head cocked, and she regarded Daire. "Different names? Two clans? Yet brother?"

"We have the same male parent but different female parents. I call him my full brother and let no one call him less. We have many different naming conventions among my people. Some take the mother's name, some the father's, some hyphenate…sorry…some combine the names.

"Untidy," Tifra said, almost as if in an internal conversation. "Disordered and confusing."

"Do you know where Stellan is?" Daire demanded. "I haven't been able to raise him since that hull section moved." She did not reach for her weapon but something in her posture conveyed menace to the alien. It raised both hands palms out again.

"Not enemy. Danger here, yes. You saw some of what haunts the passages. Come with me. I take you to where I and some live."

"I'd rather find my brother," she said.

"Not always safe here. There are others here who band together—stay safe. We will see if your brother is found. Others may know. We watch passageways for the mad or the dangerous. Come, come."

Daire hesitated. There was no way to know if this Tifra was trustworthy, but she was alone on an alien ship, with no way to find the path back to *Wanderlust*. Stellan might need help wherever he was now, and this seemed the only way to get it. One thing was certain; she would not leave without her brother.

"Why can't I raise Stellan?" she asked.

"Most communicative….communication devices work only line of sight here. Metal is very dense, many fields of force and power… passage… no, conduits. Disrupts communication."

"Surely you have intercoms. Who's in charge here?"

"No person in charge. Not a ship here. A derelict, yes, ancient of days ago. Long before my people. We are all like you… land here and not able to escape. If this thing jumps space again, you will not be either. We, the stranded, know how to work some things. There is no one who knows how to work all things. There are some places we have…internal communication… some places safer, more comfortable. I will take you.

"I will trust you," Daire said.

"Having no choice makes it easier," the alien said.

"Just so."

"Follow."

Tifra started out, gesturing at Daire to follow. She led her to a raised path of metal decking behind the fringe of tree and bush. From there it was most of a mile to the far wall. The trail branched frequently, but Tifra seemed to know the way. Daire noticed that there were splotches of color on the intersections and her guide clearly knew what those meant or knew the trail so well she didn't need them. The tall alien walked quickly. Daire was pressed to keep up, which didn't leave her much spare capacity for questions.

When they came to the partially open archway back into the more ship-like hull of the alien structure, Tifra's demeanor changed. She seemed more alert and cautious, carefully examining the hallway for danger before she moved.

"Why aren't you carrying a weapon if it is dangerous out here?" Daire demanded

Tifra looked back at her, the copper eyes reflecting the light like a cat's. "Some of us—we who wear this color," she gestured at her suit, are "speakers to all" supposed to be safe from all. Old, old custom. Most respect that, almost all. So, no weapons. But not all dangers here are from the living."

They came out into a wide space with many spoked corridors on several levels, some lit, some not. Tifra pointed upward at one three levels above where a dull red light throbbed. Something about it seemed...unhealthy. She felt her skin crawl at the sight.

"Never go that way," Tifra said. "None come back. Only screams."

They moved down a lower corridor, away from the unhealthy red opening. Tifra didn't seem to fear anything coming out of that glowing opening. But Daire kept glancing back, her hand near her laser weapon.

The passageway they were in branched. Tifra hissed at it.

"What?"

"This not always here. When here, sometimes one way trapped, sometimes both."

"What? Why?"

"What, why not always relevant here. Deal with what is." Tifra moved back into the corridor, she looked into one of the small rooms to the side and came back with two objects. They looked like a pair of free-standing lights, three feet tall, of a delicate make that once had fabric shades. She turned them on, each emitted a pale blue light then, to Daire's surprise, pitched one down the left-hand corridor. It did not smash but lay glowing about thirty feet away.

Then she pitched the other down the other hall. It flew ten feet then, as if a giant hand slapped it down, smashed into the floor. The light flickered for an instant as the lamp was crushed to the floor.

"Gravity gradient," Daire whispered. "But just in one place? What the hell?"

Tifra hissed again. "Yes, last time it was the other corridor. Also bolt of energy in the opposite one, side to side. Barely missed me."

"Traps?"

"Or maybe just bad old machinery? What difference? Acts as trap. Much of this place is like this. Random, mad, like some of the occupants. In space too long. Changed too much."

"Do we go back?"

"No. Other ways have other dangers and much longer."

Tifra led the way to the left-hand corridor where the other lamp still glowed. This time she rolled the lamp on the floor ahead of them. Twice she did this, each time apparently satisfied. They reached another corridor at a ninety-degree angle. There she set the lamp down, switching it off.

Tidy little thing, isn't she? .

She followed on the other girl's heels.

Well...I think she's a girl? Just like Stellan did. She's pretty flat up top though, possibly not a mammal-equivalent? Best not to ask, there are so many taboos about sex in many cultures and who knows what hers is like.

Considering that she was from a species Confed didn't know, we're communicating amazingly well. Someone on Alamy did me a huge favor in that regard. We might have been waving arms at each other for months otherwise. Even better luck that her job is speaking to...well it seems like there are a variety of aliens aboard. This thing has been capturing ships for a long time. Could it be it didn't notice us because we landed on the Alamy? She's still mostly exposed and even where she sank into this monstrosity, she's not well... disassembled, dissolved, whatever the hell happens.

Maybe there is a way out of here. For us anyway. And if that's the case I can't afford to let any of these know about it. I don't see any way to recover Alamy, and Wanderlust's life support could maybe handle at most twenty-five human equivalents for a jump back. Four more in the cold sleep tubes if their physiology is comparable. For now, something I keep to myself.

Right now, all I want to recover from here is my brother. Then we'll see.

She followed Tifra through the tilting mass of green gold hull and corridors and hoped. They travelled most of two hours by Daire's comm. If she wasn't lost before, she was now. But as they stepped out into one broad-passageway over an immense reservoir and what might be a water treatment plant, Tifra seemed to relax.

She looked back at Daire. "This area is safest. Unsure why, but least changes. Least dangerous equipment. We rarely see machines move about here."

She walked out onto a catwalk, more of a raised roadbed, Daire thought. More proof of the original owner's size. Tifra set a brisk pace but slowed when Daire visibly struggled to keep up.

"Area ahead," Tifra said, "is where most choose to live. Another section of plant farms, much smaller. All clean water needed. We call it the town, in many different languages.

"How do you communicate among each other?" Daire asked, still working to keep up with the leggy alien. "Do they all speak Mefal?"

"No," Tifra said, "Two biggest groups are the Pukts: small, biped, big eyes, beak-mouth and Akatis: tall, walk on three legs. Pukt language too hard to use, mouth beak sounds difficult, so we use Akati language. Easier and more logical anyway.

"There are some no talk with others. Odari like that. Unfriendly, live alone."

Another minute brought them to an area that was significantly different. The levels here were no smaller but there seemed to be more nooks and crannies and small chambers. A number of bipedal aliens were moving about. Tifra called out to two large aliens who stood near the narrowest part of the passage. Both were taller than Tifra, grey-skinned, angular, spindly creatures with three legs, something no known alien species had.

She stared at the Akati cautiously as they came up. Both wore reddish-brown clothes, apparently a uniform, and carried staves of metal with what looked like sword blades on one end. These reminded her of the martial art weapons her father practiced with. The guards gave her studying looks but relaxed visibly after Tifra called to them.

Clearly Hara-san had made the locals wary of humans. One of them went over to a wall and picked up a boxy object and spoke into it. Some form of communicator. Their arrival would not be unheralded.

"Are those weapons more than just metal poles?" Daire asked.

"No," Tifra responded. "We defend ourselves with simple weapons. Energy and projectile weapons draw the attention of the cleaners and worse, the executors, when used. Hara learned this."

"Executors?" she asked, wondering about the smashed machine he and Daire had seen.

"There are many machines here," she said, waving a hand at the massive walls and soaring arches of the area. "We seldom see them. Many are small and live in the walls and bulkheads, repairing, adding, altering. The Whisperers say that the City has grown much over the ages.

"The ones we do see are the cleaners, about the size of a Pukt." Seeing her confusion Tifra held a hand about four feet off the ground. "These have tent…" she stopped and seemed to be searching for a word.

"Tentacles?" she guessed and mimed something waving flexible arms.

Daire was certain the look she got was one of amusement. "Yes. Tentacles," she stumbled over the word several times with her help.

"Cleaners dangerous, but it is possible to defeat them. They tend most of the areas we can access, remove debris, dust and dirt and make basic repairs. They do not often come here but when they do it is usually to work on the water, waste or air systems. They ignore people for the most part. Sometimes they do not, the reason is not always clear to us. So we avoid them when we see them.

"Samplers are few, bigger than me and fast. Sometimes people survive them, sometimes not. All that is here is old, perhaps erratic, or so strangely programmed as to make little sense to us. They need not concern you.

"Executors, twice as tall as me. Shaped like people, so they can use all the passageways. They have many blades and weapons that burn or fire bits of metal. We have only seen them when someone tries to attack the City. Then they appear. But they do not even help the Cleaners when we have fought those. It as if they report to different authorities."

"Any of them ever fight each other?"

This time the look seemed one of surprise. "No. Not that I or mine know. Not a thought I have had before."

"It does sound like machine logic," she added. "In some respects very basic machine logic. This thing is a riddle wrapped in an enigma." Then she had to explain riddle and enigma. Oddly the concept of riddle seemed to elude Tifra, who eventually merely made a helpless looking hand gesture.

They passed the guards who looked down at them impassively, though one nodded to Tifra. Beyond the guard point, the passage opened out into another of the layer-cake rooms, though this one was full of noise and even some low tinkling music. A fountain gushed in the center and there were tables scaled to the most common size of Confed species.

At the closest table sat several aliens about Daire's size. They featured large bulging eyes and a formidable orange-yellow beak, talking among themselves, feather crests ruffling in an excited manner.

The bird-beaks and the tripodal aliens seemed the most numerous of the species in the plaza. She saw others, none of which she recognized, mostly humanoid. There was one life form that she swore looked like an animated bush with eyes.

"Population here always uncertain," Tifra said, as they walked forward. "Some vessels contain only one gender. Some species surgically prevented spacers from child-bearing."

Daire nodded. "That was done by some Confed species before anti-radiation drugs and therapy were developed. Not now with us."

"Most here do not reproduce. For some it is choice. Others, the conditions are not proper. Some species had only a few members to start; others have wasted down to a few. Some die naturally if they have not been through enough jumps. Others fade into wraiths, then whisperers, then random fragment of memory."

What? Daire thought but before she could ask, a voice called out.

Tifra paused as another Pukt came out of a side passage. It eyed Daire as he came up, taking note of the weapons riding her hip. The parrot-faced alien addressed Tifra in a speech that held many beak clacks. Tifra's reply was a different language Daire felt, perhaps Akati, given that she did not have a beak.

Daire waited patiently while Tifra reported to her superior. When she finished, the other made a gesture toward Daire, that she tried to reciprocate, and he walked off.

"I have told Councilor Scholl," Tifra said, "who heads the speakers, of your story. He welcomes you to the town and has had a place prepared for you and your brother should he be…when he is found. I am to take you back there. He will report to the faction mayor about your arrival.

"Faction Mayor?"

"Chief of our council. Leadership rotates among the Akati and Pukt who are most of the population. All others are grouped into a third party, and within them they rotate among the groups. The smallest groups simply do not participate and are governed. It has long been this way."

"It sounds practical," Daire ventured.

Daire followed her past what seemed like living quarters, some of which featured what she assumed were Pukt children. She was taken to a small, curtained room with some basic furniture including a cot for her and something like a futon for Stellan.

"What happens now?" Daire asked.

"Food, drink, rest. Since there are only two of you, after we find your brother, it does not cause…concern. You will be given list of rules, mostly ways to stay alive here.

"I go to brief council. Assure them that you are not a danger."

"Thank you."

"For now, we do not insist on taking your weapons," Tifra said. "That will follow if you stay here. Use your weapons and you will be marked by the City. Executors could follow. You will have no reason to use these here."

Daire nodded. "I'm a trader. I do not wish to fight, save to protect myself or Stellan. Nothing else here belongs to me, nor do I wish to take anything but knowledge from here."

Tifra's face twisted some, grimace or humor? "Knowledge of here, mostly useless elsewhere. Knowledge of us? Well, a curiosity maybe. We do not know where our places are, or if they still exist, or even if this segment of space-time dimension. Still, I will teach you if you wish.

"But trader, what will you do? Your ship joins the others trapped here. Who could you tell?"

Daire did not answer. Tifra assumed their ship was trapped but they had landed on *Alamy,* not on the device, the City as she called it.

"Would you escape here if you could?" Daire suddenly asked.

Now it was Tifra's turn to remain silent. She looked down at Daire with her copper-colored eyes. "I would. The other of my kind have been through too many jumps. Same for most here. Children exceptions, but only Pukt and Akati have those. I would see blue skies and yellow suns such as my crew did before I was born."

Daire nodded.

Tifra shook her head as if to clear it or perhaps ward off her equivalent of tears. "I go," she said, her voice notably rougher. "I will bring you some of the things Andrea, the one like you who died here, left behind. Rest now. Stay in this general area if you go out. Only I speak your language."

As she turned to leave, a small, furred being pushed aside the curtain. It bore a tray which Tifra gestured it should leave next to Daire. The tray contained a large bowl of something that looked like cream of wheat, a beaker of water and a cup.

"All is safe," Tifra said. "Bland but nourishing. We feed to sick children, so it should not cause you distress.

"This place...this part of the," she gestured which seemed to take in everything, "a little like a planet...so they tell me. We have three times.

The Bright, the Twilight and the Dark. Now comes the Dark. Most sleep."

The small, furred alien chittered something and backed out. Tifra followed. Daire sighed, looked at the warm food and decided to save her rations for another time. The meal was bland as promised, but filling. Afterwards, drowsy-eyed, she pulled off her boots and clothes and almost fell into the bed, still managing to keep her weapon and equipment belt under her, so it could not be moved without waking her.

Hours later she awoke, checked her weapons and sat up. The red girl hadn't returned, and Daire was determined to see what was around. She slowly lifted the panel. The light outside was low, this must be the promised Dark.

The small alien who had brought her meal was outside, not far away, seated at a very ordinary-looking desk with a light on it, reading some form of book. It rose slowly and walked over her small, furred hands up with her fingers spread in what looked like a placatory gesture. Daire stood aside as the alien walked in and retrieved the bowl, leaving the water behind. It gestured at Daire to follow.

They did not travel far. There was an obvious public bathroom nearby, which the alien showed her how to use. It waited outside for her to finish and return.

Daire sighed as the alien led her back to the small shelter. The mixed colony of aliens regarded her cautiously; not unfriendly, but wary, given the casualties she assumed were inflicted by Captain Hara and his crew. She was hampered by the lack of a common language but toured the area, accompanied by her small companion, trying to appear as friendly as she could. Some of the marooned spoke to her, knowing she could not understand them. But it was a start.

After a bit she decided to head back into the shelter. The chill of the area was beginning to wear on her.

Tifra returned while it was still dark, bearing the effects of the survivor who'd sheltered with them. She handed Daire documents and a data folio.

"She told us her name was Andrea Levinson. Much of what she

said was strange to us who have known no other world than this. But she was an agricultural tech, resettling on Avanzado after a divorce, looking for a new start.

"She seemed a nice person," Tifra continued. "She was very afraid of Hara, who she said was mad. She grieved for the other passengers who died, killed by Hara's men or things here. We were sorry we could not heal what was wrong with her. She sickened and died quickly."

Daire looked through the data folio. The woman had been in her late forties, with a grown daughter. Daire kept the pitiful packet that summed up a life; they'd be returned if she was able.

"What became of her body?" Daire asked.

"It is in the great farm, where most dead that the cleaners do not get are placed. She was buried by a fruit tree."

Maybe that would be a comfort to the daughter if she ever learns of it.

Tifra also brought a cube about a foot square which she placed in the middle of the room. She made a circular gesture on top, making sure Daire could see how she did it. The cube began to glow with an orange light. Daire felt a gentle heat from it.

"Many find it cold here," Tifra said. "We find these in place of machines. Circle one way get heat and light. Other way turns off. They never run out."

"Thank you," Daire said. "The chill here has been seeping into me. Is there any word on my brother?"

"We have eyes and ears working. And we have other ways to gather information. With luck, soon," Tifra said. "Some worry about how to approach him, but the first step is finding.

"For now, enjoy warmth. There are large baths nearby, very warm. Must wash before getting in but there are places for that." With that the alien girl left again.

Attractive as a hot bath sounded, Daire had no intention of getting naked anytime soon or being separated from her weapons. She'd only been shown friendliness so far, but it did not do to rely on it. Hara's people had caused problems here, and the stock of goodwill for humans was probably quite low. She sat by the cube, enjoying the gentle warmth and did the only thing she could do, wait.

Hours later, Tifra suddenly appeared at the entrance to the shelter. Her quick movements were enough to make one jump in alarm. Now the light outside was as bright as ever this space mausoleum was.

"News good," Tifra assured. "A whisperer shared news of the big one. Stellan. Seen near the great repair shops. It's decided that since he saw me and was not spurred to violence that I should find him. Others concerned. He is big, carries weapons and a dark aura."

"I'll go with you," Daire said, her heart leaping.

"No. Area he is in has dangers. Enough that I go alone, easier, faster. You stay here. We fear his aura if you are hurt."

Daire had no idea of what that was supposed to mean but sensed that Tifra would not be moved. Also, every second's delay risked Stellan's safety. "When you see him, say Aunt Shasti sent you. It will convince him that you are friendly and that I'm with you. He is by nature suspicious and dangerous to provoke."

"Good advice. I will take. Stay here. It may be many hours before I return. Others remain worried about your kind. They will not approach beyond bringing food, water. I have shown you facilities for cleaning. Have you need before I go?"

"No, just please bring him here safe."

Tifra gave a single nod and sped away in what seemed to be her default setting for movement.

CHAPTER TWENTY-TWO

Stellan sat against a wall, eating one of his ration packs. The meal, which would have satisfied most men, muted his hunger but did not eliminate it.

One of the disadvantages of being both large and Engineered. This body takes a lot of calories. Even the mad eugenicists who designed my birth mother couldn't lick that one.

After finishing every scrap of the meal, he placed the remnants in a line, making a crude arrow. His ranger marker had run out and he had no other means of marking the trail. His knife made no impression on the walls, and using the laser would be idiocy with no knowledge of what it could provoke. He was at a junction of some sort of rail network and what looked like a loading dock. The light was poor, but he felt that favored him with his enhanced eyesight.

Discouraged, he climbed to his feet. Even his Engineered stamina was taxed with twenty-seven hours gone and no sleep. He would have to find a defensible spot to hole up for at least two hours.

A whisper of sound caught his ear, and he stilled himself. Using an old hunter's trick, he opened his mouth to ease pressure in his ears. Again, a stealthy sound came, perhaps a footfall. He peered around.

The sound seemed to come from a piece of machinery that looked like a crane on a track over his head.

"Hello," a voice sounded from overhead, near the crane. "Aunt Shaztee sent me. Daire says to say this. Don't shoot at me."

No one on this godforsaken hunk of metal would have known to use those names unless Daire had voluntarily given them to them.

"Hello," he called in relief. "I won't shoot. I'm a friend. Do you know where my sister is?"

"Safe," the voice called back. "With my people. Food, water, rest, safe. She sends me to get you."

"Who are you? You can come out. I will not harm you. I am a friend."

"I am the one you chased before."

"Red skin, silver hair?"

"Yes. You chase others?"

"No. I'm sorry, I did not mean to frighten you. I just wanted to talk. To learn. Please come out where I can see you."

"Yes. Remember no shoot."

"I am putting my weapons away. My hands are empty."

Above him, the silver-haired alien appeared and looked down. She held out both her hands to show them empty as well.

"My name is Stellan."

"So your sister say. Stellan of Rainhell clan, yet full brother to her."

"Yes."

"I am Tifra il Edil. Means Edil clan, born into clan. Your sister call me Tifra. You can. It is form used between friends."

"Stellan is the same. My sister is unhurt?"

"Unhurt. We decide I find you. You see me before. Sister, say you think me female. True."

"Ah. Well. Yes, you look a lot like one of us."

"Skin, hair different."

"We have many such differences among us."

"We do not."

"Will you come down, or do you wish me to come to you?"

Tifra stared at him from her slanted coppery eyes which reflected the nearby light. "Come to the stairs at far end." She pointed into the dimness where he could see a stairwell. "Please come up slowly. I am friend. No weapons. I speak to all peoples. This is my work."

"There will be no trouble." He walked to the stairs and mounted them easily, impatient but unwilling to spook Tifra again.

At the crane's level, he paused, raised his hands and mounted the last stair. Tifra was there, standing well back. They studied each other.

She is beautiful, just as I remembered. There was a feline grace to her, as if she might flash into sudden movement. Her face was humanish, small nose, wide-set slanted eyes, long silver hair bound with ribbons, on her forehead sat some sort of circlet. She wore similar clothes to last time; earth-toned shirt and pants and a half-cape. Perhaps it was a uniform? She'd said she was a "speaker-to-all." A diplomat perhaps?

Tifra did not smile, and he, trained as a trader, made sure not to show his teeth. Only humans bared their teeth in smile.

"May I put my hands down, Tifra?"

She lowered hers. He took it as tacit permission.

"You look like my kind too," she said. "Skin and eyes different. Some of us have hair that is brown. Silver is most common."

"Do you run this place?" he gestured around.

"No. Save time. I will answer same questions your sister asked. This place ancient, unknown aliens made it, to work in space but not as a ship. Some sort of construction device blown into space by disaster," she stumbled a little over the words.

"All people now on it are stranded. Place either ate their ships, or they were aboard when it jump through space-time. Complicated, more talk later. This place is dangerous, sometimes intentionally, most times not. Still, always dangerous.

"I speak to all. Learn languages well and remember much. You will learn more why later. For now, come with me and go to your sister."

"Yes. Please." He walked slowly up to her, standing a head taller than the alien. The look she gave him was, well, he felt it was appreciative. He thought she was young, though that was a wild guess.

Get your head right! You're not here for a date.

"You speak our language amazingly well for someone, who could only have learned it after meeting people from the *Alamy*."

"Thank you. I learn fast. More on why, later, but this always my skill. Learning more all the time.

"Come, follow. Do not use your weapons in these halls. It will summon worse. Keep on belt."

"Agreed." Clearly there was some danger present, but not a pressing one. She seemed more worried that he might shoot someone or something that did not have it coming

They quickly left the vicinity of the machine. As they did, he studied his companion surreptitiously. Her movements were quick, sometimes a little jerky. She evidently had a high metabolism, and the coolness did not seem to bother her. There was a pleasant sweet-spicy scent to her that made him aware that he had not bathed for a bit. He admired her long limbs. While there was a pleasing roundness to her hips, she did seem slim up top, like a Denlenn demi-female.

She, he noted, also seemed to be studying him. "You are very different from sister. Not just gender."

"As she must have told you, we have a different female parent. Daire gave you my female parent's name so I would know I could trust you.'

"Aunt Shaztee?"

"Shasti Rainhell is her name. Aunt is a title, usually a blood relation but in our case, well, my mother is a great friend of my father and perhaps surprisingly, of her mother."

Tifra seemed to consider this. "Not unknown. So Shasti," she looked at him to see if she had the accents right and he nodded, assuming she could puzzle out the gesture. "So Shasti is "family of choice" to Daire."

The laugh that came out of him was unplanned. He was relieved it did not seem to startle Tifra. "In many ways Daire is closer to my birth mother than I am. But that is a story for later. We should be alert. You indicated there is danger here."

"Danger from the thing," she gestured around them. "Usually not intentional. Sometimes the cleaners... machines with arms." She waved her around to indicate tentacles he thought. "Sometime are dangerous. There are a few dangerous people that wander. Not many and most of them have gone mad. Also a few of your kind from the fight among the ship people but we have not seen them for months. Probably all dead. One stayed with us. She died too. Something wrong inside we did not know. Could not fix."

Stellan thought as they moved forward at a brisk pace. Tifra covered ground easily. "When we saw you the first time, were you looking for us? I'm totally turned around in this maze but that was quite a distance from here."

The alien girl looked back at him, her eyes catching the light. "No. Not for you. I...I wanted to see your ship...mean *Alamy* ship, did not know another arrived."

"Seems like a long dangerous trip alone," he said.

Tifra slowed a little. "I am restless," she finally admitted. "All of days, too the same. Time, sometimes I have too much of. The world, too small. My people mostly too old. Others, less curious or more afraid. It was a mission of myself. I wanted to see, to learn. Maybe bring back some treasure.

"Instead found you. The others of your type were dangerous. But we thought them gone. My whisperers gave me no warning of your presence."

"Whisperers?"

"Story for later. Anyway, be wary. Follow me. We have hours to walk."

CHAPTER TWENTY-THREE

Daire stirred. There were voices outside, some sort of commotion. As she stood from her cot, the same small, furry alien that had brought her food before opened the curtain and gestured for her to come out. She did so warily, but all anxiety fled when in the distance she spotted Tifra and beside the alien, Stellan, looking about at the crowd that had gathered a respectful distance away.

She broke into a run. "Stellan, Stellan!"

Her brother's head snapped around. He saw her and immediately started in her direction. Prompting Tifra to call out something urgent to the crowd, which shifted away and a few fled.

Seconds later she was wrapped in her brother's huge arms and lifted off the ground. Despite the emotion of the moment, he was, as always, careful of his strength.

"Daire! I was afraid you were lost." As if suddenly conscious of all the amused eyes on them, he quickly put her down. "Not the most appropriate way to greet one's captain."

She thumped him on the chest. "Ya big dummy. You were the one I was worried about." She hugged him again.

Tifra was still speaking to the crowd. While they had no way of knowing what was laughter among the diverse group, the murmur from the crowd seemed gentle.

Daire turned to Tifra. "Thank you."

The tall alien's expression seemed like a smile to Daire. "Doubt that you are family is gone. People afraid of the big...of Stellan... seeing him...gentle with you, reassures."

"I'm glad," she said. *Her diction and vocabulary are already better, less hesitation as she expresses herself better. How is she learning so fast?*

"I report back to the mayor," Tifra added. "Go rest and eat. Food will be brought." She looked up at Stellan who returned her friendly regard. "Much food, I think. Some spices too. I will come later for a long talk."

Daire led Stellan back to the compartment she was staying in. As she did, she noted a pair of guards trailed them this time. They hadn't been afraid of her, discounting her using her weapons for fear of these 'cleaners." But they were clearly wary of Stellan, as tall as any of them and built far more powerfully. She didn't mention it. He would have already noticed and probably expected such a reaction.

For his part, he was nodding and waving slowly to the crowd. Stellan possessed many of his father's gifts for diplomacy, which was good, as none would have come down Aunt Shasti's line. Some of the aliens waved back and all seemed comforted by his relaxed manner.

As they went in, Daire dropped the curtain and pointed to the futon on the floor. Stellan sighed in pleasure as he slipped out of his boots and flopped on the mattress.

"You can even get cleaned up later," she replied. "They have a communal hot water bath apparently."

"Ah, bliss. I could almost like this place."

Daire and Stellan sat next to the glowing cube. His sister sat with her back to the cube, seeming to soak in the heat. "I don't think I've been really warm since we set foot on this thing."

He gave her a half smile. "I feel the same way about being full." Then he frowned. "I will save our own supplies since fresh food is available here. Hopefully we can get more when we get back to our ship."

"Agreed," she said. Then dropping her voice to a whisper. "Don't tell anyone here that we landed on *Alamy* and not this station. We couldn't possibly evacuate all the people we see here."

He nodded. "How many of these here speak Gal standard? And where are the crew of the *Alamy*?"

"I don't know about the *Alamy* other than one passenger who sheltered with them and died suddenly. They don't know why. Tifra hasn't been exactly forthcoming. As for being overheard, well, she's a professional translator and she clearly learned from one the *Alamy* crew. I've seen two others with similar uniforms to hers. But if I were them, I might put someone out of uniform near us to listen in. If they all learn as fast as Tifra, there could be more ears here than they are admitting."

"Good thinking. Almost as suspicious as my mother," he said. "Keep that up. The way we are being watched; I do not believe that *Alamy* crew served as good ambassadors for our kind."

"Yet they sheltered poor Andrea. We don't have time to develop relationships with a lot of folks here. Plus the chances of establishing rapport with anyone but Tifra seem remote."

He shifted to look at her. "What are you saying?"

"There's no chance we'd survive the trek back to the ship, even if she gave us directions. This place is dangerous as hell. I think we need to take her into our confidence and that means seeing who wants to get a free ride out of this nightmare. From what she says, almost no one here can leave. They've been here too long and have been too changed by the transdimensional drive's side effects. I even wonder how many would try."

He nodded. "Tifra is the youngest person we have seen save for the Pukt and Akati children. She's very alone."

Daire gave her brother a curious look. Stellan had the normal interest in girls for a young male, but there was something more going on. He'd been fascinated by Tifra since he first saw her.

"Well for certain, she's in the small group that might risk leaving. I don't think that the Pukt or Akati would send their children off in the care of unknown aliens, especially after Hara and his bunch. The only other candidates are the Odari, off the most recent capture before Alamy. From what we've heard of them—I think the effort there wouldn't be worth the time or risk."

"Agreed," Stellan said, "Let's say for now that they are not our problem. That brings us back to just Tifra."

"And if there any survivors of Hara's group?"

He looked at her in surprise. "Why concern ourselves with them?"

"Think for a moment beyond your alien sweetheart," Daire said, in exasperation. "What do we really know? Hara led them here. We suspect some were threatened or just shanghaied, but we don't know that. They clearly were attacked by a sampler and a cleaner, maybe they thought everyone was an enemy. We also only have the word of a group of aliens we've never met for how they acted here. Beyond that —there may have been some drafted or threatened into Hara's group."

"This has not escaped my attention. But Daire, you have a tendency to see more good in people than is present. You are gentle of heart. The survivors with Hara now are only the hard and tough. The gentle, the good and the weak, were killed on *Alamy* or here. Do not delude yourself. Our job now is to save ourselves, and if she and you both will it, take Tifra with us."

"You really like her, don't you?"

Stellan looked embarrassed and for a moment much younger. "I can't deny it. I find her beautiful and more. There is something about her. I....can't explain."

Food was brought. The porridge that they had given Daire, along with some spices and baked goods and some fruit. Stellan carefully sampled everything, then, hunger getting the best of him, slowly ate it all, experimenting a little with the spices and letting Daire sample from his plate. She nibbled with a better appetite, reveling in his brother's presence.

CHAPTER TWENTY-FOUR

Tifra returned after briefing her captain and the faction mayor. "Come, walk with me. There is a pleasant place for growing nearby. One can even see stars from a panel there."

They followed Tifra out. The small furred being was not at its desk and there was only one guard who nodded to her and then resumed his easy three-legged stance. Aliens of various types, though mostly Akati and Pukt, walked about the tasks of their daily lives. All gazed at them curiously. Many called out a greeting or question of some sort to Tifra, who occasionally had to stop to answer. But they made their way through the outskirts of the settlement following the silver-haired girl. They saw another Mefal, this one walking with a cane, who waved to Tifra, who waved back.

Some small children watched them from a distance. Where human children might have thronged them, the Akati and Pukts stayed well back, either afraid, or simply not curious in the human fashion.

A long, wide, sloping passage led them upwards. As promised, there was a wide space akin to a park. The artificial lights here were more orange than yellow, but the plant life here did not seem to mind.

"Ah," Tifra said, "we have arrived at the right time and at my favorite place."

The orange lights above them dimmed to a cool blue that barely illuminated the vegetation around them. The sight above captured their attention. At some time, a great force had torn a rent in the alien machine. For whatever reason, it had been filled with a transparent material. Through it they could see a swath of stars. At that moment, the dull burning coal that was this system's sun swung into view as the machine rolled in its long slow orbit.

"Beautiful," Tifra said, as it glowed above them.

Both Daire and Stellan also gazed at it, neither realizing how much they had missed a sky until this moment. Then the orbit took it out of view.

Tifra lay back on something like grass, and they did the same, looking at a night sky. "I have spoken with the council and assured them that you mean no harm to us and were not like Hara's," she stumbled a little over the term, "crew. That you are merchants and not fighters. Some doubt that seeing you," she looked at Stellan. "But your sister and how you are with her, support this. Since there are only two of you, you are welcomed to the Town provided you abide by our laws and customs."

"Are we to meet the council?"

"Not in person for now. We learned much of your people from Andrea and in any event, only I can speak directly to you. I bring whatever questions they want answered."

Stellan and Daire looked at each other puzzled.

Tifra caught the look and seemed to understand it. "Remember, curiosity about your kind is meaningless here. All are stuck here and cannot leave. So what use is such information save as a diversion? Please take no insult, but your arrival here is not of great import to the leadership.

"We already met your people and for that reason, some are reluctant to be near you. To others, it is of no interest, or they are cautious of the new and will do so in their own time, of which we have much here.

"Akati and Pukt are mostly interested in themselves. My people are curious, and I have told them much, you will likely meet them soon. Others such as Pucari, the alien who has attended you, are friendly.

"But since food and shelter are not issues here and it is a society of the marooned, we have long been accustomed to adopting new arrivals."

"So what must we not do?" Stellan, practical as usual asked.

"As I told Daire-sister before, we will not take your weapons, but you must not use them. To do will bring the cleaners or worse against you. We will not help you should you do so. Do no violence against anyone, or face banishment for a time. We are aliens to each other, should a taboo or cultural norm be violated you come to one in a bronze uniform…well, me, until you learn Akati. A mediation will be held, and the issue resolved.

"While the City supplies basic foods, we do grow a greater variety in the fields and all serve, gather food and do such manual labor as is occasionally necessary. You will be notified of when your turn will be, but it will not be soon. We understand the need to become…

"Acclimatized, used to," Stellan offered.

Tifra nodded, pleased. "Just so."

"Your personal possessions are yours, but any other equipment becomes property of the community. I have talked to the council about leading a group to salvage your vessels before they are drawn in and disassembled but with the distance and danger there was little appetite for it. I think this is foolish and will try again."

Daire looked at Stellan who nodded.

"It's past time we were honest with each other," Daire began.

Tifra simply stared back, cocking her head from side to side in that odd way of hers. Finally, she said. "You, first."

Stellan sensing this was a negotiation like any other, let his sister lead.

"Some of this you may know from Andrea. We came here from a frontier world of the Confederation of Species— an interstellar organization that exists in an area that extends over a thousand parsecs, joined of course by the various pipelines of interstellar travels through jumpspace. I assume that is how your own people transit?"

"How we did, yes. How most of us did. Though not this place. This place we think travels in dimensions as well."

"We're a small trading ship," Daire continued, "hired to see if the fate of the *Alamy* could be determined."

Tifra waved a hand. "Obvious, small ship, else captain and first mate come into unknown place and in danger. Why no warship come looking?"

"*Alamy* is itself a small ship and privately owned. Naval vessels, even in something as large as the Confederation, are rarely at rest, or available for searching for small ships lost on a frontier."

"Same," Tifra nodded. Either she knew their gesture, or her species had a similar one. "No one searches for lost small ships. So my captain says."

"You might be surprised," Stellan said, thinking of his father. Tifra spared him a glance but said nothing.

"A probe," Daire continues, "told us that the jump *Alamy* made from a well-known point in our space into unknown space was short. We had contracted to come through and search, less for survivors than for bodies. Some of our people have burial customs that emphasize recovering the deceased's body. There was also the financial matter of the ship and her cargo. We came through hoping to find salvage and found this... thing.

"Tifra, what is that we are on?"

"Even the eldest whisperers do not truly know and some of them had contact with the last of the Originals," Tifra said. "Best we think, it was a construction device for something immense, a project in space."

"A Dyson sphere, or a Ringworld," Stellan murmured, looking about.

"Something happened and this was blown away. Maybe everything blown away, as the Originals did not seek a way back. This...thing began to add to itself, build more."

"So, there is an AI then," Daire said eagerly. "There must be."

"This we say too, but it only communicated with the Originals. None have communicated with it since. The Originals were very strange; they seem to have known no other lifeforms or even conceived of it. Perhaps in their dimension there was no other."

"Possibly an advanced alien race," Stellan said, "but without an effective stardrive. Why else would a species need a Dyson sphere or a Ringworld?

"Other reasons occur," Tifra said. "Biological ones like super-fertility. No one knows the why. But this place—it learns. Sometime, a ship landed and had stardrive. It and crew never left. Then others were captured and added. Sometimes it absorbs rock and ice. Always it grows.

"The Originals that were left never sought to escape, but made provisions for aliens that come aboard. Machines here sample new aliens. Samplers roam ship. Few survive being sampled, but after there is food and drink for the remainder. But the Others never trusted aliens. They kept all access to the AI to themselves. When they faded entirely, access lost.

"Faded," Daire asked. "Do you mean died?"

"No, mean faded. Hard to explain. If you are on this ship when it transitions through space, time and dimensions, you fade. Become insubstantial. Andrea said your word would be—wraith. Each jump more so. Eventually you are just a whisper in a mind. But some who fade become more powerful on the other side, and all hunger to be a living body.

"Bad ones force themselves in, sometime replace the person in body. I and some others make peace with enough strong ones, carrying them within us," she placed a hand to her head. "My whisperers keep others out. I remain mostly me."

Daire and Stellan stared at each in revulsion.

"We have heard no whispers, nor seen any wraiths," Daire said.

"I may have," Stellan said, surprising her. "There was a figure, it seemed translucent, wandering. One second it was there then it was gone."

"You have not been here long," Tifra said. "Not gone through jumps. You will see. They are always waiting. Too many want to be in a head."

"These wraiths…they can't die?"

"Not after they become wraiths, no need for food, light or water. There is a…stage beyond that, the Whisperer. Just a mind invisibly wandering the halls here. Eventually all go silent, maybe those ones die. We don't know. Many go mad, or mad for a while. Some speak but cannot be understood, too alien, maybe silicon life form or something even stranger.

"Tifra," Daire said, "tell me what Andrea said about *the Alamy* crew. Clearly something went wrong. Your people are suspicious of us."

"It is less and more than you think," Tifra said in her maddening way. "We are suspicious of all newcomers. Twice came aboard aliens that were carnivores or xenophobic to the point they could not be dealt with. Mostly this place killed them off and we, the Stranded, killed off the others.

"The Captain of Alamy… Haru?" she continued, struggling with the "r" sound.

"Hara," Daire corrected.

"He led the others here by deceit, threat and promises of wealth. When he realized he was trapped, his ship being absorbed, he and some of his crew came at us with weapons. He killed two of our people before we realized what was wrong. Then we fled. It was not necessary to fight. This place is huge and changes often. We led him and his to the places where the greatest changes and dangers take place, and they did not appear again.

"But Hara is not gone, old, old wraith take him. One of the very few powerful enough to subdue original person inside. We do not see him yet but wraiths and whisperers chatter in the hallways. News spreads like wind. We know he is out there. The wraiths pick up the knowledge of your language, so I learn. Not complete yet, but I learn quickly.

"And the others?" Daire pressed. "There should have been forty-three people on *Alamy*. Twenty-seven passengers and sixteen crew.

"Most dead," Tifra reported. "There was fight on *Alamy* when they realized they could not leave. Fight over air, water and food. They did not know what could be got here. The "useless ones" as Hara deemed them, were sent into space or pushed ahead in here. Sampler took one, that person did not live. Others set off traps or wandered into dangers. Andrea found by us. She helped me learn the language.

"Hara and his people went as I said. Maybe some live but we have not seen them in the ways we use."

"God," Daire said. "Those poor people."

Stellan concentrated on the practical. "You said, the sampler only took one person? He wondered if the biological mess they had seen on their way in was the work of the sampler.

"Yes, male, female, other did… does not matter," Tifra said. "Sampler only needs information for life support. You are safe from sampling. This place knows your kind now. You will find food, water suitable to you. There are slots near the far wall touch a gold cube and a basic…ration…is delivered. Most of us can use the same. Broad spectrum is what Andrea said. Some of us make quite good food out of it. Then there are the big gardens. Food grows there too."

"Well, there's that," Daire said.

Stellan wondered if he was different enough that the Sampler might see him as another species, then dismissed it.

"How many of the living, as you call them, are there on this, what do you even call this place?"

"There are many names for this place," Tifra said, "most translate as hell, purgatory, prison, usually when we need such a word, it is called the City. The part we live in we call the Town."

"It still seems odd that such a place would be so dangerous to move about in," Stellan said.

Daire shrugged. "How dangerous would a factory building with tools, elevators and such be to a primitive? Stick a finger in a socket, climb inside an elevator core or a cuber and you're crushed."

"So we think ourselves," Tifra added. "We are all space people, but the Originals had science beyond ours. Nothing my people make could last a billion years."

"I wonder where they came from?" Daire asked.

"Lost, lost in mist of time," Tifra said, waving her hands. "We know enough to know that this is not in the galaxy it came from. Oldest of Whisperers say so and they heard it from the before people.

"One in my minds saw this galaxy from outside, probably from a globular cluster. We do not have instruments, our ships long ago absorbed, but nothing we see looks familiar to any of us."

Stellan felt his skin crawl. "Extragalactic?"

Tifra nodded. "I do not know if this is my galaxy, it may still be. Galaxies are immense, mind-numbingly so. My people are so far from home. It is beyond a dream that it could be found again. Lost also in space, time and perhaps even in dimensions?"

"That could explain something about age here," Stellan said. "Each jump might take them out of normal space for centuries, millennia, epochs even.

"You have never seen or heard the like of me, or any of the species you have seen here?" Tifra asked.

"No," Daire said, "certainly not among living species we know of, but neither are we experts in xenoarchaeology."

"Are all our civilizations gone?" Tifra said as if to herself. "No, better not to know. More for others than for me. All my life is here."

"How long have you been here?" Stellan asked.

"Born here. Only of my kind to be so," Tifra said. It was hard to read expressions on her face, but Stellan thought she had a haunted, sad look. "Mother passed away. Father walked into a corridor that suddenly was not there anymore. The other females of my kind here are past childbearing. I will not give birth to a life in this place." There was vehemence in that last.

"I live through two jumps—which is much. Sometimes this place does not jump twice in a lifetime. We do not know what it means. Perhaps nothing. So much is uncertain here."

Daire looked at her. "I get the impression that you are young. So are we. Neither of us has seen our twentieth year."

Tifra looked Daire over closely. "Yes, I am young. Years means different thing, different places, and little here. But I think that we are similar.

"So I am not only myself," Tifra said, her hand stroking a yellow and green flower on a bush near her. "I am a compilation of the ghosts of this place. This is one reason I learn your language so fast. Five additional minds to learn and remember. Otherwise, it would be impossible to learn so fast. Still, alien concepts difficult.

"Do you…do you know them all?"

"It varies," the alien girl said, sitting back on the grass. "Some of them are full personalities, other times there are whispers, ideas and memories that are not mine. Those rarely manifest in me; it's more like I encounter them. Yes, I hear them and sometimes see them in my mind. But they are not inside my mind with me. Still, it can be very disorienting when it happens.

"I deal mostly with five inside me. I give them a home, and they keep out any others. One is the eldest, Khist-tok, a large fierce being, intelligent but solitary. She was a military scout. In appearance, he was not unlike these Conchirri Andrea spoke of, a large saurian.

"Visania Pulo Fan was a traveling priestess and dancer of a small, furred, omnivorous species. She is kind and spiritual.

"C'tell Ana is the opposite. She was a prisoner on a ship. "Con artist" thief, smuggler, a humanoid female similar in appearance to you and me.

"Twisel 98009 was an engineer. Member of an asexual species that reproduced by fission. Not much personality but an inflexible sense of purpose. It seldom communicates with me but likes mechanical puzzles and making things. It has been of great help with the food synthesizers.

"Cabadra-fabia, is the last, a merchant. Ollowoos are small, dark of skin and descended from an omnivore with residual flying ability. They had a membrane between arms and body that allowed them to glide for considerable distance and even fly in low gravity.

"Sounds like a flying squirrel," Daire muttered.

"I note that all the beings you…host," Stellan said, "are female or in the one case, asexual."

"It is usually easier," Tifra said. "Most find binding easier if there are similarities, given the intimacy of the association. Others prefer opposite binding but that is more difficult to achieve. Some have different versions of gender, so all different.

"Most times it is like a conversation in my head. Sometimes, like when I first saw, Stellan," she stumbled a little over his name, "it becomes reflex, and my perceptions of my body alter. Cabadra's people have flight/fight reflex, not fight/flight. We saw you and fled."

"Yes," he said, an admiring note in his voice. "You ran like the wind and that leap was impressive too."

"Tifra grimaced. "But I am still a Mefal, not an Ollowoo, my body was sore after how we used it."

"Have you ever been afraid you would be taken over?" Daire asked

"Only once," she said. "The oldest one, the least like me, Khist-tok. She used to concern me. Not long after Hara arrived, I ran into a cleaner. For some reason, it attacked me. Usually they ignore us. But this one charged at me.

"Khist-tok took over. I found a metal pole with a spiked end and fought like I was a saurian. It drove off my enemy, badly damaged but Khist-tok was angry, roused with bloodlust and pursued it. Only hours later and with the help of the others did I regain control of my body. It took weeks to recover from fighting like a giant beast in my small body. It was terrifying, even if she did save me. We have spoken seldom since. I think she may soon fade out of me entirely and become a Disrupted. She is weary of this existence.

"Some other of the disembodied will come forward and ask to be taken into me. Perhaps I will, if only to keep the Uninvited from trying to force their way in. We call those who have been dispossessed by a wraith...your closest word would be a "thing." Hara, if he still lives at all is now Hara-thing."

"Are you all like this?" Daire asked. "Multiple personalities?"

"Most are," Tifra said. "For those who have gone mad, who can tell? The Odari, from a world that circled a blue sun, hear no voices and carry no memories but their own. They are stable but stoic and not much given to communicating with the others. They moved into the far hallways and discourage visitors. Sometimes we see them in the great garden but likely we will know no more of them until they become wraiths. If then. They may die or choose to die before the jumps alter them and avoid that fate."

"How many people live in this...Town. Are there other towns?" Stellan asked.

"No easy answer," Tifra said. "Am I one person or six? But as you mean it, how many with bodies, we do not keep count, nor all live together. Most cluster in the groups that they landed with. There have been seven ships that land since my birth. One warship, two scout-ships, the others were liners or freighters attracted by salvage and discovery. So maybe seven or eight hundred living bodies wander here. About five hundred live all the time in the town.

"It's a wonder there hasn't been more interspecies conflict," Stellan said

Tifra made a queer gesture with her head a circling that Stellan took for negation.

"Cleaners act then," Tifra said. "They and other machines attack those who fight. Or executors come for the few who try to destroy the City. Disapprove of the disorder, we think, more than anything else. Rarely intervene is small fights, only against large groups or high-tech weapons.

"Remember, for most there is no reason to fight. Food and water available. Their ships are gone, reprocessed. Escape is not possible. Who can build a ship and escape to...where? The City voyages in time, space, dimension. We have nowhere to go. No way to get home even in a ship.

"Even for many of the living, the process of fading has begun. They would likely simply vanish if they left.

"The Whispers tell us that during one rare escape on a small ship that did not land, it was found that those who had jumped more than five times aboard the City simply vanished. That ship departed with only a few of us aboard along with its original crew. There was no room for more and most could not go, been here too long, too many jumps. An escape has not happened in the memory of the living.

"So we organize largely as we choose. There is also room enough for us to get away from other groups we do not like."

Daire looked around at the green-gold hallways and the circular shaft above them with dislike. "Like hide and seek in a haunted house."

Tifra seemed to think, working her way through the simile. "Yes. The Whisperers and the Wraiths are another reason. They have been here long and also dislike conflict. Most of them, anyway, the sane ones. Hard to argue all the time with those in your head. So fighting is not common."

"Amazing," Daire said.

"This is what happened to your, Hara," Tifra said. "He come aboard. Realizes he cannot leave. In anger, he attacks those he sees, holding them responsible. Also he fights with his own. So the cleaners, samplers and executors come. Those last, we seldom see, nor wish to. They are deadly."

"And only one of our people made it to your…commune."

Tifra nodded. "So far. I could ask Whisperers to look and listen. Do you wish to see?"

Daire sighed. "I want to say no but I feel we should learn all we can as soon as we can."

The alien girl seemed to concentrate. "I have asked my quintet. Well, all but Khist-tok, who is hard to rouse. They know what I know, but can hear the Whisperers or passing wraiths better than I. Let me go speak to the other Mefal, perhaps a few of the others and see what may be learned by others."

With that she stood, and they followed her back to the shelter. Daire noted that the two guards were still there. Perhaps they were different beings, it was hard to say, but it remained that they were watched.

CHAPTER TWENTY-FIVE

Stellan and Daire relaxed in their shelter after sleeping. While Daire had wandered about the area on her own, she was leery about doing so with Stellan, who seemed to worry them more, given Hara's violence. He was content to remain in the shelter, and they discussed all they had learned of the cosmic haunted house they'd fallen into. After days of cold and danger, both were glad for a rest from physical and mental strain. All their physical needs were met by their hosts who were considerate, if not effusive in their welcome.

Well, other than one detail. However she was saved from mentioning this.

"You mentioned a bath," he said. "Is there laundry as well?"

"There is." Daire rose and went to the curtain raising it. Opposite them stood the two Akati guards.

"Tifra," she said, being the only sound they would know.

The guards looked at each other and one departed. She watched its tripoidal gait in fascination, then dropped the curtain. She turned to find Stellan asleep on the futon and settled on her cot next to him.

About a half-hour later, Daire was awakened by Tifra's voice. "Hello. May I come in?

Stellan was already sitting upright. Part of his mother's heritage to him was that he always awoke sharp and oriented. Daire was not a morning person. She blinked and wiped her eyes.

"Please come in," Daire said.

Tifra brushed the curtain aside. To Daire's surprise, she'd brought robes of a light-blue fabric that she dropped on the end of Daire's bed.

"You anticipated our need," Stellan said, looking pleased.

"Of course," Tifra said, with an expression that Daire associated with her being pleased. "You are sophisticated, civilized people. You have had food and rest. Now you desire to be clean. Your exertions these past days have not been light.

"Change into these and I will take you to the baths. Leave those clothes you want washed in a pile—there. They will be attended to. As to your weapons, you may leave them here. They will not be touched. The guards outside will see to that. None of my people would use them for fear of invoking an executor.

Daire knew that would make Stellan unhappy but decided the utility of the weapons was outweighed by gaining influence here. In any event, she would not dare use one. "We will leave them here. Please be sure no one touches them, they are set to safe, but accidents happen."

They sat for a few more seconds.

"Ah," Daire said. "We usually don't undress in front of people we don't know well."

"Oh," Tifra, seeming amused. "Baths public here. Will be difficult."

"Ah," Daire said. "Oh well, when in the Town do as the Townsfolk do."

"Wisdom," Tifra said. "But I will wait outside."

"You, however," she said to Stellan, "close your eyes." He handed her the small robe and did so.

Daire undressed and piled her clothes. While she had spare undies in her pack, there seemed little point to donning them. Stellan was less self-conscious, stripping down to his underwear, but putting on the robe before taking those off.

She did say she was the only child of her kind here and none of the other aliens I've seen look that much like her or us. This might be an education for her.

"Good," Tifra said. "We go. Any instructions on this clothing?" she pointed to the pile on the floor.

"No," Daire said. "It's heavy-duty wear, damn near indestructible and should be fine with anything that your own clothes would survive."

"Come," she said. She opened the curtain. Outside was a Pucari, the small, furry alien who had brought them their meals. Tifra spoke to her briefly and nodded to the guards, who to Daire's surprise did not follow them.

Well, mostly naked unarmed people aren't likely to cause trouble.

They followed Tifra through the Town. She was surprised at how ordinary it was. There seemed to be shops and stalls. Some were tucked in openings in the walls. Others were little more than a line of tables. Had they not been buried in millions of tons of alien metal, it would have been a charming, if rustic scene.

"We have a hospital of sorts," Tifra said, "one level up. Depending on the skills of the beings that were stranded here, there is some form of medical care. Likely primitive by your standards, as we have little in the way of equipment. There is a jail as well for those who misbe-have. Banishment from the Town is the fate most feared though.

They listened as Tifra told them of the life of the Town. In a few minutes, they reached an area of broad, flat pools. The smell of heated water and humidity reached them. This area was curtained and divided with structures that had clearly been built by the townies of various materials scrounged and harvested from the City.

Attendants from several of the species greeted Tifra and eyed them, particularly Stellan with a mix of curiosity and concern.

"While we bathe together," Tifra said. "Washing is more private. At least for most of us. The Pukt do not care, but I am not Pukt." She took Daire to a curtained stall with a huge drain on the floor, sized for the original aliens no doubt. She'd have to be careful not to step on that grate, or her feet would go through. There was a bucket of steaming water, something that looked like a sponge, soap and towels.

Stellan went into another.

"Come out the back when you are done," Tifra called.

Daire took the chance to get as clean as she would be aboard ship, sighing with the pleasure of it. She wrapped a towel around herself and walked through.

Tifra stood on the other side, before a broad and shallow pool. The alien girl stood unselfconsciously naked. She was as flat-chested as Daire had suspected, though her hips were round. She seemed hairless, save on her head and the red skin color seemed uniform over her body.

Tifra in turn studied Daire. "Shall we get in? Or do you wish to wait for your brother?"

"In is good," she said. *And will save some embarrassment.*

Daire placed her towel on a nearby bench and carefully followed Tifra into the water. It was very warm but not so hot that she flinched and did not seem to bother Tifra at all. Some Pukt were on the far side of it, as well as an Akati and some of the small furred brown people. They stared at them but did not come closer.

Daire caught Tifra staring at her chest.

"Are you pregnant, or have a small child?" Tifra asked.

"No," Daire said, calmly. Questions about sex and sexuality could be explosive between cultures and had to be handled carefully. "Was there something that made you think so?"

"No offense intended but you are the aliens most like my kind that I have met. In our females, breasts only fill out when we have a child."

"Ours often increase in size with childbearing," Daire responded. "But they are always present."

"Are those large?"

"Er...not so much. I'm smaller in stature than average for a human female, by about four inches. I'm in proportion."

"And your brother?"

"He is much larger and more powerful than the average human male, almost a foot taller and as strong as any two or three strong men."

"He is special then."

"Yes, but it is a long story, and I will let him tell it."

Stellan stepped through at that moment, and Tifra lost interest in talking to Daire for a few moments.

Daire turned and noted that Stellan had kept a towel around his waist, but it concealed little. She'd gotten used to this reaction poolside from all her girlfriends in school. Her brother was handsome and built like the greatest of athletes.

Thank God he's neither vain nor callous about girls. He has my father's natural chivalry. Boy, my future husband is gonna have quite a bar to clear.

He came up to the pool, hesitated, then doffed his towel to put it next to Daire's and waded in to join them. He sat on the pool floor in water up to his shoulders and sighed in contentment.

Daire laughed and Tifra looked at her. "We do the same!"

She seems pleased to find similarities with us. That's good. It's a basis for an alliance.

Stellan looked at the arched and vaulted space. "It is hard to understand what was intended here."

"Whatever was," Tifra said, "has also changed. This thing absorbs all the time. It makes new things. The trans-dimensional drive. Even this," she gestured about. "This could not have been an original purpose. While the Originals lived, even as Whisperers, they made much change and set a pattern for...evolution?"

Daire nodded at the use of the word.

"So whatever the City once was, it is now a small world, in a way, though no one would choose it."

A sadness seemed to drape over Tifra. She almost visibly shook it off. "Your sister say...says...you are special?"

"My birth mother, Shasti Rainhell, was the work of genetic engineering and not a responsible work at that. She was produced illegally out of the genes of thousands of people selected for physical traits. She is nearly as tall as I am and stronger."

"True?" Tifra said in astonishment.

"Oh, yes. She may well be the strongest and fastest member of the human species, at least on a pound for pound basis. Her eyes are a pale green and her hair black. Her skin color is like Daire's."

They sat relaxing in the warm bath, under the lights that presumably simulated the sunlight of the Originals' world. Stellan told Tifra the tale of how he had come to be. This necessitated telling of Robert Fenaday's quest to find his wife Lisa, and his involvement with Shasti during that search. Battles across worlds and sights that were beyond anything Tifra could have experienced, seemed to almost daze the young alien.

"One has heard old tales," she said finally, "of adventures across the stars...but such a tale! Never did I imagine such a tale. The Quintet within me are astonished too."

"Do any of them tell you we are full of waste product?" Stellan asked with a small smile.

Tifra laughed. "One does, C'tell. She says that, con woman that she was, she would never have dared spin so outrageous a tale."

"Can't say that I blame her," Stellan said.

"Oh, and you need not conceal your teeth when you smile," Tifra continued. "Andrea taught us that you smile that way. So indeed to do the Ollowo and among the living, the Mesha, though it is unusual."

"Thanks," Stellan said. "It is a hard thing to remember all the time."

"We will be careful around others though," Daire added.

"I think," Tifra said, with a touch of shyness, "that you are a little like me. Restless, want to see new things, new people. Both of you could be home, rich, comfortable. Yet you choose to run a small ship on your own. I envy you what you have seen...." Words seemed to fail her, and she waved a hand at the universe.

Daire gave her brother a look. He returned it and nodded, divining her intention.

"Tifra, we came to find the *Alamy*, and we've done that. I don't think we can do much more here."

She simply gazed at them.

"Let me ask you a question," Daire said, taking a deep breath and committing to the plunge. "If there is an escape from here. How many could take it, and of those, how many do you think would?"

"Escape?" Tifra said and even across the gulf of alienness her bitterness was plain. "It has happened occasionally when the chances were…." The alien girl's head snapped around to face her. "You do not ask this…." she seemed to struggle for words in her excitement, "without reason."

"First, I must know the answer to my question," Daire insisted.

Tifra seemed to consider, looking from Daire to Stellan, then at the other aliens enjoying the far side of the bath. "Few could. Most have been through too many jumps. At least this is what we think, the information passed down. But who can say? Still most believe this. Only the Pukt and Akati have children intentionally here. Right now, I am the youngest of the other races."

"Would the Pukt and Akati want their children to leave?" Stellan asked.

"Leave? To the care of unknown aliens, with no idea of where their civilization lies, if it even exists in this galaxy or dimension? No, I am quite sure. Parent-child bond strong, almost a…"

"Biological imperative…a physical need of their body," Stellan said.

"Yes, like that. For both their species. Otherwise, why have children here?"

"Tifra, it sounds like you are the only one?" Daire asked.

"The Odari," she said, "I told you of them. They have been here only one jump. But they do not talk to others. They could be dangerous to approach."

"Let's say for now," Daire said, "that the Odari are not our concern."

"Then of the people here," Tifra said, "only I can flee this place with any real hope of surviving."

"And would you?" Stellan asked.

The girl was silent for so long that Daire wondered if she would answer at all.

"I have sometimes dreamed this," Tifra said slowly. "For the others, our Captain, the original crew, it has been too many jumps. They are all older now. Could I abandon them, who cared for me?"

"Wouldn't they want you to have a chance for a life?" Stellan asked.

Tifra's hands twisted together, water falling off them in droplets. "I don't know. I don't know."

"Tifra," Daire added. "Whatever they feel, this is your one and only life. If you have a chance to do what you want with it, you must give this the most serious thought."

"Now," Tifra said, firmly, "you must answer my question."

"When we came here, we didn't land beside the *Alamy*, which for all the fifteen or so months it's been here is still far from submerged. We landed atop it."

"We didn't tell you this earlier," Stellan said, "for fear that either we would be overwhelmed with the numbers who want to go, or that others would try and seize our ship from us. From what you say the first is not a factor. As to the second, well, sometimes others who cannot escape, might begrudge those who would."

"You should escape while you can," Tifra said, looking down at the water.

"We intend to, but we have no prospect of getting back to our ship without your help. This place is a giant and lethal maze. We are concerned that some may try to stop us out of anger or spite. It's not logical or sensible but it can be that way.

"There is something to what you say," Tifra admitted. "The people of the Town would not, I believe, impede you. It is not as if they could go in your place."

"Even if they could survive separating from here," Daire said, "we could only take about twenty or so. We have a few cold sleep chambers but no way to calibrate those for aliens we have just met."

"The bigger threat," Tifra said, "is random dangers of the City, or the Uninvited who took Hara and maybe others of the *Alamy* crew. They lair in a part of the City we do not go. When a Whisperer fails, they become the Disrupted, mere memory fragments that you can encounter. It makes you think that you are the other for a while. The Uninvited are not bothered by that and often are found nearby."

"Yes," Stellan said. "I think that happened to me. I was in a compartment and suddenly I felt like I was seeing it from someone else's head."

"It can be disorienting and dangerous. Some of the oldest and strongest of the Wraiths congregate there. They absorb the memory fragments or use them as a form of camouflage. The *Alamy* crew that were taken by the old ones, you will not get back."

"Then we have done all we can here, and it is time for us to leave. Tifra, will you guide us back at least? You do not need to make any other decision yet."

Tifra stood, and the water sluiced off her body. She looked up at the yellow-orange lights above her and at the cavern of pools, as if engraving them on her memory.

"At the least," she said, looking down at Stellan, "I take you to your ship. As for the rest, I must think on this."

CHAPTER TWENTY-SIX

They did not see Tifra that evening and whiled away their time in Town. The various aliens seemed less wary of them now, most nodding, or greeting them in some fashion; a few, including the alien that looked like a bush with eyes, avoided them.

Omo, the small, furred alien who looked after their physical wants, learned their names and began to teach them some Akati. Both of them were gifted at languages, a necessity for traders, even though Standard had evolved as the language of the stars. But they did not have the advantage of having additional minds to work on the issue as Tifra did, so they progressed slowly. But it helped pass the time until Tifra came back.

They were sitting down to what they thought of as the evening meal. While the light in most of the alien machine did not vary, in the area of Town, something like a diurnal rhythm was maintained with ten hours of strong light, ten of intermediate and ten of twilight and near darkness.

Omo brought them dinner, including some of the fruit Tifra had shared with Daire in their first meeting. There was also a fermented beverage like a wine that was palatable if not wonderful.

Daire noticed that the Pucari had placed service for three on their short table. "Tifra, come?" she asked in Akati.

"Yes," Omo responded in the same tongue. "Soon."

As if summoned, the girl appeared at the door. "May I enter?"

"Please do," Stellan said.

Omo put down covered bowls of food and more of both water and the wine, then excused herself.

"We are glad to see you," Stellan added. "The meal will be improved by the company."

Tifra gave him what Daire felt was a shy look.

I may have to warn him about that. Tifra has never had attention like that from anyone. We don't need any emotional issues to deal with too. That is unless he's the emotional issue. He's very taken with Tifra despite her built-in audience. I wonder how that would work?

By tacit agreement, they spoke of trivial matters. All seemed careful about the wine, not wishing to commit any offense. So they sat around the table, which was so low to the ground that Stellan could not get his knees under it, and enjoyed the food.

But at the end of the meal, Tifra was ready to talk. "I have spoken to my people and through the captain, to the council. The council itself has no interest a risky journey to your ship, but they do not forbid me from doing so. At my captain's orders, I did not discuss with the council that I might not come back. He thinks as you do, that neither Akati nor Pukt would allow children to go. So he thinks it best not to mention that you have a ship that could leave here.

"Even to go back to your ship is danger. My captain says the Whisperers in the halls tell us of the old one who took Hara, seeking more of your kind for his followers. It might be that he seeks your ship because the body he is now in had not jumped. He may think to escape."

"Could he?" Daire demanded.

"Who can say? Such a thing has never happened."

Stellan studied Tifra's face. "Did your captain say anything else?" he asked gently.

She met his eyes. "Yes. He said that if there is a chance for me to get away, he wants me to take it. There is no future here. He said all the crew spoke together. They love me but want me to go.

"I...I want to go with you," Tifra said, clearly in the grip of deep emotion. Perhaps Mefal did not cry, but she looked like she might. "I am afraid. Of losing all that I have, all that I know. You seem....good people but you are aliens. I have known you only cycles. What kind of a life could I have out there, alone?"

As he studied the upset girl, Stellan felt something move in his heart. Tifra wasn't a human, in some sense she wasn't even an individual, amalgamating five other aliens inside her. But from the first moment he saw her, she had held a fascination for him, and he sensed something more. Whether it was a foolish hope or not, certainty dropped about him like a cloak.

"You will not be alone," he said. "You will have a life among friends. You will be looked after in such manner as your captain would approve. This I swear in both my names, Fenaday and Rainhell."

Daire looked at him surprised but after a moment she smiled. She saw relief wash over her brother's face.

Tifra simply stared, her eyes searching his.

"Stellan," Daire said, "never breaks his word. More—his word binds me, our ship and our families. All that he says, will be done."

"Thank you," Tifra whispered. "So much to think about and things I never imagined I would have a choice in. So much confusion and no little pain. I need some time to think. For now, I will commit to daring the halls with you to get you back to your ship. Pack your things. I wish to be with the others of my kind, for a last little while. We will leave in the Bright."

They nodded and Tifra left. They packed their gear. Omo came in later. Evidently she was in the know, as she brought packets of food, water to refill their canteens and some containers of fruit juice. They mimed their thanks as best they could and the small furred being seemed to understand. She patted their arms, and it did not take a translator to know she wished them luck.

Both rested. Stellan, more than Daire, who was restless by nature. Finally in the Twilight before the Bright, the small alien returned and gestured they should follow her with their gear. But she did not accompany them, instead turning them over to the solitary guard who had watched over them. He no longer bore a weapon and only gestured at them to follow. The tripodal alien croaked out the words. "Tifra. Follow."

They walked behind him as his three legs took their steady pace forward. It made Daire a little queasy to watch. Stellan meanwhile was alert, studying everything but it was early and the town was still settled.

Perhaps Tifra's people think it best we depart quietly. Not that most of the aliens here seemed terribly interested in us. They're an insular bunch. Of course, we humans haven't shown them a very good side either. They may just be happy to be rid of troublesome newcomers.

I don't think an ambush is likely. We have our weapons, and they probably have a good idea what those can do. They wouldn't want to risk a fight here where it might bring down an executor.

With that thought she relaxed some, leaving it to Stellan to detect any trouble.

They came to a section of shelters that were sturdier than most. Daire caught sight of silver-haired beings. They were in a cluster at the far end. Tifra was among them. The girl wore her usual uniform but with a pack and belt. The small crowd of Mefals was embracing Tifra, one by one.

The Akati grunted, "Tifra." Then it simply turned and left.

Stellan looked at her.

"Let's wait here," Daire said. "They know we are here, and we don't want to step on a moment. This is delicate."

Tifra walked up to them slowly, accompanied by the older male of her species that greeted them when they arrived. He wore a faded and patched uniform, but it did not diminish his air of dignity and authority. Daire did not need to be told that this was Tifra's captain. He stopped a step away and seemed to be studying Stellan. A sudden shock of recognition hit her. She'd seen that look before on her own father's face, anytime a prospective boyfriend had been introduced.

Perhaps Stellan sensed it as well. He inclined his head respectfully.

"This is Captain Ossa of the Mefalan Scoutship, *Lossanack*. In your language, *Searcher*," Tifra said, with a note of pride in her voice. Her face however was closed and subdued. Daire could only guess what she was feeling. "He wanted to speak with you. I will translate what he says, as he says it. As I will for you."

"Greetings, fellow Captain," Daire began, sensing that Stellan was waiting on her, given the formality being displayed. "I am Captain Daire Fenaday, master of the private merchant *Wanderlust,* out of New Eire, member of the Confederation of Species.

"This is my brother, Stellan Rainhell, he is my second, and my most trusted of friends in this life."

"I am glad to meet you," Tifra said, as her captain spoke in a calm, measured voice that conveyed authority. "I appreciate your greeting to me, captain to captain, but it is to your brother that I wish to speak."

"Of course," Daire said.

He looked up into Stellan's face. "We are gifting you with our only treasure. The daughter of none of our bodies…" Tifra choked up, and the old man put a hand on her arm until she could resume, "…but all of our hearts."

"It was you who gave your word to treat our Tifra with friendship and respect. I do not know you. I wish I did. I wish there was time. But I wanted to hear this from you, face to face."

"I will repeat it gladly," Stellan said, "and add more. You need not tell me how special Tifra is. Somehow, I knew that the moment I saw her. If she goes with us, then she will live among friends, and lack for nothing material in this life. My father is a merchant prince, my chosen mother a naval war hero. My birth mother…she is a force who runs an entire world. Some would call her a queen. All this will stand between Tifra and any need."

"This you swear on your own honor," Captain Ossa said. "I must hear that, as those others do not stand here in front of me."

"And again more," Stellan answered. "You stand in her father's place. This is now a promise between you and I, as if you were her father. I will guard her life with my own."

"Stellan," Daire said, startled. Then looking at her brother's set face, she nodded.

"Rest easy in your mind, Captain Ossa," Daire added, turning back to Ossa, "she is a ward of our family now."

Ossa's face was stern but probably only from his desire to not break down in front of them. "I wish that there was more time to get to know such people as yourselves. You seem a fine male, Stellan. If I am any judge of beings, you will do all you say."

He looked at Daire. "You have given your word as a captain. I am satisfied. Sadness and joy are intermingled. I could not have hoped to provide this gift to her. To me, you are sent as if by some great power."

He moved forward and clasped arms with Stellan, then Daire. He turned to Tifra who wrapped her arms about him. Daire and Stellan stepped back and turned away, giving them a few moments of privacy for tears and goodbyes.

CHAPTER TWENTY-SEVEN

Goodbyes said, they moved out quickly. *The sharp knife cuts best,* Stellan thought. *True literally and metaphorically.*

Osso's parting gift to him had been a Akati staff with sharpened edges and a point. Tifra couldn't carry it, it violated the tradition of the speakers-to-all. Even one of the banished would not harm her, for they would then be actively hunted by all others. Daire shouldered the weapon while he carried the packs.

Tifra's path took them up and away from the town, he recognized some of it from when she'd brought him in. They walked quietly but steadily at a pace that was slow for Tifra and certainly him but one that should not exhaust Daire, who needed two steps to one of theirs.

He was glad to be away, being less trusting by nature than his sister. In a small community, bodies were valuable for labor if nothing else. While the townsfolk did not labor excessively from what he had seen, there was always a hierarchy. *If everyone at the beginning of time,* his father liked to say, *had been given a refrigerator, at the end of the first year there would be those with none and those with a thousand.* A saying as apt for a politician as a merchant but true.

They'd had little choice but to trust both Tifra and the townsfolk, but he was still relieved to be on the way back and without so many unknowns around them. *Well I'm happy about one unknown*

Tifra walked alongside him. Daire trailed but not too close, as he wore his pack and at his insistence, carried hers. The alien girl's face was closed, and she seemed lost in her thoughts. Her steps were heavier than he had seen.

She's alone in a way no one else can be. What can I do for her?

He leaned closer and she glanced at him.

"I meant every word of what I said back there."

She gave him a slight smile. "I believe you. I think, being what I am, that I am a good judge of people. My quintet believe you too. Well, C'tell Ana says she'll wait to see proof and Khist-tok is still quiescent, but you've won over the majority."

This is going to take some serious getting used to.

"I'm glad of that," he said aloud.

"Thank you," Tifra said, more animated than she had been for an hour. "Now let us walk with your sister between us. You will watch our backtrail."

She gave Daire a friendly look. "It will be most of two to three days to your ship, depending on dangers and changes. You will set the pace. Your brother does not seem to tire, and Mefals evolved to be fast of foot and enduring. I do not wish you to injure yourself."

"I can keep up," Daire protested. "I used to do cross-county."

Tifra looked at him confused.

"Long distance running," he said. "Since she weighs only five and a half pounds and exists on sunlight and conversation, she was an ideal runner."

"Are you saying I talk too much?" Daire asked archly.

Tifra laughed in a surprisingly human gesture.

"I would never say such a thing…out loud," he replied, slowing to let Daire pass him.

"Just because I don't eat like an Okaran doesn't mean I'm without energy," she returned, "and two-thirds of what we're carrying is just stuff for your meals!"

"What's this, *'we'* are carrying?" he teased. "I seem to have your pack."

Tifra laughed again as the siblings sparred. But the long and dangerous halls of the City lay before them—cold, partly lit, and unpredictable, and the sound of her laugh faded away. They fell quiet and concentrated on their surroundings and the pace. There was far to go.

Tifra's knowledge of the way back was as indispensable as Daire expected. She warned them of a corridor that looked perfectly safe, only to see two prongs extend from one wall and discharge electricity toward two glassy spheres that appeared on another. She located another gravity gradient, only this one was the opposite of the first crushing one that Daire had seen. The trip back without her would have taken weeks if they survived at all.

Daire also marveled at Tifra's quiet courage. Most of her travels through City had been done alone. She had no close companion her own age among the other species. Occasionally an Akati or Pukt had accompanied her, but only for a specific mission. Simple exploration into danger for its own sake was not in their makeup. Odd for species that had taken to space, but Daire had no idea of their sociological backgrounds, and both species seemed to have adapted to life in the artifact in a way that the others, particularly the Mefals had not.

She wondered if millions of years in the future the artifact might grow to a planetary size and be inhabited by their descendants.

Probably genetic drift will get them, she thought, depressed by being encased in the artifact in a way she had never felt in any ship. *Though maybe if some larger populations got stuck here in the far future, it might happen. Maybe as a planet it wouldn't be as mad a thing as it is as a ship. Or maybe it would become a planet-eating monster?*

She shook her head to clear it of these grim notions.

"Something is odd," Tifra said, looking around at the levels of one of the layer-cake rooms they'd stopped in. "We have seen no wraiths, nor do I or my quintet sense any of the whisperers nearby."

"Is this area known for either?" Daire asked, looking around uneasily.

"Wraiths travel where they will," Tifra answered absently, as if she was listening to her inner voices. "Though both they and the whisperers avoid the town or large groups of the living generally. Yet there should be some here in the halls, and I have heard nothing. Nor have my five."

"Do they have friends among the other wraiths and whisperers?" Daire asked, suddenly struck by the thought.

Tifra shook her head. "Once inside a person, they do not contact others. This is for my privacy. The relation is intimate. To invite others into it could break their connection to me. I suppose there are exceptions to all rules, but I do not know of one.

"Out here, they can congregate but rarely do. They have an infinity of time and perhaps most of their relationships have worn out. Also, some are from species that were solitary or where only a few arrived here.

"Still, this is strange. I do not like it."

They ate and marched, resting at regular intervals. Despite her boast, Daire found the constant climbing fatiguing even using the Akati spear-staff. They were out of the area where the light varied, so only with their comms did they have a sense of elapsed time and distance. But there were some sections in which the light levels were low and Tifra led them to one of those when she said it was time for sleep, which saved Daire's pride from being the one to suggest it.

The darkened area was a doorless room, which Stellan checked with his light before they entered. Opened containers lay in there but whatever they'd held had long ago been looted. Stellan manhandled one container to block the doorway and even Daire was surprised that he could move the large and sturdy metal container. Once he was satisfied that nothing could rush them, they selected another open container for their bedrolls. It would keep the warmth in.

Tifra was delighted with the microwave heater/pad. Warm food was a chore when she journeyed alone. She had the equivalent of Sterno cans for cooking, but the speed and ease of the small pad made life easier. They listened as she told them of the life of the Town and the history of the City, the various species that had come and gone.

Then they settled for the night. At Stellan's insistence they slept in shifts. Tifra agreed, rarely having had that option in her mostly solo travels.

"What danger are we looking for?" Stellan said.

"There are the mad out here," Tifra said, "and some living out a period of banishment. Then there are some who seek to live alone or in small, like-minded groups. Not so dangerous to me, but to you I cannot say. Sometimes cleaners are dangerous as I have told.

"Then there are wraiths," she said. "They are not ordinarily dangerous, but one does not wish to be too close to one. The disembodied are more dangerous, those that continue existing to that stage develop greater mental powers. They can force their way into a person. I can drive those off with the help of my quintet, but they could pose a threat to either of you with only one mind for strength."

The next day they marched on, avoiding some areas that Tifra warned of, even where those dangers weren't apparent. It made for some frustration, as they were not moving in a straight line, though at least for today, most of the journey was on only two or three levels.

The second night found them in another low-lit section, a broad room with a sculpture that boasted a water feature. It even had a section which could be used as a bath if one stopped the hole in the bottom. The water was warm, almost hot, so they refilled their canteens and let them sit. Tifra produced some tea she had brought, evidently planning on this. Then they enjoyed warm baths, particularly Daire, whose small size meant the cold acted more on her.

Tifra sighed in contentment, sharing a bath with Daire. She seemed puzzled by Stellan's not joining them.

Daire laughed quietly. "When we were both small, well even as a baby he was twice my size, we might have been bathed together, it would not be our custom when grown to do so.

"And well, you're a female," she continued, "while if it was the two of you, he might have been happy to join, with his sister here…it would merely be… frustrating."

Tifra looked up over the rim of the improvised bath. Stellan was lounging against the wall, spear-staff nearby and adjusting their packs.

She leaned toward Daire and whispered. "This is…embarrassing…but…my circumstances…well…I am completely inexperienced, and we are different species. But…he seems to like me. I don't want to do anything about it. Not for now. Nor would I really have any idea what to do if I did want to. We are aliens."

Tifra suddenly looked very young and vulnerable to Daire.

"Stellan has seen you as an attractive female since he first saw you," she whispered, hoping the sound of running water would cover their speech. "I know that he likes you."

"Is it alright to ask," Tifra lowered her voice even further, "if he is…experienced?"

"He is. I have never known him to be ungentle, or unkind with girls. A lot have thrown themselves at him, he's handsome, strong and wealthy, so he's developed a natural caution about giving his heart… about developing attachments.

"There was also one possessive, borderline-crazy female who caused him such trouble I punched her in the nose over it."

"You both seem very protective of each other," Tifra said. "The others tell me this is true of siblings of our kind as well, but like… other experiences, this was not available to me."

"I'm sorry," Daire said.

"Another question if I may," Tifra said.

"Sure."

"Are you…well…have you?"

"Ah, yes, not a lot, but again mostly that is my choice."

"You are attractive?"

"To my kind, yes, I'm pretty enough. Like my brother, I'm cautious about men who might want me more for money and position than for me. Mainly I'm in love with my ship and the life it offers me among the stars."

"Daire, tell me truly, am I...an attractive person?"

Daire smiled. "Yes, you are. In our culture it's not common to have relationships outside of one's species, but nor is it disapproved of. As a practical matter, only two or three of the known species would have the commonality or desirability to be with or would want a relationship with a human.

"You are a very pretty person, and Stellan does like you very much. I have never seen him take to someone quite like this."

Tifra seemed relieved and pleased. Again, she snuck a peek over to see if Stellan had moved. "Since you have had...experiences. Ummm, what is it like?"

Daire opened her mouth, nonplussed, but was saved from an immediate reply.

"Hey," Stellan called, "are you two ever coming out of there? These feet could use a good soak."

"Let's talk more after we get to the ship and have some privacy," Daire whispered back, reaching for a towel. "He has very good hearing."

CHAPTER TWENTY-EIGHT

The three days of marching from the town to the surface of the alien worldlet, had worn even on the tall rangy alien. It was always cool in the great alien artifact and this too drained energy and spirit, at least from Tifra and Daire.

"We are getting near your ship," Tifra said as they broke camp on the beginning of the third day. "We are on the topmost level, below the outer skin of the City. There are many towers and projections that go higher, but this is the level *Alamy* landed on. From here, the path goes straight. I did not reach your ships. Where you first saw me was as far as I had gotten, but from there it is not a long way."

"Good," Stellan said, shouldering a pack. "I'm already thinking of the first dinner I am going to prepare aboard ship. There is a roast with our names on it." Stellan had seemed largely indifferent both to the physical effort and the temperature. However, he'd made considerable inroads in their supplies. They'd had to ration food. All that strength and vitality came with a price.

"Me, I'm going to crank the temperature in my cabin and sleep for a week," Daire said, following behind him. "And I am going to eat every sweet thing you will make for me."

"I will make plenty," he promised. "Starting with a chocolate cake and an apple pie."

He turned to Tifra. "I hope you will find the food appetizing."

Tifra laughed. "Your sister boasts much of your cooking skills. We like similar flavors from what you enjoyed of our food, though you said it was plain. I am curious about this meat, that you talk of."

He smiled. "Meat in taste. For the most part we do not eat animals anymore. Our synthesizers make plant material taste like meat. But some still hunt, and others still enjoy true meat. For myself I am fine with the synthetic."

Tifra shrugged. "I know of animals, but we have none here. It is only a memory to me. My quintet remember meat. Some like it, some do not. I dislike the idea of killing something to eat it."

"Well, you will not have to," he replied. "I guarantee you the flavor without the guilt."

They spoke on in this vein as they walked with Daire in the middle and Tifra leading.

———

Five hours later they crossed into the area near the ship. Each of them wore their own pack but they were mostly empty now. Stellan's was loaded with most of the remaining food and was heaviest.

Tifra moved more slowly now in an area that she had seldom been in, and led them by a smaller corridor. This one was lit periodically by tiny golden lights and there were small rooms, almost cells, to each side. Most of them had doors with a switch handle, set as high as Daire could reach. He wondered if the big aliens would have had to crawl in here.

Perhaps it was made for machines? Why would it be lit then? No answer occurred.

As they walked on, Stellan began to fight a fuzzy feeling almost akin to jump sickness.

What is going on? Am I sick? That makes no sense, does it? I am current on all immunizations. There shouldn't be anything in this massive pile that would bite on a human. Germs don't jump species, even viruses don't jump totally unrelated evolutionary trees. Maybe it's this corridor? Is there something going on with it.

He noticed that Tifra seemed to be wavering as well.

Something's wrong. But his foggy brain refused to focus. Better say something

A smell of unclean bodies reached him just as three humans, shouting in some alien tongue plunged out of cover of doorways and some machinery at them. Each bore a spear-like weapon. One face he knew, he'd seen it often enough.

Hara.

How could they get so close? Damn it, why can't I think?

Tifra went down. Not pierced by any weapon but collapsing as if she were a puppet with cut springs, her backpack tumbling off her as she dropped.

Pain exploded in his head. He thought himself hit by some weapon but even as he staggered and dropped his own spear-staff, he realized his pain was not from a physical wound.

He sensed that the emanation of his pain and confusion was from Hara, furthest away from him.

Got to reach him.

But as he gathered himself, one of Hara's men, wild-eyed, bearded and stinking, speared Daire. His sister, in the act of shooting the third man with her forbidden laser, gave a choked scream and was flung against a wall edge falling, laser spinning away. The other man fell, a smoking hole in his forehead.

With a roar, Stellan changed targets from Hara to the spearman and reached him as drew back his spear to stab Daire again. His hammer-fist blow landed atop the man's skull and stove it in. Blood, brain and tissue erupted from every opening in the crushed skull.

Stellan could see that while the spear had struck Daire's armor, there was no blood. He turned to kill Hara.

The dreadful white light lit up his skull again. This time he knew he could not fight through it, and the floor came up at him. He had strength for two last words as consciousness swirled away.

"Daire, run!"

CHAPTER TWENTY-NINE

Daire followed Stellan's order and ran. Weaponless, she could do nothing against Hara-thing. Hara-thing had a long, wicked spear, and she had lost her stunner and laser in the battle but accounted for one enemy.

Why did Stellan fall? Nothing hit him. Tifra, too.

She realized it must be some force of the old Whisperer that inhabited Hara. Some mental power. Tifra had said that some of the disembodied were strong enough to force their way into at least some of the living. Clearly it has done so with Hara and his companions.

Dammit, we weren't wary. We were tired but much as they stank, we should have smelled them. At least Stellan would have. They must have blanketed us with some sort of mental fog. No three men could take Stellan otherwise, not with a spear. My father is a master of ancient weapons, and he taught Stellan.

Daire felt sick as she staggered on.

Why didn't it get me? Maybe overcoming Tifra and us together was too much for it. She's familiar with wraiths and she has those five Whisperers in her. I may have been one too many.

God, it's got Stellan. What can I do?

I need weapons. Got to get back to the ship. I need something big. Some-

thing that could maybe break the hold he has on Stellan and Tifra. Maybe something explosive. It might distract it. Stellan is strong willed. Tifra knows this sort of fight. If I can break his hold, maybe they can keep free of it. He took us by surprise before.

First, I have to get back to the ship.

The sickness in her gradually settled as she made her grim way forward.

Hara-thing is smart, whatever it was. It waited for us at a point we had to pass through to get back to the ship. The others were too dangerous, too chancy. It must have realized that Tifra would take us back by the most direct and safest route and laired there waiting for us. We walked right into it.

But I'm still free and it's only Hara left. I shot one and Stellan smashed that... for a second she had to fight nausea at the memory of the man whose skull Stellan had crushed like pumpkin.

The only good thing is that I'm not far. Stellan was making his ranger marks here. I can get to the ship.

She staggered forward, the pain in her side made her bend a little to ease it. The body armor had stopped the spear thrust, but she'd been thrown against a projecting corner of metal from something, and the edge had penetrated at the join.

Gotta stop getting hit in the ribs. Keep pressing on. Aunt Shasti wouldn't be slowed up by something like this. Dad took worse fighting Pard and managed to kill him anyway. Mom managed years as a POW. Are you the weak link? Are you unworthy of being a Fenaday? Move, goddamn you. Move faster.

Ranger marks guided her, and her vision narrowed to searching for just those. She spotted their piled spacesuits where they'd left them, it seemed like forever ago.

I'm close. Gotta keep on my feet and keep going. Another mark, yes that way.

The tables that Hara had used came into view as did the bulk of *Alamy's* ramp, sunk noticeably lower into the alien artifact. Gathering up her strength, she scrambled aboard *Alamy*, glad to see the gray walls and low white lights of Confed tech. Then it was a painful climb through the decks of the dead ship to the welcome sanity of *Wanderlust.*

As she made the boarding tube, Daire placed her hand on the persona lock that would open only for her or Stellan's living hand-print. The hatch opened and she stumbled in gratefully. The warmth of her ship, set for a normal human temperature, was a welcome embrace after the cold of *Alamy* and the alien monstrosity.

God if only Stellan was with me, we could blast off from this hellhole right now.

She paused at the galley long enough to grab a tube of emergency rations from the locker. The tube of liquid contained restorative and easily digested energy. She waited a few seconds after she twisted the cap for the heating element to bring the contents to a pleasing warmth which spread through her as she downed the contents. Then she filled and drained a tall glass of water.

Autodoc now. Got to get patched up enough to fight.

Their tiny sickbay was adjacent to the galley. She staggered in, stripped off her jacket, shirt, and bra and lay on its bed. The machine activated instantly and began searching her body with scanners. A slight pinprick indicated vitamins and other medicine being injected. Then came the familiar hum of a regenerator playing over her ribs.

"Fractured ribs are being knitted together," the AI's calm female voice sounded. "Hematomas and abrasions are being reduced. You are in no danger. Twenty-four hours bed rest is indicated."

"Negative," she replied. "Ship in a ground combat and space emergency situation. Next twenty-four hours critical."

"Acknowledged," the AI said, with no more reaction than if she'd told it the weather was poor. "Additional support bandage being sprayed on, and topical anesthetics and stimulants added."

The pain receded and she felt alert. She waited impatiently for the regenerator to stop and the various sensors and umbilicals to release her. As soon as they did, she headed for the arms locker. Her custom laser and stunner were lost aboard the City, all that was left were standard stunners. She grabbed one and belted it on.

Then she headed for engineering. There, she used a chemical

synthesizer to come up with essentially a satchel charge explosive. She set a ten second fuse for it and made a detonator. Perhaps between it and the stunner she might be able to break Hara's grip on her brother. She had to get Stellan, or at least Tifra, free of Hara-thing's influence. If she simply stunned them, there would be no way she could carry her huge brother back to the ship. Even with Tifra's help, it might be impossible.

She considered her detonator. If Hara-thing saw her, he could probably prevent her from triggering it, considering how he had dropped Tifra. So she opted for a grenade-type switch. Once pulled, if he made her drop it, it would go off. It was risky but she knew that both of them would choose death rather than be used by Hara or his ilk.

Stellan will fight but these things can force their way in. Maybe it's already in Stellan. Maybe as we blast away from here, separation would kill that thing, but all those plans mean I have to get Stellan here.

She found a small spare pack, added some e-rations, a med kit and canteen, then loaded some flares and recharges for the stunner in her pack. Her old clothes she dumped on the floor and selected new ones for more warmth.

She quickly returned to the bridge and broadcast a message. She would be either home, or long dead before anyone heard it, but there would at least be word of their fate.

"This Captain Daire Fenaday of SS *Wanderlust* out of New Eire to any Confed vessel. The alien object you are approaching is dangerous. This thing has traveled both intergalactically and inter-dimensionally. It is ancient, erratic, and dangerous in itself. Do not land directly on it, or your vessel will become stuck fast to its surface and absorbed. Landing atop another vessel is safe for a period of time, albeit how long is unknown.

"There is a marooned population of unknown aliens aboard. They are friendly but cannot leave or they will die. There are other beings aboard... well, they are like ghosts or wraiths and can possess the living.

"My brother Stellan is a prisoner of one of these wraiths, who took over Captain Hara of the SS *Alamy*.. As far as we know there are no other *Alamy* survivors. I am going to free my brother or die trying.

"I have set this message on periodic broadcast. If you do not pick up a further broadcast within a week of hearing this, you must presume we are dead. Do not land. Please report our loss to Robert and Lisa Fenaday on New Eire and Shasti Rainhell on Olympia."

"Captain Daire Fenaday signing off."

With that she shouldered her pack and sped out of the *Wanderlust*, again locking the persona lock against any intruders.

Daire made her way quickly but carefully, stunner in hand. The danger from the cleaners and executors less in her mind than the threat of Hara-thing. Perhaps the nonlethal weapon, which would pose no threat to any ship-system wouldn't trigger the City's defenses. She sped back to the area of the fight, grateful for the ranger marks that Stellan had made in their first days here, otherwise she would be lost. There were a few other roadmarks for her, notably the fountain room.

Hara was lairing here for more than one reason. With Stellan under his control, he can get into Wanderlust. There's a wealth of supplies there that can make life comfortable, plus an autodoc and the ship itself. Hara-thing is in a new body, maybe he thinks he can escape in Wanderlust?

I bet he hasn't gone far from where we fought him. With his minions dead, he can't move Tifra and Stellan. Probably couldn't move Stellan in any case.

Then she reached the scene of the ambush. Peering around she looked for any sign of Stellan or Tifra. But only the two bodies of Hara's men lay there. One shot through the chest with her laser and the other his head misshapen by the blow Stellan struck. Both stank as badly did as they had alive.

To her surprise she found her own laser and stunner there, along with Stellan's. All had their magazines ejected but none were nearby. Hara-thing apparently had a morbid fear of the Executors.

They haven't come for me yet, maybe because I got off their deck and onto our ships. But if what Tifra told me is right, I may be marked for elimination. Even using the stunner might bring them down on me.

She gathered up their weapons and dumped them in her pack. But a quick search didn't show the magazines. She switched the mag in her standard stunner for her custom one which fit her hand better.

He can't be far ahead, she thought, hoping she wasn't fooling herself. *He'd have to get them moving. That means that he has to be exerting some sort of mind control on them. Otherwise, Stellan would get that spear out of his hands and impale him on it seconds. No regular man is a match for my brother.*

Whatever this thing is, it has limits. It couldn't control all of us. Stellan is strong-willed and Tifra has multiple personalities. It can't be easy.

But which way to go? There are three passages out of here. Which one did he take? Think Daire, he didn't go toward the ship, or you'd have run into them. Would they have gone the way we came? Probably not.

Daire committed to the third path, moving forward as quickly as she could. The path was straight and upward, on a textured flooring. She passed another opening and flashed her light down them, putting a ranger mark on each passage. As she jogged, she fought a rising sense of despair.

A glint from her light brought her to her knees to find a button on the floor. It was the same as one of hers, only larger. They'd bought their clothes from the same supplier, and she recognized the button, matching the ones on her own shirt.

Now Daire sped forward, quiet and grim. She was on the right trail, and the enemy was ahead.

She came to an air shaftway—huge and irregularly lit. It faded into the darkness above and below her. A bridge crossed it, but the railings had been made for the huge unknown aliens. The lower rail was actually at her hip height and the upper well over her head, so they offered little comfort or protection. Like most spacers, Daire could handle heights but there was a strong wind going across it and she crossed carefully, cursing the need to go slower. Finally, she reached the far side and resumed her run.

A sense of oppression grew in her mind, reinforcing her feeling that Hara was close. She slowed; the way ahead split but she had no doubt. The feeling of oppression emanated from the leftmost way.

CHAPTER THIRTY

Stellan regained consciousness feeling like his head was in a vise. He tried to control the waves of pain by breathing in for four and out for eight, the way he would do when about to enter a tournament. It helped some. His vision, blurry from when whatever it was that struck him, began to clear. He realized he was on his feet and had a dim memory of walking, carrying Tifra.

"Obey" said a voice in his head.

The words were in Galactic standard, but he instantly felt that the mind behind them was not human, or any alien he knew of.

He realized he was lying sprawled against a wall. A man, no, something that had once been a man stood over him, holding a spear of some sort. Hara's body wore its old uniform, soiled and bloody, but what looked out of his eyes was totally alien.

He remembered the fight now and the two dead humans. *Probably the last of Alamy's crew. Daire's laser shot had been true. I crushed the skull of the one who speared her. He must have compelled me to carry Tifra into this antechamber.*

Tifra lay on her side. He could immediately see that she was not dead; her eyes seemed glazed, but they moved.

Daire.

"Where is my sister?" he growled, trying to stand.

A blast of force lit up his skull. He found himself on his back against the wall again. Gasping. Tears ran down his face.

"Where?" he demanded.

"Not your concern. Obey."

"If you've harmed her, I'll carve a hole in your belly and slowly pull your guts out through it." He felt something pressing against his mind. A force, a presence, and he knew the debased thing in front of him was the source. But the communication allowed him to sense something back: unease, surprise, and a sense of strain.

"Where?" It came out as a roar of sound and mind.

The strain against him increased but his fear and anger over Daire and Tifra was white-hot. "Where?!?"

"Escape," Hara-thing admitted.

This told Stellan two things immediately. That Daire might be safe, and that Hara-thing judged the strain of struggling with him was enough of a danger to allow a concession.

It struck me with something. Bolts of mental force. But I was not aware and alert then. I'm both now. If I can cross the space between us, I can kill him in seconds. But how to do it? He put me back down quickly. I'm not sure he's aware of my thoughts, but he probably gets some sense of it through this link, just like I'm getting some sense of him.

Can Tifra help? Is she fighting in her mind like I am? Hell, there's six of her.

God, that might be it. I thought he was concentrating on me. It might be that he's using most of his force to hold her and her quintet down.

But why not kill us? Hah, bastard wants our bodies. If not for himself than for his fellow ghouls. He lost two taking us.

He must have wanted Daire too, but she fought free somehow. He had a dim recollection of a laser flash, maybe two. It seemed that the cleaners and executors hadn't reacted to it, at least not yet. Well, they hadn't attacked the City, just each other, so perhaps the recent additions hadn't been added to the City's roster.

Machines move at their own speed and logic. It might also be why Daire got away, because she's marked now by the City for using a weapon. Hara-thing might not be able to make use of her now.

She broke away as I wanted her too. But I know my sister; she will be back. Say two hours to get back to the ship, get weapons. She might need the autodoc.

He glared at Hara. *Your men hurt my sister. I will kill you with my own hands, this I swear.*

But for now, he had to delay Hara-thing. Their enemy may have been surprised by the resistance offered. Stellan suspected that Hara had planned to have each of them controlled by a minion. Perhaps to have even invaded his body on the spot. But they hadn't reckoned on Daire using a forbidden weapon and his speed and power.

Now it's just him. He must be using most of his force on Tifra, or why would I be awake?

It must be hard to work my body and his own and he hasn't tried to switch. Might be too risky. It thinks it can control me and make me carry her. He probably let Daire get away, that was one too many for just him. Maybe he's calling other ghouls here too.

Fuck you. My mother was so strong that not even the Evolvers could overwhelm her mind, her soul, her determination. I am of her genetic line. I am aware now. You will not bend me to your will. Death first.

"Pick up female," Hara-thing ordered.

Stellan gave a wolf-like grin and simply stared back. "I like her where she is."

Pressure built in his head and he growled like a trapped animal. Pain followed. More pain than he had ever felt.

Whose child are you? he screamed into his growing agony. *Shasti would laugh at this. She would laugh at me. Pain? She would say she had felt real pain. You're a weakling.*

The pain relented. He realized he was face down on the deck, drooling. For a second he feared his bladder had let go. No, he was just wringing with sweat.

Now it was Hara-thing's turn to smile it seemed. "This is my power. I can repeat it. How many times can you battle me?"

"One more time than you can do this," he hissed.

Hara raised his spear. "Female can die. One less to control. Harder than you."

Stellan had to hope that his interest in Tifra did not carry across the mental battlefield. "Kill a speaker-to-all?"

"I do not care for rules."

"Others here do, Outlaw. They may hunt you. This alien monstrosity itself may hunt you."

Perhaps that gave Hara-thing pause. He couldn't tell.

"I sense that you like this one," Hara-thing said slyly.

Stellan forced his feelings down. *Just like in a fight, just like tournament. Breath, control, center.*

"She's a nice female, met her only days ago. Not even my kind. I hardly know her."

He hoped to catch some flicker of uncertainty from Hara-thing, but it seemed to have taken a page from his book and calmed and focused.

It leaned against the wall of the chamber they were in. "You will weaken. All do. And others will come. The word now whispers through the hall. I have time."

"What are you?" Stellan demanded.

"You do not know my kind," Hara replied, his mouth twisting oddly as he spoke. "I was strong, clean, not this pallid flesh. Ancient of days ago, a prince. An explorer. I remember another galaxy, endless blue stars. Old, old, old, so long ago. So far away. Only I remain. Others were weak, they faded entirely. One sailed off into the deep dark, hopeless. Just a light sail but wanting to die elsewhere. Died quickly. Too many transits.

"This place," it looked about and even across the gulf of alienness and the mental battlefield, its loathing for this place flooded him. Hara-thing's defenses were suddenly disrupted, he felt age, loneliness, despair and anger. The thing before him longed for home, longed for a female of his own kind vanished in the mists of space-time. It was utterly and completely without hope or happiness.

Tifra said that many call this place Hell. Hara-thing surely would.

The wall slammed down brutally on the flood of impressions.

Hara's black eyes glittered, and the mouth moved. Curses in some alien tongue? Who could know?

"Do not seek to bargain with me," Hara-thing said. "Do not offer me riches, or service, or escape. There is no meaning here. All that there is to have here is a body."

"Yeah? Well learn to take care of your toys. For a body-collector you don't do a good job of keeping things up. You stink enough to make my eyes water. Whatever you've been feeding the face you stole, isn't doing much for the corpse you're wearing."

Hara-thing looked down at itself, raising its arms and seeming to contemplate itself.

What the hell would it know of maintaining a human body? Probably has vitamin and mineral deficiencies already. He's wiry but underweight. Bet those teeth haven't been brushed in months.

Either Hara's personality isn't in there with him, or it's so submerged that he doesn't regard it. It's picked up our language, that's so imprinted on our brains that it's probably easy for it. But memories and the details of being a living human...

Tifra is a mass of symbiotes. This is a parasite.

"No matter," Hara-thing said. But there seemed little conviction in the words.

Daire's nose warned her first and this time there was no mental fog to deaden her awareness. She felt something as well, almost like a mental itch, an awareness of some power ahead of her and to the right. She tried to keep her own mind a blank lest it give warning.

I bet it has its hands full. It somehow made them move or made Stellan carry Tifra. I wonder if he or she's awakened. I've got to get close.

She heard voices, and recognized her brother's deep voice, again she savagely choked down her reaction of relief. Now to close the gap. Step by careful step, Daire advanced, grateful for once to be small and light. Now she could see by the light of a small yellow light that there was one of the cells similar to the others they'd passed before.

Damn, no way to get a long-distance shot. I'll probably have to jump into the room, spot and shoot. A crappy situation as Dad would say. I could wait but can that thing in there pick up the emanations of my brain?

She heard a voice she did not recognize, probably Hara's but the words were not clear. The cry of pain from her brother decided her. She lunged into the room to the right.

Her eyes took in everything in a second. The room was larger than the other cells she'd seen. Stellan lay on the floor writhing in pain. Tifra lay motionless, facedown a distance away.

Unfortunately, Hara-thing was facing her as she leapt into the room. Either he had sensed her at the last second or it was misfortune. Before she could fire, Hara's mind struck at her, and the stunner fell from nerveless fingers. Daire gave a strangled cry and sank to her knees. As Hara stepped forward with his spear, Daire drew her belt knife with her free hand.

Her cry galvanized Stellan who made an animal sound and began to climb to his feet. Hara whirled and faced him. Stellan staggered back to fall against a wall, teeth bared, staring murderously at him. His clothes were covered in sweat and his face was strained with agony.

Tifra also stirred. Hara looked like he might throw the spear at the prone girl, but he hesitated, looking at Stellan. The need to battle both of them diverted enough of his attention for Daire to turn, leap and hit the closing switch on the door. The panel closed slowly with a whisper. She slammed her belt knife into the switch, hoping to jam it. They were locked in.

Hara's attention turned back to her, but the oppressive power did not strike her. Evidently, he didn't perceive the threat she posed. He was concentrating on Stellan who had sunk to his knees. Her brother's eyes glazed over, and he slumped, unconscious.

He's knocked him out to concentrate on me. I'm next.

Daire wrapped her hand around the detonator switch and pulled off the safety tab. She flung the satchel with the bomb in it at Hara's feet. The man nimbly leapt aside, with a contemptuous expression on his face. The bag fetched up against Tifra, who for the first time seemed to focus. The eyes that had been vacant a second before filled with intelligence, but it seemed like movement was beyond her.

"It is hard work to stun one so powerful and another who has so many within her," Hara-thing said, breathing heavily. "I may simply have to destroy her. Now at least I have you." He changed his grip on the spear weapon.

Daire looked at the thing that had been Hara, at the dark eyes that contained a malign alien intelligence from some unguessable time and place. Hara twitched with the body mechanics of something that had never been human, making him even more horrible.

"I'm leaving this hell hole," Daire said, holding the detonator she'd made close. "And my brother and Tifra are coming with me. You can keep Hara, you two deserve each other."

"No," the thing that Hara had been hissed at her. "My followers need bodies."

"Ten pounds of satchel charge says no. I've pressed the detonator; if my hand comes off, It explodes. You're locked in here with us. That door won't open quickly enough for you to get out."

"Your kind clings to life," Hara-thing said, aiming his spear at Tifra. "I know your people. You bluff. Leave, these others stay. I need them. I will let you go." But his look at the satchel held worry.

Daire felt her spirit settle within her. Resolve hardened her eyes. *I'm sorry Mom, Dad, Aunt Shasti, Wulf, Emma. But I couldn't let them have Stellan.*

She smiled at Hara-thing. "You won't have us. But you'll share death with us. You're overdue."

"You will die," Hara-thing said, eyes widening. Suddenly the spear was pointed at her.

"As will you," Daire said, teeth flashing. She raised the detonator and opened her hand. "You've got ten seconds to contemplate the end of it all."

Hara-thing moaned and lunged at her with the spear. Daire used the second she had to shrug off her pack and use it to block the thrust. He thrust again and impaled only the pack.

Got to hold him in here.

Hara swung the spear at her. Her pack and the armor on her shoulder protected her. but it knocked her away from the door. He dropped it, lost precious seconds trying to get the knife from the door control, twisting it.

"Too late," Daire screamed at him.

Hara banged furiously at the slowly opening door. Then it turned back to face her standing there—arms akimbo. It gave a great scream and Hara toppled over slamming into the deck in fall like a dead body. The thing within him fled.

Tifra snapped out of her trance, followed a moment later by Stellan. Daire threw her arms about him.

"Sister, no," Stellan managed. "You shouldn't have come back."

"Never," Daire cried, bracing for the blast. "Both or neither."

"Tifra!" Stellan grabbed her into their embrace as if his body could shield them somehow from the explosion.

Which never came.

They looked at each other, but the expression on Tifra's face was not hers.

"What?" Daire gasped, staring about.

Tifra laughed but the sound in her voice was alien.

"Who are you?" Stellan growled, looking Tifra in the eye.

Tifra's expression twisted into something that looked contemptuous. "C'tell. Someone had to stop you from immolating yourselves. I pulled the wire while Tifra personality was stunned by the Old One."

"You mean you wanted to save yourself," Daire all but screamed, "even if that thing hollowed us out for its use!"

"Not likely," Ana said. "You were very persuasive, human. You were sure of the blast. Old One sensed it in you, sensed your resolve to kill and die for your kin. The blast would destroy the Hara body. It did not want to be in a dying body, maybe to have to die with it. The Old One disminded itself and in a hurry. It will not recover soon."

"And Hara?" Daire demanded, looking at the sprawled body. Hara lay like a broken toy, eyes open and unseeing.

"Dead," C'tell/Tifra replied. "Leaving so fast left nothing behind to control the body."

"A pity that," Stellan growled. "I had promised myself his death at my hands."

"Let's get out of here," Daire said, standing, "before something else happens."

"Where is Tifra?" Stellan demanded, struggling to rise.

"Tifra, the little girl," C'tell/Tifra sing-songed. "Tifra, the inexperienced? You'd have a better time with me, strongman. I was a female and admired by many."

"Bring back Tifra!" he said, seizing her.

"Or what?" Ana said. "Will you break Tifra's body with those big hands? You can't pull me out."

Daire placed her hand on his chest. "Not now, Stellan."

Suddenly Tifra gave a great shudder. Her expression smoothed out and she gasped in air. "What? What happened?"

"You weren't—"

"C'tell, you bitch!" Tifra lapsed into her own language to apparently curse the whisperer at greater length.

"Come on," Daire said, pulling at them both. "We've got to go. Tifra, can you lead? Are in shape to do it?"

"Yes," Tifra said. "C'tell is back in her place: sulking and cursing us for being ungrateful. Says she should have let you blow us up."

"I do not like that one," Stellan said.

Tifra stumbled and Stellan had an arm around her in a moment.

"This way," Tifra said, visibly shaking off the disorientation of what had happened. They fled down the hallway.

"Stay alert," Tifra said, her voice suddenly deepening, perhaps it was the Saurian Khist-tok. "This place is never safe."

A sudden pulsing shook the air about them.

"No," Tifra moaned. "The jump engines."

"Tifra," Daire said, "We have to get to our ship. Are you coming with us?"

Tifra's eyes met Stellan's for a moment. "I am coming with you. This way," she gestured, "faster this way but watch for the cleaners."

They raced pell-mell down the corridors of the City as the throb of the jump drive sounded, changing and deepening. Lights flashed and even the walls seemed to move. They exited a hallway and came to the narrow-railed bridge across the terrible drop.

A cleaner reared up in front of them, cutting them off. It headed straight at Daire.

With a roar of sheer rage, Stellan leapt at the machine in a flying kick, slamming into it with both feet and all the power of his engineered body. The machine, tentacle arms flailing, flew into the railing and under it, disappearing soundlessly.

Stellan, unable to get his feet under him in time, hit the deck hard but bounced up in an instant. "Run!"

They fled across the bridge as another cleaner came out of the hallway they'd just vacated. But for whatever reason, the thing did not chase them across the bridge.

The nightmare race seemed to have no end. Daire was too small to keep up with her giant brother or the gazelle-like alien. Her abused ribs burned, as did her shoulder where Hara-thing had struck her.

Stellan simply scooped her up when she flagged, throwing her across his broad shoulders without slowing. All the while the engines thrummed, and the City seemed to come alive in its malign desire to leap into the unknown. If it jumped, they would never see home again.

They raced past the layer cake room with the first fountain they had seen. Daire could only barely cling to consciousness, the pounding her ribs had taken was a flaring agony.

"Look—our suits," Daire cried from on his shoulders. They lay where they had cached them against further needs days ago.

"We're almost there," Tifra screamed and put on a burst of speed that taxed Stellan. But ahead of them lay *Alamy's* open deck. It had sunk noticeably into the City in the days that they'd been aboard. Tifra and Stellan both had to stoop to get into the open dock. Then it was a pounding run up through the doomed ship to where *Wanderlust* lay alongside *Alamy's* upper dock.

Stellan placed his hand on the persona lock before putting Daire down and he practically shoved both girls through before the lock cycled open enough to admit him. He hit the seal command as he reached the far end of the umbilical. "I'm in."

"*Wanderlust,*" Daire screamed, "emergency undock. Full lateral thrust."

"Acknowledged," the AI's voice came urgent and fast in accord with the order. The AI blew the umbilical behind Stellan. They were all thrown from their feet as *Wanderlust* surged away from *Alamy.* The AG field stabilized in a moment.

"Course 270 relative. Max burn on engines," Daire further ordered as she scrambled off the deck, heading for the bridge. "Override safeties for thirty seconds."

"Done," The AI stated.

Again, acceleration pulled at them, not fully, or they would have been smashed into the bulkheads, but *Wanderlust's* barely-stabilized AG field had not been made for fighter-like turns and could not cancel all the energy so quickly. Alarms sounded and red lights bloomed on the status panels around them as the safeties were cut.

"Can she take this?" Tifra asked, looking at the cream-white and silver halls of *Wanderlust* as if she was about to come apart around her.

Which is not impossible, Stellan thought. All he could do was pin his hopes on how well his sister knew their ship.

Stellan followed Daire as her feet disappeared up the companionway to the bridge with Tifra holding onto his jacket. Daire struggled into the captain's seat, as he vaulted into his. Tifra, he was pleased to see, was smart enough to grab the third seat and figure out the webbing. Daire was looking at her instruments and the receding but still vast bulk of the City, which was now shimmering as strange bolts of dark-blue energy ran around its exterior.

Daire looked at her readouts then back at the City. "*Wanderlust,* fifteen seconds additional full thrust then reinstate safeties."

"Acknowledged."

The strain against their chests continued. The seconds of full thrust ticked by. There was no way to know how far was far enough. Stellan knew that Daire would push the ship to her limit but not beyond. It had to be enough. On screen, the City shimmered and convulsed in flowering of silver light and was gone, like a nightmare yielding to sudden dawn.

Daire's hand cut the thrust and the pressure lifted. They both snapped around to look at Tifra. Stellan was seized by the sudden fear that the City had somehow reclaimed her.

The alien girl was weeping, staring at the space where the City had been.

Stellan leapt out of his seat. "Are you alright?"

"Yellow suns, under blue skies, oceans and mountains," she said, looking up at him, "I'm going to see them?"

"Yes," Stellan said, kneeling next to her and taking her hand, "and so much more."

Behind him, Daire smiled gently, then turned away. "Wait until I tell Aunt Shasti about this!" she whispered to herself.

The End

ABOUT THE AUTHOR

Edward McKeown is the author of fast-paced space opera adventures, best known for his Confederation Space Series. His work includes the Robert Fenaday and Shasti Rainhell novels, chronicling the voyages of the privateer starship *Sidhe* through war-torn stars, alien conflicts, and the struggle for survival in deep space. Set in the same universe, his Maauro Series follows Wrik Trigardt and Maauro, a 50,000-year-old android, as they battle governments and the ruthless Thieves Guild in their fight for freedom.

Beyond science fiction, McKeown explores urban fantasy with *Knight in Charlotte* and *Oniichan*, blending modern settings with myth, magic, and supernatural intrigue.

Whether writing epic space battles, futuristic adventures, genetic engineering sci-fi, or found-family starship crews, Edward McKeown creates stories filled with rich characters, sharp action, and unforgettable journeys across the stars.

When not writing, Ed practices Kung Fu, Tai Chi and specializes in ancient weapons. He also enjoyes ballroom dancing and drawing.

ALSO BY EDWARD MCKEOWN

Fenaday/Rainhell

Was Once a Hero

Fearful Symmetry

Points of Departure

HIdden Stars

Between Two World

Prviateer Sidhe (Omnibus)

Maauro Chronicles

My Outcast State

Against that Time

The Lost

All the Difference

When Fighting Monsters

Maauro Seachanges

Legacies

In an Evil Land

The Deep

Journey Interrupted

Resolutions

Jeremy Leclerc Urban Fantasy

Knight in Charlotte

Oniichan

The Drear (upcoming)

On the Case